THRESHOLD

THRESHOLD

JANET AND CHRIS MORRIS

A ROC BOOK

ROC
Published by the Penguin Group
Penguin Books USA Inc., 375 Hudson Street,
New York, New York 10014, U.S.A.
Penguin Books Ltd, 27 Wrights Lane,
London W8 5TZ, England
Penguin Books Australia Ltd, Ringwood,
Victoria, Australia
Penguin Books Canada Ltd, 2801 John Street,
Markham, Ontario, Canada L3R 1B4
Penguin Books (N.Z.) Ltd, 182-190 Wairau Road,
Auckland 10, New Zealand

Penguin Books Ltd, Registered Offices:
Harmondsworth, Middlesex, England

First published by ROC, an imprint of New American Library, a division of
Penguin Books USA Inc.

First Printing, August, 1990
10   9   8   7   6   5   4   3   2   1

Library of Congress Cataloging-in-Publication Data

Morris, Janet, 1946–
    Threshold / by Janet Morris and Chris Morris.
        p.   cm.
    ISBN 0-451-45022-1
    I. Morris, Chris, 1946–   . II. Title.
PS3563.O87435T48   1990
813'.54—dc20

90-30581
CIP

PRINTED IN THE UNITED STATES OF AMERICA
Set in Times Roman
Designed by Leonard Telesca

This novel is dedicated to Herbert L. Ort—mentor, business manager, spiritual guide—with love and respect:

Without your wisdom, kindness, and unceasing care, Herb, life would not be half so sweet.

CHAPTER 1

Déjà Vu

Past a sprinkle of asteroids in the foreground of his synthetic-aperture lidar screen, beyond a red crescent that ought to be Mars, was the blue-green dot of Earth.

Or so the pilot's astronics were indicating. Captain Joseph South, U.S. Space Command, had learned to distrust his artificially intelligent "expert" astrogation system on this bad-luck test flight. Nothing had gone as planned during the maiden interstellar spongejump of the X-99A testbed he was piloting, beyond the mission being—so far—survivable.

But the X-99A had never outright lied to him. And lidar returns, any test pilot knew, were as trustworthy as radar returns. South shook his helmeted head and rubbed his eyes under his raised visor. Better rephrase that, since radar and lidar could spoof you if you let them, and South was fresh from a jump through a spongelike space whose prolonged effects on human beings were part of what this test flight was testing.

The laser-driven imaging system could only show him what was out there to bounce light back.

So something like Earth was out there, even if the expert system was telling him that the micro-match didn't fit any template of the home solar system for the next five hundred years.

The AI-expert had been giving South enough trouble on this flight that he'd promised himself, when he got home, to pull it out of the X-99A *STARBIRD* so that he could take it up into the hills around Vandenberg and shoot it with Grandpa's six-gun.

Since it was too soon to put a lead slug through its charge-coupled brain, and he didn't like the readout below his lidar screen, South did what any red-blooded American test pilot would do in his situation: he whacked the offending meter, hard, with the flat of his gloved hand.

The digital readout didn't even shiver. The date on the meter didn't change. The heads-up display reflecting it on *STARBIRD*'s windscreen didn't, either.

With a sigh, South slapped down his helmet's visor and pulled up all the relevant data through his suit's system, reading the results of his Extravehicular Mobility Unit's redundant command and control display. The projections on the inside of his visor showed him the same pictures and numbers that the master system had, only now he had to scroll and tap and voice-command his way through a full astro error search, because the suit's helmet could show him only four data pulls at a time and still give him a vision window in the center of his visor.

And South needed to keep an eye on his flight deck—especially on the lidar screen—to see if anything changed while he was doing the equivalent of telling *STARBIRD*'s AI that it had its silicon head wedged up its outputs.

But nothing changed. The planets on his lidar were still telling *STARBIRD* they were five hundred years decayed in their orbits from project ETA, this system. South pulled up a standard return template and superimposed it on the real-time lidar return. It didn't look that damned different to him. So maybe the AI itself was out of kilter.

He hoped not. *STARBIRD* was going to be a real handful to dock if he had to do it from his suit's astronics—or manually.

Still, he *had* to do it. "Give me the quickest plot to

docking, Birdy. Send it with ETA, our call signs, to Station." He flipped onto monitoring mode. STARBIRD's AI would run the message by him before it burst it by laser carrier toward the U.S. Space Station in orbit around the earth.

The AI's voice once gave him the creeps, but now he was used to it. The mission had eaten fourteen months out of Joe South's life. Even with STARBIRD's capabilities, it would eat four more before he docked. There were better than twenty light-minutes between him and the station, and not even STARBIRD could chance anywhere near half-light speed among the complex of gravity wells that made up the inner solar system. She'd be torn apart.

South's message would get there at light speed, lots faster than he could, but at least they'd know he was on his way. You could say "mission accomplished," at this point. He listened to the AI's communication and added those two words: "Tell 'em, mission accomplished, Birdy."

It sounded funny in his ears. Maybe because of the helmet's close confines, visor down. He clicked his faceshield up, and the flight deck was suddenly less polarized.

South was rubbing his eyes again, still blinking. He was seeing a ghost image of his own, haloes around letters and numbers, toggles and keys, when he looked at them. But that had been happening for a while.

It was thinking about the mission, maybe, that made his voice funny. The mission was accomplished, you bet. But every time he thought about it, he kept itching in the back of his brain. His heartbeat would race, and his suit would get all concerned and jab him with mood elevators and its damned physiology package would come to life, recording his galvanic skin response to stress and he didn't know what-all.

Yeah, he did know what-all. On take off, his pulse rate in STARBIRD had been fifty-eight. He'd been proud of that. Jumping into oblivion—the first guy to do it for real, rather than a quick in-and-out punch that wasn't any more than a roller-coaster ride for a couple of chimpanzees—he'd racked up a hot eighty-eight.

But every time he thought back to his flyby of X-3, the star system in question, his pulse rate shot to one-twenty, he began to sweat, and his ears rang. The evaluation team was going to have fun with that set of responses when he got Birdy parked. He'd had a long time to think, and he figured he'd skip telling them about the memory blackout parts, since he might be imagining them. Like the bad dreams he'd had out there (dreams of walking on a planet when he'd never left the ship), the blackouts were phantasms. Had to be, because otherwise, he wouldn't be spiking his physiology meters.

Joe South was a great test pilot because nothing—nothing whatsoever—spiked him. Except weird sponge dreams and old dreams about the Central African war—dreams about being shot down in his ATF and running around in the jungle trying to evade the Africans, and getting caught, and being a POW and, finally, being traded out. You didn't let your Space Command pilots waste away in the detention camps. . . .

The jungle on the planet in his dreams was sort of like that African jungle, but the alien detention camp was lots nicer, and the dream aliens had bigger eyes even than the blacks in Mozambique. But Mozambique had really happened, and nothing had shaken him since then, except dreams about it.

Joe South should have died in Africa. He'd known it then. He'd never forgotten it. Test pilots were made from fighter pilots who figured they were indestructible because they were on borrowed time, should-be-dead men who were sure that God had given them Get-Out-of-Jail-Free cards, and South had won Test Pilot of the Year three years running.

He'd win it again, if he could just get through the physical on the other end of this mission and get back in the game. This one mission would put him way ahead in the standings.

And he had plenty of time to practice biofeedback controls of his erratic pulse rate and whatever else he needed—months of easy cruising toward the little blue-green ball on his lidar.

So maybe he should get some sleep, give Birdy her head, and see how he felt once the transient jump effects wore off. If he had the dreams again, complete with flowers and sunsets like he'd never seen in his life, and soft-skinned aliens with wide eyes and sad mouths, then maybe he could get used to it. Ten years as a fighter jock and five more as a test pilot had taught South that you could get used to most anything.

"Birdy, I'm going off-line. Maintain present heading." He didn't have to talk to the AI, he'd just gotten used to doing it. He canted his couch back, not bothering to take off his suit, or even his helmet, let alone go aft where he could shower and shave, and sleep in his bunk. You could get used to anything.

He wanted to let the suit's system, rather than the bunk's system, monitor his condition while he slept. You personified, in space. He'd personified the suit into a buddy, and the ship into a command chain, representative of Space Command. He knew it, and he knew it was a little wacky, trusting your suit more than your ship. But it had been a wacky mission.

Part of the trouble with his memory, which the medics had predicted, was remembering the jump phase stuff, and the directly post–jump phase stuff. You were in a different time dimension than your biology was built to handle. What was good about that was that he hadn't come back an old, shriveled, incontinent geriatric. What was bad, everybody at Mission Control was waiting to find out.

One bad thing was going to be coming home eighteen months later and seeing everybody again—seeing his buddies with promotions, his retraining on new equipment because the tech improved so damned fast; seeing his folks, who were getting old now; seeing Jenna, who'd probably waited for him this time because she'd always waited for him before, even when he'd been a POW.

Everybody would be glad to see him, on the surface, but you were a stranger after so long. Being a stranger to your friends, to your wife and family, was something that hurt every time, and there wasn't any regulation that could make the dissociation into something else.

Now that he was almost home, he could feel the tension of the inevitable reunions seeping into him, even from such a great distance, while he tried to fall asleep.

So he thought, when he heard the alarm blare, and saw the red light strobing beyond his lids, that he was dreaming. If he had a problem, out here, he wouldn't have to worry about what it was going to be like reentering society. His mind was giving him a quick and easy out: a dream of not making it home because of systems failure.

But the strobing wouldn't stop and the alarms hurt his ears, despite his helmet. Even as he was returning the couch to operating position, he was pulling up scans on his helmet system.

It was the plain old fusion pack, nothing exotic. But a runaway reaction or a shutdown could get him just as dead as anything more obscure.

He had a schematic on his visor that wanted him to add liquid to the system. Well, if worse came to worse, he could urinate in the emergency feed tank.

But worse didn't come to worse: there was emergency coolant available in a backup tank, and Birdy was telling him not to worry about it.

He sat up for three hours watching the digital readout cool down and stay down. Birdy wanted to move the system back up to speed.

He didn't. It was a gut reaction, and South always trusted his gut. Let STARBIRD tool along at lower power for a bit, at least while he got some sleep.

The AI had no way of testing whether the malfunction was a heat sensor or the system itself, or whether the additional coolant had done the job, unless he pushed the burn enough to hot things up.

"How long to Station dock, at this speed?" he asked it, the first thing he'd said aloud since the trouble started.

Birdy's uninflected, precise voice told him.

Too long.

"Crap." The damned thing was right. He didn't want to spend three years extra getting home, not when he was already hyped about it.

He sat back in his couch, crooked one knee, and reached for the autopad on his armrest. With it, he banished the synthetic aperture lidar and replaced it with a real-time forward view.

Staring at it, he thought he saw something move.

He really was tired. They'd told him to watch the psychological effects on either side of a jump. First he'd seen spacemen, dreamed of other worlds when he'd never left *STARBIRD*, now he was seeing moving blips of light out here where nothing was.

Joe South took off his helmet carefully. Holding it between his knees, he ran his gloved hands over his face, then scratched his scalp all over. Time for a haircut. He looked toward the real-time view and caught his reflection: beard-shadowed guy in his mid-thirties, eyes a little large and radiating concern, perfunctory nose, and a mouth that seemed, today, like it was a little too large or a little too loose for his oval face, though women said he was sexy because of it. He was just an average guy with an above-average need for adrenaline and a naturally athletic body that, trim and under six feet, was better suited to piloting than to professional sports.

If he was going to get dead out here in *STARBIRD*, he was going to do it in some above-average way, not starve to death or freeze to death or go quietly mad waiting for his life support to run out.

So maybe he ought to power her back up to her redline and see what happened.

He was about to do that when he saw the flicker in his forward view again. He cursed it, told Birdy to put it on the scope, and put his helmet back on. Inside his personal cocoon, he felt a little more in control.

He kicked back once more in the command chair, nearly horizontal, taking all the feeds on his visor display and letting himself get pumped up. He always felt better when he'd defined a threat.

He hoped to hell this was a real one, and not a phantom, like his dreams.

But Birdy had it, too. After giving him coordinates and zooming the lidar image so that he could read numbers on the sides of spacecraft such as he'd never imagined in his wildest nightmares, the artificial voice said calmly, "Un-identified spaceborne objects."

"You bet," he confirmed. "Let's say hi, nice and polite: All hailing frequencies you can imagine, Birdy, our call signs, and make sure they know we're U.S. Space Command." American affiliation ought to be worth something, unless these were Creatures from Outer Space.

He didn't think they could be: the numbers were Arabic, there on the spacecrafts' sides, and the armaments looked like futuristic railguns on turrets, supplemented by under-belly cannon that were the direct descendants of the sort of Kinetic Kill Devices that Space Command had been testing for orbital deployment when South had left the solar system.

If they were KKD cannon, and whoever was on those ships decided to shoot *STARBIRD*, there wasn't a thing that Captain Joe South could do about it. The X-99A wasn't armed. She was a testbed.

He hoped to hell she wasn't going to become a deathbed as he toggled himself into the com system and began identi-fying himself and sending a mayday in English, pidgin Rus-sian, French, German and Spanish.

After all, he was having trouble with his power plant. As for what kind of other trouble he was getting into, he couldn't see any way to avoid contact with whoever was out there.

They were headed straight for him, armed and dangerous.

Unless he'd stumbled into somebody else's test program, something was terribly wrong out here.

Either there was a war going on that had pushed tech parameters at an ungodly rate and Joe South had just stumbled into the middle of it, or the lidar return and his AI's reading of it was right.

And if that were so, it was goddamn five hundred years since he'd left, local time, and Joe South was going to have one hell of a lot of explaining to do.

If those guys out there would let him, not just shoot first and the hell with questions later, the way those battleships told South they might . . .

CHAPTER 2

The Relic

Consolidated Security didn't take chances. The ConSec ship dispatched to take the Relic craft in tow was armed to the teeth and prepared for the worst. The tug and backup patrol cruiser alongside the *Blue Tick* were there if the *Tick* needed them, but that didn't make Reice, at her helm, feel all that much better.

Five years ago, Reice, now a lieutenant, had been the poor fool of a sergeant who'd decided he could go one-on-one with a Relic pilot. Reice had ended up in the Stalk hospital for a week, and the Relic had killed himself anyway.

That prior brush with history in the person of a pilot from the early days of interstellar space flight had qualified Reice, above all others, to deal with the next Relic who came along.

If he'd been lucky, there never would have been another Relic encounter in Reice's lifetime. There didn't have to be. It wasn't as if these crazy coots came popping out of the spongeholes of the universe every day. And it wasn't as if they all had to be as crazy as the last one Reice had dealt with. But you could never be sure. Early administrations, especially the American, Japanese, and Soviet governments, had sent test craft with human pilots into temporally anomalous hyperspaces with only the slightest inkling of the nature of spongespace, T2 effects on biological systems such as human brains, and the most primitive of technological assistants.

It was a wonder the damned galaxy got colonized at all. Most of these old ships had primitive fusion power plants, no zero-point apport packs, no asymptotic spacetime navigational aids—nothing.

They'd send the guys out to push a button. The pilots would do that, and come out . . . somewhere . . . wherever chance and their tech level dictated.

Most of them never made it back at all. The one Reice had grappled with had been certifiably mad, paranoid and full of stories about advanced cultures with impossible attributes that couldn't exist, or somebody, somewhere, from one of the three hundred colonies man had established among the stars, would have run into them.

Reice had nearly lost his ship the last time, when the Relic had tried to ram it. That first Relic was sure that Reice, too, was part of the advanced, hostile, alien civilization. Hard to convince someone that he's come home when that someone's crazy and home's a whole lot different.

Reice had no intention of losing his ship this time. He was proud of the *Blue Tick*. The G-410007 *Blue Tick* insystem cruiser had a top speed of 3/5 light and a temporal reorientation module; she was a 1K-ton, mini-pursuit ground-to-space vehicle, search and rescue capable, with kinetic armament and surveillance/cratology packages. He'd just gotten her. And he was a lieutenant, now, with a certain degree of autonomy that a sergeant just didn't have.

But Reice had gotten strict orders, from the desk of Secretary General Michael (Mickey) Croft himself, to bring in the Relic ship with no fuss, no violence, and if possible, no fanfare.

Threshold, which normally housed about a quarter million souls out here between Mars and Jupiter, had swelled to capacity with the influx of Muslim pilgrims in for the hajj and the attendees of Croft's high-voltage diplomatic conference.

Croft's office hadn't minced words: Keep things calm at all costs. The Muslims were likely to take any odd event as a sign, and any dead Relic might become a martyr.

So Reice had to find a way to finesse this antique craft—and, if possible, whoever, if anyone, was in it—home safe and sound, according to regulations.

By the book. The book allowed Reice to shoot in self-defense, however. He was considering going aboard the ship and shooting whoever, if anyone, was alive inside, just to simplify matters, when a squawk came over his com and he found himself listening to a voice from the distant past with what sounded like an American accent.

If the pilot of the craft ahead had found Reice's hailing frequency, then he'd found the tug's and the backup cruiser's. Worse, he was sounding rational: a U.S. Space Command pilot, identifying his craft as X-99A. Somebody would look that up in the history books back home on Threshold.

Reice cracked his knuckles in one flex of interlaced fingers. No use shooting the ship out of hand, not with a recorded contact to explain.

Probably no use shooting the pilot, either.

The pilot of the X-99A, a Captain South, was claiming power plant trouble.

Before he responded to the Relic directly, Reice called in to Threshold Terminal's Port Authority. When he got to the traffic controller he wanted, he said, "Jack, we don't know what this guy's mental state is, or what shape his ship's really in. I'm going to ask him if he'll shut down his power plant—everything but emergency life support—and let us tow him in cold. That way, we minimize the risk of this antique going bang in our docking bay. But towing in somebody who doesn't want to be towed is no picnic. . . . Got a better idea?"

The controller came back with a laconically delivered set of instructions, including a docking bay designator: "They really want to look at this ship, Lieutenant. I'll clear the way for you. Keep me advised. You're clear to dock anytime after 1800."

"Gee thanks," said Reice. That gave him more than enough slack, timewise. He could sit out here and argue with the Relic for an hour or two, and still make his window if this Captain South would agree to the tow.

Then it occurred to Reice that he didn't have to wait for South to agree to the tow, and a slow smile spread over his dark, sharp-featured face. He called the tug and said, "Begin making the derelict fast. I'll do the rest."

And he called his backup: "Sergeant, let's have you on this baby's tail. It gives us any trouble, put a five-pounder up its ass. If we have to, we'll tow it in dead."

A five-pound lead slug would immobilize the power plant, but not cook off a fusion plant, which this X-99A had, if Reice remembered his history of spaceflight correctly.

Only then, feeling much cheered, did he call the Relic pilot and say, "Threshold Consolidated Security vessel *Blue Tick* to X-99A. Lieutenant Reice here. Captain South, if you'll shut down your power plant, we'll tow you in to Threshold with our tug, here. We can't mate with your air lock." That was a lie. "It'll only take a few hours, and you'll be safe in the Trust Territory VIP lounge."

X-99A's com sputtered back: "I dunno anything about this Trust Territory. And I don't need to be towed. I need to talk to somebody from U.S. Space Command. If you can't manage that, how about you just escort me where somebody can . . ."

Oh boy, this was going to be a long day, after all. At least this South didn't sound too crazy. "X-99A? Look, South, Space Command's consolidated now. You've been away a long time. We're taking you to the Trust Territory of Threshold, population approximately two-hundred fifty thousand souls, including Sol Base Blue. We call it the Terminal. The local government's administered by USA/UNE—United States of America and United Nations of Earth, jointly. TTT is policed by UNE Peacekeeping, Consolidated Space Command, and Threshold ConSec—Threshold Consolidated Security. I'm your ConSec representative, Captain South, and the officer in charge of your case until we get you into the loving arms of the Stalk—Threshold—bureaucracy. That make you feel better, Captain? Just like old times, I bet."

He hoped it did. The only way that Joseph South, Captain, U.S. Space Command, could talk to anybody in his direct chain of command was by going back in time, a service that nobody in the twenty-fifth century could provide.

There was a long, long pause before Captain South answered. "Yeah, okay, I get your point, *Blue Tick.* But I still don't need a tow. Why can't—"

"Look, Relic, we don't want a malfunctioning fusion power plant in our docking bay, or maybe you don't realize we're not going to give you a parking slot in nice empty space where, if you blow yourself to bits, you won't hurt anyone."

The tug was almost alongside the X-99A. The backup was already in position, sighting up the X-99A's butt. In a couple of minutes, the situation was going to degenerate markedly—as soon as the captain of the Relic craft heard the grapples hit his hull, if not before.

And South wasn't responding.

"South? X-99A, this is *Blue Tick.* Do you copy?"

No reply.

Maybe the Relic pilot had some sort of weapon aboard after all. Reice's palms began to sweat. For the first time since he'd sighted the antique craft, Reice's own safety, and that of his ship, became a focus of his concern. He uncrossed his legs and stretched on his flight deck. His fingers trailed over a panel above his head, touching emergency recording and broadcasting procedures to life.

Then again he called his traffic controller: "X-99A doesn't want to be towed. We're trying it anyway. You've got constant feed." He got off the circuit.

The *Tick* itself was now on priority alert. She would defend herself against any weapon that matched weapon parameters in her banks, including an attempt by the X-99A to ram her.

More than that, Reice couldn't do. So he got back on the horn to Joe South, trying to convince the crazy Relic that it would be better to be towed in willingly than unwillingly.

". . . willingly means, Captain, that we don't put a slug up your ass. Unwillingly means that you're coming in with five pounds of lead in your tail or your power plant kills you while we're trying to incapacitate your ship—with our apologies, of course."

"Screw you," said the Relic pilot.

But, at the last possible moment, the *Blue Tick*'s sensors told him that South had shut his systems, including the power plant, down, all but emergency life support.

Sucker didn't want to die, that was something. And he was smart enough, though that didn't prove he was sane. With the fusion plant shut down, the chances of any mishap resulting from a KKD impacting the rear of the X-99A were nil.

As a matter of fact, the need for a KKD was nil.

Reice called the backup cruiser and told him to follow along, ready to shoot if X-99A powered up.

Then he called the tug and confirmed his previous orders, keeping in contact during the whole grappling operation.

Then he called South again, but nobody answered.

Maybe emergency life support didn't include ship-to-ship communications. Or maybe the captain was just sulking.

Or maybe the Relic was another psycho, like the last one, running around inside that ancient ship trying to turn it into a fusion bomb or planning to ram the cruiser or find some other way to make Reice disobey orders and lose captain, ship, or the much-desired low profile this mission was supposed to be keeping.

Reice kept trying to contact the X-99A and her captain long after the tug started hauling her into port. All he got from the Relic ship was maddening silence.

Maddening.

The X-99A was cold as a grave to all sensors, except for emergency life-support readings and a heat signature from one human body that could be dead and still giving off readings, if South had killed himself in some crazy gesture.

Again, Reice tried to raise the captain of the X-99A.

Again, he got no answer.

So he called the data in, personally, to Mickey Croft's office and waited for a response, even though he was sending a constant data feed up through channels.

He hated to do that. He really did. But it was Croft's office staff who'd insisted on picking up the Relic ship in the first place. If Reice had had his way, they'd have let it go on by Threshold. Its primitive astronics would never have picked up something it wasn't looking for.

Then the X-99A wouldn't have been anybody's problem until it crashed and burned in the electromagnetic shield around the Earth, or suffered some handy mishap in the months it would have taken to get that far, or Captain South tried his high-handed tactics on Consolidated Space Command and got himself and his ancient ship blown to component atoms.

But you couldn't tell Croft's office anything. And you couldn't go on the record with suggestions contrary to Threshold policy. Ever.

Trust Territory of Threshold made the rules out here. Captain Joseph South was going to find that out soon enough.

CHAPTER 3

Some Days . . .

No matter how you try, or how good you are at your job, some days are just magnets for events. Whatever action's around, it'll surface on one of those days. You'll get a block of time where everything's nice and controllable, smooth and low-key. Then you got a day like today, when everything that Mickey Croft and staff could do on full power wasn't enough to keep things on an even keel.

So it followed that today would be the day that some ConSec lieutenant decided to tow in a Relic from humanity's past, whether that Relic wanted to be towed in or not.

Michael Croft was Secretary General of the Trust Territory of Threshold, therefore human rights were high on his list of prioritized concerns. All he needed was for some Threshold Civil Liberties lawyer—of which they had a surfeit right now, because of the conference—to decide that the Relic's rights were being violated, or decide to make himself a star by choosing to define the gray area in which the rights of Relics currently existed.

Croft turned from his littered desk to the window behind him, looking out over Blue Mid, and Central Stalk's administrative district, and "down" on Blue South. If Croft unwound his lanky person from his chair and went to stand by the window, with his forehead pressed to it, he could just glimpse a triangle of star-dusted space from his office. Everywhere else, the Central Stalk and its proliferation of modules occluded his view of the stars.

It was easy to forget, on days like this, that he wasn't working in Manhattan. But he wasn't. Michael Croft was a forty-five-year-old widower frustrated by an unstoppable proliferation of red tape in his attempts to be a "good bureaucrat" (not, to his way of thinking, a contradiction in terms). He'd been born on Threshold, schooled at Exeter, Oxford, and Harvard, and migrated back to his home when the UNE shifted its headquarters out here, between the orbits of Mars and Jupiter.

Croft had the long bones and apparent fragility of the space-bred—a fine, horse face; lank, thinning hair as pale as the rest of him. His ancestors had been "Air Barons," who'd mined the moon and asteroids and gotten rich supplying the expanding need for liquid oxygen. Latter-day blue bloods such as Mickey Croft seldom were idle: his fortune was only four generations old and the responsibilities that went with opening the stars were his real inheritance.

The only true luxury, in his own terms, that Mickey Croft possessed was a psychometric sampler-modeler, which allowed him to create a simulacrum of a person and interact with it, interrogate it, pose problems to it, and practice his own diplomatic performance on it.

But he couldn't use the modeler on the Relic, even if he'd had the leisure to try: you had to have data to model a personality. There was almost no data on the Relic. And there was no time to be concerned with the Relic, one Captain South, and the possible problems he represented until they became real problems.

Not today. Not with Threshold full of confreres from the diplomatic community and touchy Muslims who'd rather be on Earth for their religious ceremony, but couldn't get any closer than Threshold by UNE decree—a decree that Croft had helped create.

Staring blindly at his window, but not out of it, Croft pulled on his long nose and touched a button on the curve of his chair's arm. "Get me Remson."

His assistant's voice came immediately from the grillwork on his desk. "Remson's out with the Muslim VIP group, sir." The young voice was vainly trying to hide its wonder that his Fearless Leader had forgotten something.

"Get him for me anyway, Dodd. And see if you can postpone my meeting with the head mullah and his daughter . . . until, say, tomorrow morning." On a different day, things would go better.

"Ah, sir, they're coming up from security now. I just had confirmation."

"Well, that's that. Still, have Remson check in with me. Patch him through whenever. I want to talk to him about this Relic mess. And you be ready to squire the mullah—" Croft spun his chair and looked at his calendar screen. "—Beni Forat, and his daughter, Dini, on a quick tour of the offices if Remson calls while they're here."

Dodd said, "My pleasure, sir. Nobody—not Lieutenant Reice or anybody else—has called with anything else about the Relic, sir. . . ."

"Let's hope nobody does." Croft toggled off the intercom and began clearing his desk for the Forat meeting.

When Dodd buzzed him, he expected to be told that the Forats were outside or Remson was on the line.

Instead, young Dodd said, "It's Riva Lowe from Customs, sir. She says she has to talk to you privately, it's urgent."

Now there was a sullen tone in the youngster's voice that conjured up an image of the fat-faced boy whose father had been a friend of Croft's father, complete with set jaw and petulant mouth drawn tight.

"Put her on my vid," Croft said, and braced for whatever the woman had to say that needed a secure line.

The vid cleared to an image of Riva Lowe, whose feral magnetism never translated well to video, and who was so intensely troubled that her face wasn't pretty at all right now, just haughty and deep-eyed and fierce: "Mickey, I've got something so sensitive I'm not even going to chance describing it this way. You've got to come down here."

"No I don't. Customs is your barrel, you roll it around. I've got more on my plate today than ten people could handle, and two Muslims from Medina on their way up here right now—heavy hitters." He saw her frown but didn't pause for breath. "But I'm glad you called. Remson's got a tour group on his hands, and I need somebody to take charge of Reice's Relic."

"Whose what?"

"Reice—Lieutenant Reice of ConSec is towing in a Relic. Meet them at the docking bay. Avoid attorneys. Keep it civilized. Bury the whole thing in paperwork until the conference is over and the pilgrims leave, and I'll take you to dinner with your whole staff, anywhere you say."

"Give me your modeler for a couple days, and it's a deal," said Riva Lowe, who might have been his type ten years ago, before he'd fallen in love and gotten married and lost his wife in a quick and intense tutorial on what emotions can do to a man. Riva, quick on the uptake, was no longer looking for aid. But not yet finished with him: her face had changed; now it was canny and somehow bold. She brushed back a wisp of brown hair that had fallen over her forehead. "And give me carte blanche with the unexplicated problem I called about, as well."

"It's a deal," Croft said airily. "Just let me know as we go along if I'm in danger, personally or professionally, because of anything you're doing with my authority."

"I told you we can't talk about it on the comlink," she said, and again the sharpness was there. "I'm assuming this make-no-waves mode of yours will continue to take priority for, say, the next forty-eight hours or so."

"Indeed it will. Give me a hint."

"Come see me, big fella." She nearly smiled.

"I'll try, but there's no chance of it before twenty-one hundred hours, so I'll call first."

"By then," Riva Lowe told him solemnly, "we'll be committed."

"Terrific. I must say, this mystery is truly lightening up my afternoon."

"You know where I am, sir. And you have a meeting, so I won't keep you. . . . I'm rather going to enjoy exercising my new power." Now she did smile, but it wasn't a fetching smile. It was a grim one. "Bye."

She rang off only seconds before Dodd told him his appointment had arrived.

The mullah was in full, archaic dress, but his daughter, Dini, was in a modern version of it that made Croft's pulse pound: Dini Forat was a breathtakingly beautiful, gravity-raised teenager with amazing muscle tone clearly obvious through a translucent robe, under which she wore a form-hugging purple one-piece that Croft would see in his dreams for years.

How could a fifteen-year-old have the body of a twenty-five-year-old temptress? And the hungry lips of destruction?

Her father had a beard and a turban and Croft was hard-pressed to penetrate his accent or keep his mind on what the father had to say. Dini's hip-long black curls kept tangling in his thoughts.

Squiring this pair on a tour of the facility was going to be a mixed blessing, but one that Croft suddenly decided he couldn't very well avoid.

The thing about this sort of day, when too much was happening, was that good things overcrowded your schedule, as well as bad things. Progress could be made with these two, if Croft could convince the father that keeping the faithful on Threshold was to everyone's benefit. And if he could do that, Croft could get on to the dicier subjects he needed to bring up with Medina's head mullah: the human rights problems that the UNE saw in Medina's slavelike underclass, and the question of defining "human" in relation to that underclass.

Human/subhuman/alien rights abuse issues were at the center of Croft's conference, and the center of his concerns. The sect that ruled on Medina considered all nonbelievers as soulless infidels, and thus subhuman. The indigenous species on Medina, and its bioengineered bodyguard class, complicated the problem.

But reasonable men could do wonders together. Croft held his hand out to the mullah, and said, "I'm so pleased to have this time alone with you, Ayatollah Forat. Shall we begin our tour with the hajj facility?"

"It's the hajj facility only if I say so, Secretary Croft," growled the squat, bearded man, who sniffed through his hooked nose before he took Croft's hand.

"We hope you'll find it to your liking," Croft said with more aplomb than he felt. Forat's hand was rough and the grip was challengingly, almost painfully, tight.

"Inshallah," said the daughter softly, which made Croft turn his head.

"Excuse me?"

"Inshallah—it's the hajj facility, Secretary Croft, only if God wills it. Surely my father remembers that."

Fire in those eyes. Shoulders back. Mickey Croft had to remind himself of what a good diplomat he was, to get his mind back on business. But he couldn't help worrying that a young girl such as this was bound to get into trouble on Threshold if someone didn't take her in hand. And obviously she was looking for one or the other—either some trouble to get into, or someone to take her in hand.

Casting about for a way to assure the young woman's safety without seeming overly interested, Croft maneuvered them toward the outer office.

There was always Dodd. He was young, and discreet, and available.

But Dini Forat's lip curled when she looked at Dodd, and Croft was too good a diplomat to force matters obviously.

Still, nothing ventured nothing gained. As he always did, he introduced his assistant formally, and said, though his heart wasn't in it, "Mr. Dodd will be available to show you around this evening, Ms. Forat, if you choose."

To his surprise, the girl looked up at him and said, "With my father's permission, I'd enjoy that very much."

The mullah sized up pasty young Dodd, nodded, and said, "This is acceptable, with a bodyguard, of course."

Croft's eyes squeezed shut of their own accord. It was too

early to discuss bodyguards. "Perhaps your schedule will permit you to let me show you around this evening, sir."

"Sir" obviously wasn't sufficiently honorific, but Croft needed to assert at least parity, if not primacy, here on his home turf.

The little mullah said, "Of course, with a bodyguard." And smiled, showing big, yellow teeth.

Croft wasn't the only one in this room who knew that the bodyguard matter was about to become an issue. Well, Croft would consider it research. Having seen for himself what the bodyguards were like and how they were treated, he'd be in an authoritative position, not a compromised one.

So he said, "That would please me greatly." And the battle was joined.

This was going to be one marvelous evening. For a moment Croft had a vision of changing places with Dodd, and escorting the teenage temptress to some of Threshold's more exciting nightspots. But it just wasn't in the cards, not for him.

And Dodd's father, whether he knew it or not, now owed Mickey Croft one bottle of fifty-year-old Scotch when next they met.

CHAPTER 4

$$\triangledown$$

Pilgrim's Progress

Dini Forat was sure that Threshold was paradise. It was full of bright lights and dizzying, glorious vistas. Everywhere was beauty, everywhere was excitement and luxury and bright-eyed, young people with unveiled faces and marvelous clothes.

Nowhere was dirt. Nowhere was squalor. Nowhere was pain or misery or want. Here beggars did not sit with their bowls beside your palace. Here people were never without an eye or a hand. Here it never rained or snowed, the wind never howled with the wrath of Allah. Neither frogs nor hail pelted from the sky.

And here were the men of Threshold, like Secretary Croft, pale-skinned and blue-eyed and tall, so tall. Trailing along in the wake of her father and the Secretary, she found herself wishing that Croft was her parent, that she had been brought up in the secular, decadent world that Croft inhabited, a world of colored lights and turbo lifts and shiny electric cars.

Even the watchdog beside her, first in the car and now on the streets, didn't bother her. Much. This Dodd was short and squat and dark and ugly, like everyone she knew at home.

Dini wanted to get away from the other pilgrims so much

that she could taste it. As their party encountered another made up of turbaned men and veiled women, she lowered her eyes in shame. She wanted to pretend she wasn't one of them. She wanted freedom. She wanted to cast off every veil and run about in pants, alone, wearing neon jewelry and carrying a bag full of wonders the way the laughing blond girls she saw on the streets were doing.

Nowhere she had ever been was as cosmopolitan as Threshold's Rec Level One, where Croft had seen—must have seen—the gleam in her eye when he turned in the car to see how she was faring, and allowed that they could walk instead of ride.

She could shop, so Croft said. Her father fumed, but his conversation with Croft took precedence: low, diplomatic fencing, not meant for her ears. She didn't care. She would shop, with the watchdog Dodd in tow like any bodyguard.

She treated him as one, handing him packages that Dodd would pay for, showing a credit card her father had sourly handed him—not her—when it became clear that *not* shopping would be a sticky matter, if not a breach of protocol.

Dini Forat had never felt such power. At home, she was hardly ever with her father, let alone with him in a situation where her good behavior must be bought. Their own bodyguards, she saw when she turned and looked past a rack of scandalous clothes, were on their heels, nostrils wide, dumb eyes shifting from possible danger to possible danger, always ready to leap upon their charges with superhuman speed and shield them from harm with their bodies.

She hated bodyguards. They were horrid machines who thought they were human, and bled like humans, and yet had no souls or even the will to live.

Like the warriors she had met at home, the right death was all that really mattered to the bodyguards.

Dini Forat was committed to the right life. Life coursed in her more demandingly than ever, tingling up and down inside her as she strode to a fitting room with a handful of garments that, at home, she never would have dared to buy.

Her father was glowering at her, when she came out clad

in tight white pants and a shirt with ballooning sleeves that cupped her breasts and thrust them forth, unveiled.

She said pointedly to Dodd, "Do I look like a Threshold resident of good breeding?" and turned around once as if she were still in belly-dancing school, arm above her head and hips swaying.

Dodd said, "You look . . . amazing. Perfect. I could take you to a club I know, a private club," he added hastily. "Very chic. Later. If your father and the Secretary are going to be talking all night . . . ?"

She said (nearly squealed, playing dumb but knowing exactly how to put her plan into action), "Oh, yes! I'd love that. Here, have them wrap up my old clothes and I'll wear these. And this." She reached over and grabbed a sling bag, into which, as she followed Dodd to the counter, she put everything she thought should go there: a little portable phone, an electronic makeup artist with a cosmetic pack, a wallet, and a *Guide to Threshold Nightlife*.

Dodd paid, and when he had, she took the card from him and put it in her new wallet, smiling.

The dizzy watchdog was too excited at the prospect that later he might get his nose between her thighs to realize how outrageous it was that any of this was happening.

She snuck a look at her father, who was talking animatedly to Croft. Was his face darker than usual? Suffused with rage? She didn't know. She didn't care. Threshold awaited.

"Let's go now," she said, when Dodd came up with her old clothes. (She was veilless in free society! Her head was totally uncovered, her throat and neck and breasts as well!) "They're just talking government, as old men will always do. Show me a place to get music, and vids, and then let's go find a coffee, and pastry, and . . ."

Little, fat, dark Dodd was giggling. "Well, that's a tall order, but let me see if I can't prevail on the two of them to turn us loose now on my recognizance."

She pretended to be looking at yet another outfit while Dodd, unknowingly, asked the impossible. Her father would not wish to seem parochial, nor to offend by questioning the propriety or the security of Croft's hospitality. Dini had been waiting for such a chance so long she had thought out every nuance.

Off she would go, with a bodyguard or two behind and this short, ugly—but free—infidel beside, into the wondrous world of Threshold. And beyond.

She had her credit card in her own purse. She had clothes that made her unremarkable. She had, for the first time, a chance to let some of the urgency in her body and in her soul escape.

Dodd had a mole on his lip and those lips were not thin enough for Dini's taste. She wanted a man like Croft, but younger. A bold, tall, fair stranger who believed in nothing at all but life and living it, a techno-wizard, an outlaw baron of the sort she saw on vid shows.

She wanted a life. A real life, with real risk and real pleasure. She didn't want to hurt Dodd, not his feelings or his career, but living life meant breaking rules. She had been living by rules long enough to know that for a certainty.

When the fat lips told her, "Okay, but we have to stay in touch. Your father's insisted on sending a bodyguard, of course, but I imagine he'll stay out of the way. I have to get you back to your rooms by eleven—by twenty-three hundred —but that doesn't mean we can't have fun, even before the dark clubs open."

"Dark clubs?"

"Places that open at Zero Zero Zero time: nobody knows how they got their name exactly. Remember, Threshold was military, at first. Sol Base Blue still is, really—all the Blue North to Blue South modules on the Central Stalk are ConSec, ConSpaceCom, Peacekeeping and Administration, and military slang's probably the best place to look for the term's derivation. Spacers still say oh-dark-thirty when they mean half past midnight. . . ."

The watchdog rattled on, and Dini made interested noises without really listening. She was watching a miracle, the first real miracle she had ever seen.

Her father and Secretary Croft—looking so ill-matched,

tall and short, dark and light, fat and thin—were getting into their car and pulling away; behind them, all but one bodyguard, Ali-4, followed.

And so it was done. So she had dreamed it, but never had she expected to succeed.

She turned in a full circle: There was not a pilgrim on this street, nor one for as far as her eye could see. Everywhere were gleaming windows full of wonders and lighted squares towering into a bright hologram of ceiling that seemed to go up forever, though she knew it did not.

"And now, Ms. Forat, your wish is my command," said Dodd, sticking out his arm, bent at the elbow. Ali-4 was watching attentively, so she took it.

"Wish?" she smiled. "What may I wish for?"

"A tour of more shops, a go at the galleries, a VIP look at Sol Base Blue, a museum or two, something to eat or drink—"

"Drink. I would like a drink. Somewhere there is music and dancing."

Dodd raised a too-thick eyebrow. "It's a little early, here, for music and dancing, but I'll do my best. We can certainly find prerecorded music, and later I'll get a concert schedule. . . ."

Dini Forat went arm in arm through a nearby doorway with the ugly young man, who was beginning to seem less ugly because he was so worldly and wise. There was nothing within but a great twirling escalator, with a shining rail that wound its way out of sight. "You'll like this place. Best on this level for French wines."

Praise be to Allah, she heard herself think, and stopped the thought with a superstitious chill. She was going to have her first taste of alcohol. She was going into a bar, unveiled, with a man she hardly knew. Her knees shook as she stepped onto the escalator with the stranger.

Her life was beginning. She'd known she would find a way.

When, at the head of the stairs, an implacable robotic headwaiter demanded a club card for entrance, she knew she was truly free: the bodyguard, Ali-4, had no such card.

He was discreetly behind, and Dodd didn't think to bring him past the robot-attended barrier.

The door closed, and Ali-4 was outside it, while she, cut off from all restraint, faced a room full of young, sophisticated people who did not know the heavy burden of sin that she always had, and were laughing because of that.

When she found a way to shake off this Dodd, this watchdog of her father's friend, then the transition would be complete.

Dini Forat was never going back to Medina. Never. Not if she had to stow away on a ship bound for a new colony. This had been in her mind forever. It had been the reason she'd contrived to accompany her father, while making sure he could not guess her motive.

It was the reason that she had not killed herself long since. Her body knew what she needed, and knew that on Medina it was not possible.

Here she would find all she had been denied: she would taste wine, and freedom, and love.

Somewhere among the men of Threshold, she would find a man. The right man. A pale, fair man who would teach her of love and fall in love with her and marry her and then her father would not dare to try to force her home, deflowered and disgraced.

The most important thing had been getting free of her father. The next most important thing had been getting free of Ali-4. Now the most important thing was getting free of Dodd, the lackey watchdog. Then the most important thing would be getting free of her virginity.

With that gone, she could begin to make a life on Threshold, or even among the stars.

Dodd and she sat at a mirrored table and wine was brought in tall, graceful glasses, wine with bubbles in it, which tickled her nose.

Soon enough, he had drunk and she had drunk and everything was beginning to seem much sillier than life had ever seemed before.

But she held firm to her purpose. She had read about

alcohol. She had watched vid. She knew that if you became too drunk, you could not think.

And she must think, to make good the rest of her escape.

But first, she must find a place to relieve herself. She stumbled over her tongue, asking Dodd for the "woman's room."

"Oh, yeah—waiter." And he asked a man where such a place might be. She was truly shocked. She felt herself flush.

Dodd squeezed her hand as she got up to leave and she was astounded at his forwardness. She'd shaken off the touch before she realized he meant no harm. Nor was he trying to restrain or detain her.

He was just . . . a person of Threshold.

She said, trying to be clear because the drink had befuddled her tongue, "I am going to relieve my water like any other person of Threshold. Right back, I'll come."

"It's fine. Take as long as you like," said Dodd.

She would do just that.

And when she found the place marked for women's use, in it was another woman.

This woman had a white-and-black outfit and was very helpful, telling her "The back door's easy to find, honey, if you want to just go through the kitchen."

The woman asked no questions about why she wanted to find a different way out of this place.

Dini volunteered nothing, used the stall, and then left quickly.

Her heart was pounding. Would Dodd see?

It seemed he had not, when she reached the kitchen and hurried through it, eyes down to avoid catching stares from cooks in white.

Then she was out of the place and climbing down manual stairs, and going through a door that opened before her, so that she was on a street.

And it was not the same street on which the building fronted, not the same street at all. This street was an interior place, with no dazzling lights, just many back doors.

A sign to her left said LOADING ZONE/FREIGHT ELEVATOR.

She walked down it, and a door opened.

She got in the lift and punched a destination at random, too excited to take out her Threshold guide and try to figure out where she might be.

The freight elevator door closed. She hugged her arms. When it opened again, she would be somewhere Ali-4 could never find her.

She would be alone and abroad on Threshold, with a credit card and a new life ahead.

She knew that using the card would give her away, eventually. But before then, she intended to fall in love. And after that, everything would be different.

With luck, she would find a credit machine right away, get scrip out of it, and not need to use the card again for days, perhaps not until it was too late for her father ever to be able to drag her back to the prison world of Medina, among the pilgrims.

Perhaps she could evade him until after the hajj!

The lift settled, sighed, and opened its doors. She blinked at a dark street with a less pleasant sort of light, bars of it, illuminating hulks of ships and huge trailers and cargo modules.

But then she heard laughter, and saw a man and a woman unsteadily climbing the steps to a place called BAR.

This would do. This would certainly do for a start.

CHAPTER 5

$\triangledown$

A Little Courtesy

Normally, the Flangers that Richard Cummings III was bringing to Threshold would be quarantined by Customs for three weeks, no matter how much clout Cummings, the heir apparent to NAMECorp, tried to apply.

But these weren't normal times. The Flangers were mansized chimpanzee-faced marsupials newly discovered on Olympus, a planet under NAMECorp administration. The species was being considered as possible med-experiment replacements for terrestrial animals. This made having some samples available during Croft's Life-form Rights conference a North American Exploration Corporation priority.

Aboard the *Beau Vista*, Rick Cummings had three Flangers, two females and a male, comfy in his cargo bay. As the ship he'd leased from his father's company powered down and settled into its docking slip, the freighter's AI did all the work. So Cummings had plenty of time to worry about whether his scam would work.

He'd ram the Flangers through Customs, he was almost sure. He hadn't trekked all the way from Pegasus's Nostril (the space habitat NAMECorp had put in orbit around Olympus) to fail in the eyes of his father, Richard Cummings, Jr.

No, the Flangers weren't what was worrying him. That

agenda was overt and arguably to the benefit of everybody on Threshold, including NAMECorp, one of Threshold Terminal's major stockholders.

Rick Cummings's dry mouth and knotted stomach were the direct results of the little somethings he had stashed in the marsupial-type pouch of each Flanger—things he didn't want discovered. Secreted there were Leetles—half-inch-long beetles that tasted like lettuce and had an unmatched psychotropic effect on humans when ingested.

Leetles were already contraband, even back on the Pegasus habitat. But Cummings had to have the Leetles, even if it was risky smuggling them in here. Without the Leetles, the real smugglers' prize, a third Olympian life-form he'd dubbed Brow, would die before he got one into the NAMECorp Lab Base. If you were the first to bring a new life-form to any NAMECorp Lab Base, the reward was staggering, and the no-questions-asked policy would protect him from embarrassing charges.

After all, NAMECorp was his father's company. And bringing the Brows to Threshold was so outrageous, so amazing, so audacious and so lucrative that Cummings III just couldn't pass up the chance. The reward would augment his trust fund nicely. The coup would force his father to stop treating him like a teenager.

And the Brows were . . . well, once you'd had one around, you didn't want to be without one. When Dad found out what the Brows could do, he'd understand why Rick hadn't taken them to a lesser Lab Base. Only the top levels of NAMECorp bureaucracy could be trusted with the secret of the Brows, and that ruled out long memo chains and interstellar communications nets.

Rick Cummings needed to display the raccoon-pelted telepathic Brows to a select group, because a Brow who'd just eaten a Leetle could affect the mental processes of humans in any way its master chose. So this master was going to be very careful about which humans received a demonstration.

It was too bad that the Leetles were contraband. It was clear that humans shouldn't be eating them, but it was necessary for Brows to eat them. Otherwise, the Brows would die.

So Cummings's hands were sweating as he watched his flight deck put itself in neutral and waited for the green light. Then it was Show Time.

One of his Brows sensed his nervousness and tried to climb into his lap. He had the three Brows on the flight deck and three Flangers in the cargo bay because, if he left the Brows to their own devices back there, they'd find some way into the Flangers' cages to get at the Leetles, eat all the Leetles in one sitting, and be sick.

He couldn't have that. He'd fed each Brow one Leetle, and they were at peak performance levels, right where he needed them.

He wasn't going to try to hide them. He was going to use them. That was the whole point of this exercise.

He let the Brow climb into his lap. It looked enough like an Earthly raccoon to fool most people, who'd never seen a raccoon except on vid. So that was a help.

With closed eyes, he stroked the Brow behind it ears and under its snout, which was shorter than an earthly raccoon's. While he did, he closed his eyes and visualized what he wanted the Customs official's visit to be like. He wanted to shake hands with the Customs official who came aboard and he wanted to sign his paperwork and he wanted everything to seem unremarkable. He wanted the one Brow to pass for a raccoon and the other two to be unnoticed—unlisted on the manifest. And he wanted the entire maneuver to proceed flawlessly.

The Brow stretched out on his lap and began to whistle softly in pleasure, blowing little bubbles where its black lips met.

He knew enough about working with Brows by now to be sure it was going to try to give him the result he'd shown it. Everything would be pleasant, friendly, and the Brow would ride out of here on his shoulder.

When a Customs officer in blue uniform showed up with a

computerized clipboard and asked for permission to come aboard, Cummings felt almost relieved.

Either it would work or it wouldn't work. If it didn't work, and the Customs man insisted on quarantining the Flangers or discovered the Leetles or the Brows, then the Brows would starve to death and Cummings would be in jail for smuggling. He tried not to think about it. You projected the result you wanted to the Brows, and they matched it.

But the Brow on Rick's lap sensed his concern that the man coming aboard might be a possible enemy. It climbed up on his shoulder, wrapped its ringed tail about his neck, and stopped whistling.

Instead, it hissed once.

In back of Rick Cummings, where the flight deck ended and the bulkhead began, something rustled: the other Brows were alerted by the hissing of the first.

Onto the flight deck came the blue-uniformed Customs officer, and Cummings smiled at him.

The man, eyes on his clipboard, smiled, too.

"Richard Cummings III?" said the florid official, still smiling absently as he looked up. Welcome sparkled in his eyes. "We hope you had a pleasant flight."

"Flawless, Officer," Cummings said, nodding, still exuding as much happiness as he could manage.

"Anything to declare, sir?" asked the Customs man diffidently, nearly chuckling, as if he'd made a joke.

The Brow's tail tightened around Cummings's neck as he stood up. "Nothing that's not already on the manifest I transmitted." He stroked the Brow's tail. "My pet, of course, who's had all his shots, and the Flangers whose paperwork we expedited. They're here for the conference, and I'm certainly happy to be delivering them in person." It didn't matter what he said, as long as it was nonconfrontational.

The other Brows were simply not going to exist. Neither were the Leetles. Cummings was determined to win this one.

"Well, I'll just have a quick look back there, sir, and you're on your way."

"Let me come with you," Cummings offered and, still with the first Brow balanced on his shoulder, led the official back to where the Flanger cages were.

In the cargo hold of the 300T freighter, the cages looked tiny, lonely, insignificant.

"See?" Cummings said, pulling down one peepscreen with a touch: "Safe and sound."

The Flanger stared at the peepscreen with mournful eyes and bit its nails. But it seemed to smile as it did so. Cummings smiled until his face ached. The tail of the Brow on his shoulder was twitching.

The Customs man said, "Seems to be good condition, sir," and then walked on to the next cage.

When the officer had peeped into the remaining cages and determined that the other two Flangers were alive and well, he handed Cummings the manifest to thumbprint.

Cummings checked it, pushed his thumb against the touch-sensitive square, and was rewarded with another official smile.

The Customs officer then pulled a hard copy from the handheld's slot. He offered it to Cummings with a flourish. "Here you go, sir. Have a nice stay on Threshold. We're rather overrun lately, with all these folk in for the conference and the Muslim pilgrimage at the same time. So you don't need to take this to the office. We're waiving a pro forma interview, since your documentation's impeccable and I've done my on-site."

"Wonderful, Officer. The sooner I have these Flangers in the Lab Base facility, the happier I'll be."

Happy was the key word, after all. He paced the Customs official out of the cargo hold and all the way to the outer lock, where he stood, stroking the Brow's tail, as the man waved a jaunty farewell before he got in his open truck and drove away.

Free and safe, home at last. Cummings looked up and down the NAMECorp docking bay. No other Customs people or troublemakers in sight. He checked his chronograph:

the NAMECorp truck would arrive any minute, to pick up the Flangers and take them to the Lab Base.

And he, his three Brows, and the Leetles in the Flangers' pouches were safe on Threshold, with duly executed entry notations in their Customs file and hard copy to boot.

As Cummings saw one of his father's trucks approaching, he put away the hard copy that allowed him to bring in "life-forms—4/type: flangers (3); raccoon (1)."

He could almost feel the fat reward slide into his bank account. He could almost hear his father's amazed admiration when the Lab Base techs told him what the Brows could do.

This was going to be more fun than eating Leetles, although he might do a little of that, too, once the gravid mothers hatched up a new crop.

CHAPTER 6

Scavenger's Horde

Riva Lowe took one look at the scruffy Relic pacing back and forth behind a one-way mirror and closed her eyes.

Customs was a stinking job sometimes, like now when you had real trouble and not enough priority to deal with that trouble effectively. Riva Lowe should have been high in the diplomatic service by now, dealing with people of consequence. But she wasn't.

And it must be her fault. There was something she'd done, consistently, to limit her options. She was smarter than most, more dedicated than most, but she was also underperforming compared to most of the people she'd gone to school with. She was as hard on herself as she was on others, and if that—her knack for calling things as she saw them and demanding competency in exchange for respect—was what was holding her back, then there wasn't much she could do about it.

She opened her eyes and the five-hundred-year-old pilot was still there. She should, at least, be working on the truly sensitive matters at hand. This beard-shadowed, shaggy-headed fellow in a museum-quality uniform ought to be the concern of some other department—any other department.

But she'd let Mickey Croft push this Captain South onto her desk in exchange for . . . what? A favor owed, and some time with his modeler. She'd scrolled the file on this South, and there wasn't any reason to hold the Relic if he could pass a physical.

Not, that is, if you discounted Reice's abrasive first encounter. Riva Lowe knew Reice better than most, and that meant that she was willing to give South the benefit of the doubt. Reice would hash out the pecking order with an automated waiter in a coffee shop if you left him to his own devices.

"Reice," she said absently, not taking her eyes off the man pacing like a zoo animal before her because, like an animal, he seemed to know that she was there. Throughout his ten-stride circuits of the room, his eyes never left the wall between them, which was mirrored on his side and reinforced high-impact glass on hers.

"Yeah, boss," said Reice in his inimitable fashion, managing to lace the words with provocation.

Still she didn't turn. "Get this man to the medics and have them do a full physical work-up. If he's plague-free and not a carrier of any small organisms restricted here, give him a provisional ID card, some sort of work permit with a low credit advance against whatever his back pay will turn out to be. Check with ConSpaceCom and get them computing that number."

"A work permit?" Reice sounded as if he thought she'd lost her mind.

"A work permit." Her nails dug into the briefcase she held. "With a parole notation so he'll have to check in every two weeks. There's no telling how long it will take ConSpaceCom to find a way to fleece him out of however much money he's got coming."

"These Relics can be dangerous, Riva. Are you sure you want to—"

She turned on Reice. "I can be dangerous," she told Reice as she brushed past him. "Don't forget that. Especially when I'm this busy." She headed for the door leading out of the gray cubicle, from which prisoners could be viewed while being interrogated beyond the mirrored wall.

She hated police stations: They were all alike; the presumption of guilt by the mere fact of presence was so strong, she could taste it.

That poor Relic was in for a very hard time. She didn't see any reason to make it more difficult.

But Reice wouldn't let things stand: "Ma'am, I'm not sure that's all we need to do about Captain South."

"That's for the medics to decide, isn't it? Whether he's competent. If he's not, he'll be in therapy for a bit and you and I can discuss his status at leisure." *When I get my more pressing matters attended to.*

Croft had told her to bury the Relic in paperwork. Giving him a full med work-up would do just that. "I've discussed this with Deputy Secretary Remson," she said warningly, "and he concurs. We don't want to attract any attorneys, if you get my drift."

"I do, but—" The ConSec lieutenant wasn't convinced.

Riva Lowe resented the need to discuss this any further. There were always lawyers lurking in police stations. Everyone who was brought in for even the shortest detention deserved representation. Croft specifically wanted to avoid legal tangles where this Relic was concerned. Reice should be savvy enough by now to understand.

"Be nice to him, Reice. If you can't remember how, fake it. We don't want him upset with the way we've treated him here. We don't want to charge him with anything. We want to get South over to Med without wasting a single moment more than is absolutely necessary, and with no police record, not even a parking ticket. Is that clear?"

"Clear." Unhappy. Unconvinced.

And Reice's footsteps said he was going to follow her out the door and argue.

So Lowe turned to face him one more time. "I've got to go now. Check back with me at the end of your shift. I'll be done then and you can report your progress over a cup of coffee."

Reice's tight, dark face relaxed. But they were still both on duty.

"Yes ma'am," he said, with only a hint of a smile.

And she left him there, fleeing through the busy station with its auto-debriefers and its criminal processing cubicles full of unhappy people, to find her blue Customs car waiting.

She told it to take her to her office at Blue Mid Wheel, Spoke 8, where she'd instructed her real problem to meet her twenty minutes ago.

It probably would have been faster to use a vacuum tube, but she already had the car. In it, she could catch up on some paperwork and tell her office to update her. Which it did. There was an early notation of a strange reading during a preliminary scan of an incoming NAMECorp ship, but it wasn't substantiated by the subsequent inspection by one of her best officers. She signed off on the document and then on the next, and the next, hardly reading them.

When she was done with that, she asked for the results of the scans she'd requested on her real concern: a scavenger's spacedocked salvage.

The scans made no sense whatsoever, not in ultraviolet, infrared, heat, X-ray, or any other signature mode. Not unless there was nothing at all within the skin of the salvaged remnant. But the skin wasn't any kind of alloy that Customs equipment could identify.

"Wonderful," she said aloud. Then she read on: none of the cratology programs had found a shape or a density inside the salvaged container. None of the signature readers reported anything. No available technology could indicate anything whatsoever about the container except that it was there, about a metric ton of it, and that it was spherical and that it reflected light waves in a manner consonant with a class of metal alloys.

Oh goody, the mystery was deepening. She hoped to hell the plot wasn't thickening. If the scavenger in question was going to be pushy about his importation rights, this wasn't the time for it. If this was some kind of trick by a faction hopeful of disrupting the conference, or some Muslim scam to avoid the decree that kept off-world pilgrims from trekking any further in-system than Threshold, Mickey Croft would have her head.

But before that, she'd have the scavenger's head. One thing Customs could do, if it wanted, was take a very long time processing something. She didn't need to make a determination one way or the other about this scavenger's find. She simply had to begin examining it and let that examination take as long as possible.

She ought to be able to handle that; she had a strain of inscrutable Oriental cunning in her ancestry.

But scavengers could be difficult. She reached to her right, without looking, and fingered the autobar. Into the compartment below the bar dropped a caffeine/sugar drink with a mood-stabilizing component.

The drink would do the work of a three-course lunch, and she'd be ready for the scavenger.

But she wasn't, when she got back to her office to see him.

Something about the South case was bothering her, more than it should, if it were simply Reice overreacting to a possible threat and doing his courtship display at the same time. Reice was the last sort of entanglement she needed, as long as she was still considering herself upwardly mobile. Which she was. And South was . . . what?

Sad. Lost. Pathetic. Volatile. Reice hadn't been wrong about that. She could still see the ancient captain pacing behind that glass, looking like some tiger or lion, all coiled tension and wasted energy.

Med would deal with him. Riva Lowe knew what a sick man looked like, and Joe South wasn't sick. He was . . . primitive in a disturbing way that no medical exam was going to pinpoint. . . .

Faced with the scavenger waiting in her office, she pushed thoughts of South away. South wasn't going to take up another picosecond of her time.

This man was.

In the Blue Mid Customs office, with its government-issue standards and flags and pictures of Mickey Croft shaking her hand, the scavenger before her desk was like something that should have died with Captain South's century.

He was . . . dirty.

He was old and dirty.

He was old and dirty and raggedy and he . . . smelled.

The scavenger had a huge head with a yellow-white pony-tail and red ears. His face was craggy and either tanned or flushed from excessive alcohol consumption. The dirt smeared so thickly on his coveralls made it hard to read the mission patches on the coverall's arms.

It must be grease, Riva decided, as she realized that she was staring at him wordless and openmouthed.

"I'm waitin' fer the D'rector," the scavenger said, swivelling from his thick waist in the visitor's chair to look her over. "But I sure would appreciate a cup a' somethin'."

His shoulders reminded her of a wrestler's. His eyes were watery and pale. His lips were so chapped that they had actual cracks in them and the cracks were bright red under big brown flakes of dead skin. Behind his lips, his teeth were yellow, and green, and spotted with black.

Riva Lowe looked away, at the nice, clean UNE flag to one side of her desk, and then at the Customs standard on the other side. Then she took a deep breath. "You're looking *at* the Director. And I'm sure my man outside will be glad to get us both some tea."

"Tea?" The scavenger blinked at her. "Okay, tea."

She circled wide of him to get behind her desk. The stink was of grease and oil and perspiration.

How long had this scavenger been out there? Long enough to have come up with whatever it was. She sat primly behind her desk, then decided her body language was wrong and leaned one elbow on it, picking up a stylus with which she punched up his file.

"You've been working your way upchain to me for . . . sixteen hours, Mister . . . Keebler. That's fast work in any bureaucracy." She was scrolling his past data. This wasn't an uneducated person. This was an eccentric person, some sort of psychological misfit. A hermit with three Ph.D.'s and no assets but his salvage ship, his membership in a powerful union, and whatever it was that he had outside at spacedock.

"Well, D'rector, I been at this job a long, long while. I know when somethin's worth fightin' about."

"Oh yes?" She leaned back. "And what makes you think there's anything in that . . . container . . . you have out there?"

"You've got my statement. Statements. You've got your own people's reports—eleven of 'em, by my count, if everybody I talked to filed one. Whaddya think that is, came outta a white hole in an area that ain't been explored since the early days o' spaceflight, and then wasn't followed up because the ships sent out there didn't come back?"

"A piece of one of those ships?" she said hopefully. "Who knows what the stresses of collapsing into a black hole and then being spat out of a white one can do to metal?"

"Ma'am, no offense, but you don't know diddly about physics." The scavenger sat forward. "If that thing'd been part of a ship, an' fallen into a so-called black hole, by the time it got pushed out the other side—if ever—it'd be the size of a pellet of buckshot."

"Oh, well, then you don't think it fell into a black hole and was expelled out the white hole concomitant?"

"I don't think it was no ship o' ours, or anything o' ours, that got sucked into a black hole, no. And as fer what comes outta white holes, this hole o' mine—the richest hole me or anybody I know's ever fished—the stuff just comes outta it. There's more things in nature than people've got catalogued. And this here piece o' salvage is one o' them. Actual alien artifact from some advanced civilization. Gonna make me rich and famous."

Riva Lowe rubbed her forehead. It was damp. She couldn't have this unsavory person running around Threshold making waves. Or telling such stories.

"Well then, Captain Keebler, I guess you won't mind taking me out there to have a look at it."

CHAPTER 7

Out on the Streets

South kept stifling the impulse to fight somebody—anybody who was doing this to him—and his hands were trembling from the strain of not breaking loose.

But there was nowhere to run. He kept trying to convince his body of that, first during the towing phase, then when three big guys who were obviously cops "escorted" him into a futuristic paddy wagon; then again when, after interrogation, even bigger guys in white coats took him by ambulance to a hospital of some kind for more interrogation.

Where did you run when you couldn't get home from here?

Intellectually, he'd known that he had no place else to go by the time the ConSec lieutenant had ordered the tug to tow him. Emotionally, he'd known it when he first caught sight of the huge space habitat called Threshold.

He'd just sat there in his powered-down testbed and started to shake. Even in his suit, visor down, cooling system on high, he was sweating so badly that his eyes stung.

Threshold was a giant version of the space station that had been the dream of South's time, a dream you fought to keep. The design parameters of the first station weren't so different from Threshold: Threshold looked like a huge antenna strung with geometric shapes the way the first station had, but Threshold was an Escher rendering.

One look had convinced South that Lieutenant Reice hadn't been kidding when he said a quarter-million people lived out here. South saw things he guessed were processing plants for minerals and oxygen dug out of the nearby asteroids. In his day, you were talking yourself hoarse trying to convince Congress that the best way to supply man's needs in space was to put a permanent base on the moon and dig your raw materials out of the lunar regolith.

So it wasn't the technology that scared him. It was linear enough, from what he could see. The technology made sense. So did his feelings: they weren't crazy; they just didn't seem endurable.

Everything he'd known was dead and gone, mostly forgotten. It was too big a realization to digest. It had stuck in his craw. And so did the way these people were treating him.

There was something wrong, somewhere. He wouldn't have been hustled into a police station, then into a medical facility, in the old days. Where was Space Command? How about a technical debrief? Didn't anybody care about his mission? When South had demanded to go home, he'd been told that Earth was cordoned off, permanently off-limits to all but its caretakers and a privileged few—one of which, he wasn't.

Currently, Captain Joseph South was sitting in one more white room with recessed lights that mimicked sunlight so completely that he'd patted his coveralls for sunglasses he must have left on the ship. He'd answered dozens of stupid questions, none of which seemed relevant.

Now he was about to answer some more. The door opened, and in came a woman. He hadn't seen a woman for eighteen months until today, but his body was too scared to give the standard salute. He just crossed his arms and his legs and looked at her from his chair. "When can I go back to my ship? Where's my MMU—my spacesuit? I need to see somebody from Space Command." He kept saying the same things to everybody who came to talk to him.

They never answered any of his questions, so South didn't really expect this woman to help him. He was just reciting his version of name, rank, and serial number (all of which they already had).

This white room didn't have anything loose in it except Joe South, test pilot from the dawn of time. No bed, no table lamps, no desk drawers that pulled all the way out. (He'd checked.) Even the chair he was sitting on was bolted into a track. So was the one behind the clean and empty desk studded with electronics.

The woman came to sit behind the desk. He watched her hands, not her face. In them was a folder. She took documents out of it. Then she cleared her throat. "Mission Commander South, I'm your—"

"Captain's okay."

"Excuse me?" She peered up under her brows at him.

"Captain South'll do."

"Do you mean we've made an error?" She was frowning and when she did, her square face seemed to fold in on itself, as if she were a hundred years old. "Because if we have, we'll need to correct that right away." She tapped a stylus against pale lips. "Before the error chain gets any longer."

"I mean, yeah, I was mission commander of a one-man testbed, but so what?" He looked closer. Her mouth seemed to extend too far over to the sides of her face. Her eyes were like that as well, as if she were some film star who'd had too many face-lifts. "You're not going to understand. I need to talk to somebody from Space Command."

"I am somebody from Space Command, mister," she said. "Or as close to it as we can manage. I'm your reintegration counsellor. I've been sent over here to get your signature on some documents. Standard Relic procedure. We'll want you to check in with us twice a month. We'll need an address as soon as you've got one." She started moving papers from one pile into another as she spoke.

"You'll have to sign a few waivers." Three sheets went from Pile A to Pile B. "You were MIA for twenty years, then presumed dead, so you'll have some back pay coming, once we get things sorted out." She looked up at him. "Sign these, please, and push your right thumb against the sensitivity square beside your name."

He almost said he wouldn't be signing anything until somebody told him what the hell was going on. Instead he said, "Don't you people do standard mission debriefing?"

"Not when the mission's five centuries out of date. Sign here, spaceman."

He was so shocked, and her order was so direct, he stood up and did as he was told, going through a pile of papers blindly, scribbling his name and pressing his thumb against the squares beside his signature.

He couldn't focus on any of them; his vision was blurry. After he'd signed the last one, he stared at it. It was a request for retroactive discharge.

He picked it up in trembling hands. "I don't want a discharge." He folded it and put it in his back pocket.

"What?"

"You heard me," he said. "I'm . . . retrainable." His voice shook. He was supposed to be smart. He'd always managed to fight his way through paper wars before. They weren't chucking him out on the streets somewhere more alien than Africa. They didn't do that to you. This was some kind of mistake. "I want to see somebody in my regular command chain. I want a list of options. Maybe I'll go back to flight school. . . ." The last was barely audible.

The woman was looking at him with an icy expression. "We'll get you an appointment with someone who'll explain things to you. It'll take a while. Meanwhile, you'll check in with me twice a month. Here."

"Yes, ma'am." He had his hands clasped behind him. That way, she couldn't see them shake.

"Here's a temporary work permit, a low-ceiling credit card, which ought to serve your interim needs." She slid them across the desk toward him.

He didn't take them immediately. The whole room was swimming. The armed services weren't what they used to be. Not if they were just tossing him out the door like so much garbage. South wished he knew whether what they were doing was by the book, but their book was centuries ahead of his.

And they were giving him something. Maybe he was being foolish to look a gift horse in the mouth. They weren't going to let him starve. He just wished they weren't in such a damned hurry to get rid of him. "I'm going to sleep in my ship," he said because he wanted her to know he figured he had that right.

"Your ship's in quarantine."

"And I'm not?" He had wanted out of here. Now, he didn't want to leave.

"Here's an immigrant's handbook. We'll have to get you citizenship papers, you realize?"

"Huh? I'm a U.S. citizen in good standing. . . ."

"Threshold citizenship." She stood up, shook her head once at him, and tapped the little pile she'd pushed toward him. "Take your things and leave, mister. Get hold of yourself. In a couple of weeks, we'll talk again. Use this opportunity to orient yourself. I'm sorry I can't stay longer, but I have another case waiting."

"Another . . . Relic?"

She was walking toward the door. "Hell, no. We haven't had one of your kind for years. You're dismissed, space-man. Go find yourself some R and R. And don't end up in jail. It'll make everything much more difficult."

"Yes, ma'am," he said.

She hesitated at the door and he realized he was supposed to leave with her. He picked up his pile blindly and walked out first.

In the hall, which was as white as the room they'd been in, she seemed to unbend. "Here's my number. My card." She handed them to him.

He took them and stuffed them into his back pocket, with the discharge papers. "Thanks."

"Try the Loader Zone if you want to work some of it off," she said.

He didn't know what "it" was, but she'd given him only that one piece of advice.

"How do I get there?"

"Out the front door. Turbo lift's on the corner. Level SB1, Red or Blue ought to do it. And, spaceman, good luck."

"Yeah, thanks."

She strode away on soundless, rubber-soled shoes. "Follow the red arrows to the front door," she called back before she disappeared down a corridor.

He did, thinking he was going to need all the luck he could get.

He found the street entrance, after asking several more people, who must have thought he was odd-looking. He'd had a shave and a haircut, so it was either his mission coveralls or his eyes. He knew in his heart that he wasn't going to be able to get his suit back, any more than he could bunk in his ship. He was beginning to wish he'd bought it out there, arguing with the ConSec lieutenant. He missed his AI, which was the damnedest thing of all. Birdy wasn't much, but at least they were contemporaries.

The Loader Zone was a welcome change from white and clean and sterile, and he drew a deep, shuddering breath when the lift opened on the raucous commercial cargo area. Here at least his adrenaline level was appropriate.

Men were guiding transports up to aprons, waving light wands, dressed in colors that probably still identified their function down here, the way your colors told your job description on an aircraft carrier.

The men were big and rough and there was a lot of yelling. There were also men who obviously weren't entirely human: he saw a couple of faces that might have belonged to upright-walking camels, and one that was actually scaly and green.

Nobody'd stare at him down here, that was for sure. He'd

stuffed the wad of orientation material in his pocket. Now he realized he was hungry and got out the little card.

Credit card, just like in his time. He followed his nose to a place that served food and most of the menu was in English, so he ordered at the bar. There was still beer in the world. He didn't know why that made him feel so relieved. Most of the brands weren't familiar.

But he had a beer and some chili, and halfway through the chili, somebody came up next to him and jostled his elbow.

South had almost been able to forget that this wasn't just another foreign port—this was a foreign time.

The bar had neon and bottles and something that looked like wood and felt like wood under his hands and elbows. So when the guy jostled him, he told him to fucking watch his ass, and wasn't prepared to be grabbed by the shoulder and spun around.

Etiquette was different here, South realized when he saw how angry he'd made the fellow with the single, shiny earring and the long braid.

He'd been told not to end up in jail. He put up both hands and said, "Sorry, I'm sorry. I'm not from around here, and I've had a bad day. I don't want any trouble. Can I buy you a drink?" as quickly as he could.

The guy with the braid couldn't have been over twenty-five. He looked almost disappointed as he rubbed his jaw and said, "Yeah, awright. Where you in from, spaceman?"

"Uh—it's a long story."

"Gimme what he's having," said the longhair to the bartender. "They're all long stories. I'm Sling. I'm aftermarket. What's your trade, Joe?"

He hadn't told Sling his name. "I'm a test pilot—was."

"Was?"

"Long story, remember?"

"What you testing?" The keen interest under Sling's wispy brows was unmistakable. It was also clear that this guy couldn't raise a beard if his life depended on it.

South rubbed his jaw and felt the quick-growing stubble

there. "X-mission." Maybe the jargon had changed. "Experimental. Black. No talkee." He smiled his most winning smile.

"Well, like I say, I'm aftermarket, if you need anything interesting."

"Aftermarket what?"

"What?" Sling leaned back on the bar. "I can take your average buggy and give you an additional light; I can drop a zero-point power plant into a fifty-year-old wreck. I can do other things, too, for the right price," he confided, after looking over his shoulder and then beyond South's to make sure there was no one within earshot.

The bartender was talking to his only other customer, down at the curve of the bar.

"Other things?"

"Come on, sport, you're not down here looking like that and talking about no-talkees if you're straight-up legal. You need a little extra firepower, I'm the man to see."

"Okay, I gotcha. I wouldn't mind a look at what you can do." At least he'd learn something. He had to start somewhere, and he knew from experience that a government pocket guide to wherever didn't tell you one hell of a lot.

"Eat up, then, Joe."

"How come you know my name?"

"Ah—oh, an expression, that's all. So you're Joe?"

"South."

"Sure thing. I like it. Has a real directional ring to it."

When they'd finished their beers and South had polished off the chili, he paid the tab with the credit card, which worked without a hitch and should have proved to Sling that he was who he said.

Maybe nobody down here was too free with information. The place had that feel about it. At least it had a recognizable feel. So did the aftermarket shop of the man called Sling.

It wasn't exactly a chop-shop, but it was surely the cash-up-front, no-receipt-requested sort of place where you had your transportation needs attended to if your cargo had to be handled delicately, and you needed to be able to outrun a police cruiser such as the ConSec one that had found South's *STARBIRD*.

He heard lots of terms he didn't know, and saw lots of bits of ship and armament he wouldn't have dreamed could exist outside of a government facility. He saw iridium and beam weaponry; he saw countermeasures packages for stealthing spacecraft; he saw what was supposedly an "a-potential weapons system" and "zero-point, scalar-pulsed jump drives, if you've got the cash. What's your limit on that card?" Sling pulled on his mousy braid.

"I don't know. Somebody just gave it to me." South smiled weakly and knew he sounded like some kind of outlaw.

Maybe he was. He couldn't be sure yet. But he was sure that he wanted to go back to *STARBIRD*. So he said, "I want to get back to my ship but it's in quarantine. Got any ideas?"

"Let's get drunk and think about it, on you."

There didn't seem to be a better option.

Sling's drinking tour of the Loader Zone included a running commentary. The Loaders had a union. They employed "subhumans and biogenetically engineered humans as well as purebreds. So lots of stuff happens down here that doesn't officially happen. You're in the right place, space-man, for whatever you aren't doing."

Sling obviously thought that South was a heavy hitter doing something illicit and profitable. Well, that was usually drugs or guns or illegals. Things couldn't have changed more than that. This was still a human society.

They drank in four bars, then they drank in five more, and South began having difficulty with the zipper on his coveralls.

He knew he was in trouble when he couldn't quite recognize Sling, among the patrons of the joint he was in. Rather than yell and see who turned around, he sat in a corner.

That was a mistake. He began thinking about his dead

parents, and his dead lady love, Jenna, and his dead culture. And he was feeling pretty dead himself. A girl came up, and this one was identifiable as a member of the opposite sex to his various inboard sensing systems. She had a head of blond curls like a halo and she was obviously in it for the money, but she took credit cards. He made sure of that right away.

So he wasn't really all that surprised when he found himself lying behind a truck with huge wheels, his head pounding, and his credit card and ID missing.

Well, at least he hadn't ended up in jail. And he still had his pocket guide, though he didn't have his discharge papers.

Figuring he could walk where he was going, he tried to stand.

He couldn't do that, not just yet. He slid back down, onto the cold surface of the street. The MPs would find him eventually, he thought, still so drunk he was thinking like a Space Command officer.

Which he wasn't, not anymore, he told himself in a savage burst of clarity, just before he passed out again.

CHAPTER 8

$\triangledown$

In Search of
Harmony

Mickey Croft was feeling much older than his forty-five years when the three-hour session on the "Regulation of Commerce in Life-Forms and Controlled Substances" drew to a close.

As protocol demanded, he stood by the dais from which he'd been chairing a panel discussion that kept threatening to degenerate into a shouting match. Now Croft was shaking the black, white, yellow, brown, purple, mottled, webbed, clawed, and mechanically cold hands of every conference member who wanted to congratulate him or stroke him or tell him (very politely) that he was an asshole.

He'd been sure that the human/subhuman/alien rights conference was going to spontaneously abort, at least three times this evening, which made his average that of one crisis per hour.

He was getting too old for this crap. He was also getting tired of being called "Honorable Sir" and "Your Excellency" and "Mister Secretary" and "Sirrah" and "Croft-San" and "Mahlik" by men with lasers in their eyes who'd prefer to spit on his corpse, and women who'd like to do so after they conquered him sexually, because as the most powerful man in the room he had a certain deadly attraction for both sexes.

He was getting along best with the bioengineered, the computer-designed, and the provisionally admitted alien "subs," because at least they didn't feel this peculiarly human need to challenge him for dominance or co-opt him. The nice thing about subhuman and alien races, as well as the technologically derived mules in attendance, was that all of them lacked the human need to count coup.

The not-so-nice thing about them was that, to a person, they all longed for human status, for acceptance, for recognition, for protection under laws never designed to protect them. Croft was working at his job today. Humanity needed every wile at its command to keep the interstellar expansion rolling on without tensions exploding into energy-wasting, expensive conflicts.

Exploration and expansion had proved to be the only antidote for humanity's addiction to warfare, and with the present technological level of the human race, wars could obliterate entire planets. So you had to solve your problems. You couldn't let interstellar or interspecies relations degenerate. A diplomat's task was a difficult one.

Secretary General Croft sighed and turned from the last admiring Epsilonian, who was lisping his praises through furry, camel-like lips. Somebody human was calling his name.

He searched the thinning throng, nametags firmly in place, headed for the UNE buffet. Somewhere must be a familiar face, to match the voice he couldn't quite place.

Then he saw Riva Lowe threading her way toward him and admitted to himself how tired he was, not to have recognized her voice.

He'd been on the go since well before he'd had Medina's head mullah dropped in his lap. Since then, he'd been a court magician and jester rolled into one, trying to finesse the mullah into attending the evening session.

Croft hadn't thought of anything else since it had appeared that he might have a chance to do the impossible.

Now, having not only brought the mullah with him to the session, but survived the session without an irremediable break in interstellar relations, exhaustion threatened.

He vaguely recalled telling Riva Lowe to keep him informed about her progress, and that he wouldn't be available until now.

Croft straightened his shoulders as the woman approached, a determined look on her face.

"Hello, sir," she said, herding him toward a corner.

"Good evening, Director Lowe. Come for a snack? The buffet's open."

"Come to tell you what I'm about to do." Riva Lowe reached into her purse and pulled out a little privacy generator. She flicked it and everything around them disappeared. They were then in a silvery tube of excited atoms that blocked out sight and sound, although Croft could have pushed his way out of it with no more than a tickling sensation to mark his passage through the security measure.

"I hope this is necessary, Riva. We're making quite an overt display of ourselves," he said disapprovingly.

"Sir, do I look like I'm dressed for dinner and drinks with the high-and-mighty?"

She didn't, of course. She was dressed in a black pressure suit liner, but Croft wasn't much on women's fashions and, for all he knew, Rowe's outfit was some nouvelle fashion statement. Government functionaries tended to run about conferences of this sort with their status blazoned on their sleeves (as hers was) whenever possible. This separated them from the rank and file and made sure that no visiting dignitary accidently snubbed them. Purposeful snubs could then be evaluated.

The hardest call in intelligence, or diplomacy, was intent. He wished he could make a stab at calling Riva Lowe's, right now. Croft blinked at the woman awaiting a response and said, "I'm sure you realize you look perfectly appropriate, and that I'm a bit too harried at the moment to evaluate domestic nuances. Can we get to the point, please? Your mystery, which is justification—let's hope—for a privacy shield here and now?"

One had to keep one's staff under control.

The woman licked her lips and raised her eyes to his. "Sir, I've got a scavenger—member of the Salvagers' Union in good standing—who has a unique and possibly dangerous artifact he's towed in as far as spacedock. He wanted to import it. I want to impound it, at least until this is over, if I understand your guidelines. I need to know that you'll back me if my actions cause a flap."

"We don't want a flap, Lowe. We can't afford one right now. I thought I'd made that clear."

"Oh, you did, sir. But I can't make this one go away. I have to deal with it." Riva Lowe had slanted eyes with a hint of epicanthic fold. They gave her an exotic aura, especially since she didn't in any other way resemble a Eurasian mix. Right now, those eyes seemed sinister. And the posture of the body forcing her pressure suit into a distractingly female shape was too challenging.

Whatever this was, Riva Lowe was even more upset about it than she'd been earlier. Croft said, "Then deal with it, Director. I told you before, you have my authority."

"Yes, all right. I talked to Remson about the other matter— the Relic. That's containable. But I'm going out there to spacedock, to look at this other thing. If anything odd happens, I need to make sure you understand that I'm considering this . . . object . . . as possibly dangerous to Threshold. . . ."

"So that if you disappear, I'll not just assume it's an accident?" People tended to wax theatrical when they knew you were too busy to pay attention if they didn't. "I promise, I'll look over any file you'll be so kind as to send me, Director. If you're concerned about your safety and yet insistent on going yourself, why don't you take some of your staff, or even Remson or young Reice with you?"

Riva Lowe blushed. "I don't need help that badly. Remson's got his hands full, and Reice's Relic still needs to be watched. I just wanted to report, the way I said I would, if things were escalating."

"Well, now you have. And you've gotten a reiteration

from me that you have full authority to deal with this . . . thing. Whatever it is, unless it's directly threatening to disrupt my conference, I won't need to hear from you again about it until you've something more in the way of hard evidence. Until, one hopes, this conference is safely ended and all the attendees packed off to their respective solar systems. Isn't that so?"

"Ah . . . yes, sir. Unless a threat is imminent."

"Your job, my dear, is to make sure that doesn't happen."

"Yes, sir." She retreated a step, her face immobile.

"Good. Then we're done. Unless you'd care for a shrimp cocktail or a drink before you leave to risk your life examining the unknown?"

Croft didn't wait for the intense young woman to respond to his dry invitation. He stepped through the privacy tube and back into the ken of the folk remaining in the conference room.

A little knot of people had gathered before the tube. Remson was with them: tall, hefty, bull-necked Remson was unmistakable, with his shock-white hair and his youthful face and his welcome knack for holding things together, no matter the difficulty of the task at hand.

Croft's aide plucked an imaginary speck of lint from his dinner jacket and said, "Ah, here's the Secretary now, and just in time. We were all ready to go ahead to the buffet without you, sir."

Mickey Croft seriously considered putting Remson in his will.

Behind him, the privacy tube disintegrated, and he saw, out of the corner of his eye, Riva Lowe striding determinedly toward the other exit.

Infuriatingly officious woman. But good at her job. Croft, freed from the privacy tube and greeting Remson's handpicked clutch of lesser mullahs and other distinguished guests, was willing to wait and see whether her concern was justified before he marked her down for a reprimand later.

If and when, of course, he ever found the time.

CHAPTER 9

$$\triangledown$$

Love Will Find a Way

Dini Forat was having more fun than she'd thought possible. She had found paradise, here on Threshold. She had found herself.

She was dancing with someone in a club, someone whose name she had forgotten. This someone had picked her out of a group of girls she'd met, and whisked her off in a round of sightseeing the like of which, she was sure, short, fat Dodd could never have provided.

This someone was tall and blond and he had access to "all the best places, m'lady." He was blue-eyed and his smile was as wide as her heart.

He was a marvelous dancer, and obviously a person of impeccable breeding. And yet, he was no boring law student or diplomatic scion. He was adventurous.

Then she remembered: his name was Rick. He had found her and coveted her and now, she was sure, he would truly claim her.

He had his own car, a great car as fine as Secretary Croft's, with a human driver. In it, not long ago, he had shared a treasure with her: they had eaten a strange fruit that tasted like lettuce and now her head was swimming and the air was full of colors.

Rick had said, "Now, don't tell anybody we did this,

Dini. It's not legal, but all the best fun isn't." And he'd winked, while his arm slid around her shoulders and his fingers trailed against her heaving, uplifted breasts.

She was on fire. She was light-headed. She danced, now, with this boy again and he was incandescent against her. The music was special, here. The people were special, here. Her father couldn't find her here.

She'd warned Rick about Father, with her head on his shoulder as the music played: "My father is very strict, the head mullah of Medina. You must understand. If we're caught together . . ." She'd let it trail off, exchanging a confidence for his earlier confidence about the little fruits called Leetles.

"So we're both breaking some laws?" He shrugged and leaned back to look at her without breaking step. "I'm not afraid. You're worth it."

And he'd kissed her, in public, right on the lips.

Her heart was going to break out of her chest, she was sure. She no longer had any idea of where on Threshold she might be, but she was in the arms of the man of her dreams, and nothing else seemed to matter.

Not the time. Not the danger. Not anything but pressing herself against him.

Eventually, he wanted to leave. She was suddenly disheartened. What had she done to offend him?

In his car, out on the strange level where the roof showed the stars above, she said, "I'm not going home, so you can drop me anywhere there is a hotel."

"Of course you're going home," he said. His eyes were very wide and as blue as the sky on Medina. "I've just met you. You can't go getting in trouble until we've . . . well, until we know each other better."

"Then let's get to know each other better, for by dawn, everyone on Threshold will be looking for me. They mustn't find me." She crossed her arms and slid against the car's doors. "I'm not going home. I'm running away. I shall stow away on a freighter and make a new life on a new colony, where no one's ever heard of Medina, or my father, or—"

Rick reached out and put a finger to her lips. "Let's think about this. If you don't want to go home yet, perhaps you'd let me show you my place? Just for a few minutes, of course. A tour, a coffee to sober you up . . . And we'll talk."

He was so much more knowledgeable than she. His eyes bored so deeply into hers. It was as if he'd known her and she'd known him forever.

"Talk, yes. You'll tell me all about Threshold, and about how I can evade my father's henchmen."

"Sure thing," he said, and talked to the glass beyond which a human driver—not a bodyguard—waited for instructions.

Then he turned back to her. "I've never met anyone like you, Dini. I don't want anything bad to happen to you. And I'm good at figuring things out. I want you to tell me as much as you can about yourself, and I'll think of some way you won't have to go back to Medina, if that's really what you want. I promise."

"Oh, that would be—"

His mouth silenced hers as he pulled her across the seat. One of his hands held the back of her neck. The other stroked her thigh, then kneaded it. It was as if he were a magnet, pulling her to him.

And then, somehow, everything disappeared but the track of his fingers against her skin.

When the car stopped, she was gasping and his hand was under her blouse.

Nothing else was real but that touch, and when the touch was gone, she felt suddenly exposed, foolish, vulnerable and cold.

"You're shivering," he said. "Come on, we'll fix that." His nostrils were flaring with each breath he took.

She hardly noticed the building into which he brought her, past a doorman who bowed and greeted him as "Meester Cummings."

She didn't care that his apartment had a clear roof and through it she could see what he assured her were real stars.

She didn't care about the beautiful art on the walls or the coffee he made her.

She wanted him to hold her.

When he brought the coffee, there was an animal on his shoulder, a big, masked cat. He smiled at her and the animal seemed to smile, too.

He said, "Let me show you the rest of the place," and with the animal still balanced on his shoulder, held out his hand. She took it.

A thrill ran through her.

In the bedroom, the animal hopped onto the bed. Rick sat down beside it, stroking its fur. "Pet him. He likes you. See?"

She stroked the furry, ringed tail, and the animal reached for her hand with black, manlike fingers.

As it took hold of her, she became suddenly very tired.

Dini leaned back, then lay back on the bed and stared up at the stars beyond. There were no stars on the ceiling of her hotel suite. Staring at these, the points of light seemed to rotate. The motion made her dizzy. She closed her eyes.

She heard the animal chitter, then the bed sank a bit as Rick lay back beside her.

"Rick," she said. "I wish to stay here. I don't want to go home. Ever."

He rolled toward her and his breath tickled her ear. "We'll stay awhile. Then I'll take you home. You'll go, for me. We don't want to cause an incident. Then tomorrow night, we'll meet again and by then I'll have something figured out. Trust me, Dini. If you knew me better, you'd know I'm as good as my word. And I can't resist a challenge."

His hand closed on her throat.

She opened her eyes in surprise.

He was staring down at her. "Any challenge," he said, and started unfastening her blouse with his other hand while he watched her face through blue, half-closed, beautiful eyes.

She was late getting home, but home she went, a changed woman. A woman at last.

Rick Cummings himself drove her, and all the while he was telling her not to be afraid, not to let on that anything out of the ordinary had happened, and especially not to mention his name.

"But you don't understand," she tried to tell him. "I'm so late . . . and I ran off without my bodyguard—my escort. My father will be furious."

"Your father will pretend nothing is wrong. He's got more at stake here than a teenage daughter's curfew," Rick Cummings predicted with worldly certainty.

She wanted to believe him. He was the man she was going to marry. She cuddled against his arm as he stopped the car a few yards short of her hotel. "You get out here. Walk in smiling, as if nothing's wrong. You've memorized my number. Repeat it."

She did. She'd never forget anything about this boy—this man—who'd made of her a woman. His vidphone number had seared itself into her brain the way his manhood had penetrated her heart.

She thought he loved her. He must love her. They were risking so much together.

"Great," he said, when she'd successfully repeated the number. "This is going to be tricky, but it'll be worth it. You do just as I say, and everything'll be fine."

Dini could feel his passion. He, too, knew that their love was worth the risk. He was excited by it, not frightened. Even though she'd told him how dangerous it was to help her, he was not afraid.

Truly, this was the man of her dreams. She had been right to let him make love to her.

She had been right to come to Threshold.

"One kiss, Dini." He reached for her. "Now, remember, don't mention my name."

She could hear his heart pounding as she kissed him one last time. "Say good-bye to your kitty for me," she said, and got out of the car.

She waited until he'd driven away before she walked on unsteady legs toward her hotel and up the stairs.

Rick had said that the risk was worth it. He said he loved the idea of helping her. Tomorrow he would say he loved her, not just the risk and the challenge. She was sure of it.

But the closer she got to her father's suite, the more Dini worried that she'd never be let out of there again, except to board the ship that would take her, deflowered, probably pregnant, and obviously defiled, back to Medina where execution in a public square would be her lot.

She had defiled herself with an infidel, and she was sure everyone could see. Dini Forat closed her eyes in the lift and tried to recall his face. But all she could see were Rick's blue eyes, and the eyes of his ring-tailed cat, which were as deep as the night above his bed and as filled with twinkling stars.

She could still taste the lettucelike fruit she'd eaten, when she got to the floor where her family's suite was. And she could still see colors in the air.

If not for Ali-5, who saw her as the lift opened, she might never have gotten out there, but run and hidden somewhere until it was time to call Rick Cummings's number.

But Ali-5 did see her, and then it was too late. Her dream was about to become a nightmare. The beautiful colors in the air all turned dark and menacing as the bodyguard raced forward to grab her out of the lift before it could close.

CHAPTER 10

$$\bigtriangledown$$

Other Side of the Law

All South wanted to do was report his stolen card and ID. He didn't see any reason for the local cops to treat him like a criminal.

But they did.

"Look," he nearly snarled in frustration to the sergeant behind the desk when the going got rough, "I came in here of my own accord, because my ID was stolen. How the hell can I show it to you?"

Then there were two uniforms behind him, and they put their hands on him, and all the rage he'd been working so hard to keep in check came boiling out of him.

One cop wanted to handcuff him, and South wasn't about to let that happen.

He knew damn well that you didn't take on a couple of uniforms in a station house, but when he wouldn't put his wrists behind him, the second cop tried to put him in a choke hold. South hadn't been in Africa for nothing. He leaned back into it, elbowed the cop behind him in the gut, and pushed back, kicking out at the second cop as he and the first one fell.

He happened to catch the second cop under the chin with one booted foot.

That dropped cop Number Two. But by then there were half a dozen more helping, and he was lying on his stomach with his hands jerked up hard behind him. So he didn't know who hit him or who kicked him or who used the taser on him.

When he could see something more than the blood rushing into his eyes from a cut on his head, he was looking at a chickenwire-inlaid-glass detention cell about three feet wide by five feet long.

At first South was relieved that it was private, from the look of the fellows in the cells on either side. But then he watched while three men came in and wrapped a struggling prisoner in something that looked altogether too much like a wet canvas shroud.

It probably wasn't. This was the future. In Africa, they used to bind guys up in strips of wet canvas and wait for it to shrink. As it shrank, no matter who you were, you remembered whatever they wanted to know.

Considering that there was somebody sitting in there with the bound guy; and that somebody had either a pocket recorder or a clipboard; and there was a discussion going on—something very African was happening next door.

On South's other side was a roughneck with a greenish cast to his skin and what looked like a bad case of eczema. This guy kept throwing himself against the glass, head first.

The cubicles were soundproofed. The silence began to get to South. Finally he said, "Shit, I gotta get out of here," out loud, just to prove he could still hear.

And a voice from somewhere above said, "Name, please."

It was some kind of AI, a mechanical voice. He looked up, saw a speaker grill in a ceiling he couldn't reach if he jumped for it, and gave his name.

Then he sat on the floor, scrubbing the clotted blood out of his eyes as best he could, and had a long discussion with the AI about who he was and where he'd come from. He didn't have his watch any longer, but the dialogue must have gone on for better than an hour, with him and the AI talking in circles about how he could prove who he was, when he remembered the card that the lady reintegration counsellor had given him.

If he still had it, maybe she'd prove that he was who he said he was.

They obviously didn't bother with fingerprints, but he remembered retinal scans, so if anybody cared to try, and could contact the lady, she could ID him.

So, for that matter, could Lieutenant Reice of ConSec, but the AI wasn't programmed to react to that set of sounds. Or else Reice wasn't gettable. Or somebody figured to just let South sit awhile and cool out before they sprung him.

He'd been told not to land in jail.

Oh, well, maybe the card would work. It was there, crumpled, in the bottom of his hip pocket when he reached for it. But it hurt like hell to reach back there. He'd cracked a couple of ribs or something, during the brawl.

What the hell was wrong with him, starting a fight he couldn't win?

There were tremors running all over him, and his forearms burned as he tried to hold the card steady enough so that he could read it. He had to use both hands.

He read the name aloud: "Lt. Commander Lydia Jones," and what else was on the card: "PSYOPS/J2/CSC/UNE MEDICAL INTELLIGENCE OFFICE." And then he read out a phone and office extension, telling the AI to "Get hold of this officer, or when they find out what you're doing to me, holding me without cause, there'll be trouble."

Of course, they had due cause: he'd been pretty rowdy back there.

The AI crackled and he had a sense that it had gone off line.

So he said, "Hey, power on. Request legal counsel. Request phone call." Couldn't hurt to try.

The AI burped back: "Requests denied."

That was nice. At least he knew how to get it to respond to him. Now if he could only figure out how come he didn't have basic legal rights, he'd be on his way out of here. He hoped.

After too long staring at the crumpled business card in his hand, he remembered the woman who'd given it to him saying that he didn't have Threshold citizenship. Well, from the full cells around him, he wasn't the only one. When he got out of this, he'd have to look up Sling again and get another tutorial.

When he felt a little better. His head was pounding, what with the scalp wound he'd taken and the drinking he'd done. He had a bump above his eye the size of a golf ball. And he hurt from his butt to his shoulder.

Worse, he couldn't do anything but sit here until somebody decided what to do with him. And that meant he had too much time to think. He closed his eyes and leaned his head carefully back against the glass wall, and up popped those funny eyes from the spongejump, looking at him soulfully. So he opened his eyes again.

He didn't want to go to sleep here. If you thought you might have a concussion, you didn't let yourself go to sleep. He levered himself up against the wall, welcoming the jabs from his ribs and spine. Then he turned to the wall and put his hands flat against it. He used to do calisthenics in his cell in Africa, even though there wasn't room to lie down flat.

You just had to use some ingenuity. He slid his feet out three feet from the wall he was facing, and did push-ups against the glass, eyes closed, until his heart was pounding as fast as his head and his mouth was so dry that it felt as if he'd been eating needles.

Then he opened his eyes and the green guy next door was staring at him, flat nose flatter against the glass.

The eyes facing his had oblong pupils.

The sight scared the hell out of him and he shot back against the far wall, hitting it hard.

This just wasn't his day.

He kept trying to put together how he'd gotten himself into this mess, and decided he must have still been drunk.

Some of those unprounceable beers, especially the blue and red ones, must have more kick than he'd been expecting.

He started perspiring, then shivering in the empty glass cell. Then the shivers got worse, so that he had to cross his arms and tuck his hands into his armpits, and finally slide down the wall again.

Nausea swept over him in waves and time lost all meaning. Everything pinwheeled and there were disgustingly sweet pink whorls in the pinwheels. He kept trying to open his eyes and stare at his feet to quiet his stomach, but they wouldn't stay open.

Somehow, he had to keep from vomiting.

Right about when he was deciding to let his stomach do its worst, he heard a voice.

He was slow to look up, so whoever it was had already come into the cell and was leaning over him.

South heard a grunt. Something pricked his upper arm, and he thought maybe the grunt might have been his.

Then he was being lifted by one arm, without much gentleness, and a black guy in white was frogmarching him out of the cell.

He'd have complained but he couldn't find his mouth. But if you couldn't find your mouth, you couldn't vomit. He was sure that the black guy in the white coat had given him a shot, because otherwise, why were the peppermint pinwheels subsiding?

Nothing seemed to matter very much except that his stomach was feeling better and his head didn't hurt as badly, not even when black fingers pressed an envelope into his grasp and black hands helped him through the police station and down the steps.

He thought he heard a velvety voice say, "And don't get your ass busted again, fool. Next time, you'll find yourself on a work gang."

But he was definitely free, and on the street.

He could feel a building against his back, and he leaned there, using all the strength he had to maintain an upright position, and hopefully a posture that said he was more fully conscious than he felt.

He kept trying to open the envelope in his hands. He didn't want to lose it. He needed to see whatever was in it.

In it, when he finally could focus, were his credit card and ID. Or another credit card and ID. And some actual stuff that looked like cash money: coins and engraved papers.

He put them inside his coveralls, this time, all except for the cash. Then he tried walking. It looked like staggering and lurching, and he had to keep one hand against the wall.

He knew he was attracting attention, bruised and cut up. But he kept moving. Eventually he found something he could recognize as one of the tube stations, and asked somebody where the ConSec docking bay was.

The person with the blurry face told him what tube to take, and pointed him in the right direction.

The rest wasn't hard. You got on the train, or something that looked like a train. It went like hell. You put your head between your knees and took deep breaths to keep from retching.

When it stopped, you got off.

The main gate to the docking bays had an AI entry post, but that was all. It never occurred to him that if he put his ID in the slot, he couldn't get through. So he got through fine.

Every thought that he had was concentrated on survival, and survival was Birdy, his own bunk, a little bright spot called *STARBIRD* to which he was drawn with the single-minded determination that had gotten him through Africa alive.

There weren't many people around, on the docking bay. Maybe it was whatever cycle passed for night here. Maybe everybody was busy with some emergency.

He got lost in the docking bays. There were lots of them.

Finally he found the ConSec bay, and there he ran right into a stone wall—actually, a metal wall.

This one wouldn't open for his ID. Wrong service. He walked all the way around the enclosure, craning his neck.

Either the wire on the top of it was electrified, or it wasn't. There was only one way to find out.

He jumped for it, fell back, and jumped again, his pulse making his whole skull reverberate.

No good. Too high. He walked around some more, looking for something he could use to get over that wall.

He couldn't find anything. Then he thought of something. He went back to the gate and, at the same time he chucked his ID into the slot, he told the AI he was supposed to meet Reice of ConSec inside to inspect the Relic cruiser.

Something made sense to the AI, either the phrase "Relic cruiser," or Reice's name and service, because it let him through.

You had to use your head. It was too bad his hurt so much.

The AI wouldn't give his ID back, but that seemed like some kind of standard procedure: you got it back when you left a restricted area. Instead, it gave him a pass with his entry time logged on it.

If his face didn't hurt so much, he'd have grinned as he walked down the docking bay looking for *STARBIRD*. It was difficult to see clearly. The flesh around his right eye was contused; the eye was almost swollen shut. And his head hurt so badly he was squinting in the overhead lights.

But *STARBIRD* wasn't hard to find. She was off by herself, wide open. Some quarantine.

He nearly bolted up the ramp. Inside, he flattened himself against the bulkhead and said, "Birdy. Secure all hatches. Full life support. Ready systems. Engage."

The ship came to life, her lights rippling on, her hatches sighing shut. Her breath spilled over him. He said, this time in a quavery voice he was barely able to control, "I gotta get some sleep, Birdy. Repel all attempts to gain access. Repeat, no access by anybody outside, no matter what you hear. Wake me if there's any forcible attempt to board."

What was he going to do about that, if it happened? The testbed didn't have so much as a flaregun aboard.

He was stumbling toward his bunk, wishing he had his

suit. In his suit, he could have repelled a hell of a lot more than he could without it.

But *they* had his suit. And he had *STARBIRD*. Not such a bad trade, if you really thought about it. He flat-palmed his way to his bunk, needing to feel the ship around him as much as he needed her bulkhead's support.

"Damn, Birdy, it's good to be home. Can we get out of here? Give me a projection on our chances of flying out—or punching out—of this fucking place and finishing our mission."

"Course to Earth?" Birdy asked him for clarification.

"Set course to Earth. Don't execute until I say. Include any measures necessary to break free of this obstruction."

Birdy didn't know what the hell they were stuck inside. He didn't have armaments, but he had sponge capability. Nobody'd ever tried to sponge jump from a standstill. It might not work. It might kill him. It might take all of Threshold with him, if he punched into spongespace while in a Threshold docking bay.

Weapons at hand were just that. Birdy would plot him a course. That was what the AI did. "And, Birdy: If anybody comes around here asking for me while I'm sleeping, tell anyone making inquiries that I demand to talk with somebody in charge—somebody I can negotiate with. And don't take any orders from anybody but me, no matter how those orders come to you. If our survivability is threatened, ignore anything else I've said and blast us out of here or jump us out of here. Clear?"

"Yes, Captain. Calibrating . . . please wait."

Sitting on his bunk, South put his head gingerly in his hands. You bet he'd wait. He was going to get some sleep, and he didn't care if he dreamed that his mother and father were big-eyed, sad-mouthed aliens.

Then he was going to wake up and take control of his goddamn situation: Either find somebody he could reason with, or get Birdy to break him out of here.

The worst thing that could happen was he'd get himself dead trying. And he already was as good as dead. According to Threshold's bureaucracy, he'd been dead nearly five hundred years.

So he didn't have a whole lot at risk, what with his head pounding like this. Even feeling so bad had its up side: he wasn't afraid to go to sleep anymore.

Nothing waiting in his dreams could be worse than what he'd just been through while he was wide awake. Anyway, his bunk physiology package was already clucking at him, anxious to get to work analyzing and normalizing his chemistries.

He woke up once, when Birdy roused him to say that she'd had a communication from outside the ship, in response to South's message, which Birdy had duly sent.

Birdy reported, "Their response is as follows: 'Port police will maintain status quo until Director Rowe can come on-site if no aggressive action is taken.' "

"No shit," South said through sticky lips, rubbing his eyes and wincing because he'd forgotten how beat-up he was.

"Transmit Captain's response?"

"No. Let them sweat it."

And Joe South turned carefully over on his side and went back to sleep, to find his family there, alive and well, welcoming him home after a successful mission with Jenna beaming at his mother's side. Everything looked just the same, and he was so happy to be back home that he didn't even mind the aliens clapping their hands among the little crowd who'd turned out to welcome him at his hometown airport.

CHAPTER 11

$$\triangledown$$

A Ball of What?

Riva Lowe had commandeered Customs' B300E *Adamson* for the trip out to spacedock to view Keebler's artifact. Her choice of vehicles spoke loudly of how nervous she was about whatever the scavenger had towed in from the back of beyond.

The *Adamson* was a six-place high-speed pursuit ship with aggressive capabilities such as scalar pulse and neutral-stripped particle beam weapons, as well as kinetics and fifth-force grappling. The ship had a blown air-breather mode for high-speed pursuit even into atmosphere. It had ground-space-sponge capabilities, temporal realignment and classified snooper packages, and electronic warfare pods. In short, it had the capability to blow Keebler's unidentifiable ball to either hot or cold smithereens, or punch it out of human spacetime unharmed.

Lowe wasn't planning to destroy the thing with the big Customs ship. She was planning to bathe the ball in so many crippling wave baths that it couldn't remember its name, if it had one. Once its systems were jammed, she wanted to snoop it. Once she'd snooped it, she was going to find some reason to impound it right where it was, even if she had to fake one.

She'd told the pilots up front to employ all their AI systems, and the ship's seven artifically intelligent experts were feeding the master AI their best guesses at how to arrive at the scenario that Lowe had demanded without Keebler noticing anything.

She had no doubt that she could run the ruse past the old scavenger. She wasn't worried about the human pilot and copilot keeping their mouths shut. She was worried about the unimaginable: the errors that killed you were the ones you weren't prepared to prevent, the ones you hadn't thought to protect against.

And this ball of unidentifiable alloy reeked of the unimaginable. In one of the observation stations behind the flight deck, Lowe was monitoring the snoopers' progress. Every time a scan came back from the ball, it either made no sense at all, or contradicted the information collected by some previous sweep. This newest scan she was initiating wasn't coming back at all.

It was as if the ball was eating the k-band she was trying to use to scan its innards.

According to the best sensing packages that Customs had at its disposal, the ball was empty but inert, without even so much as standard 3k emanations. So that meant, if you wanted to think about it reductively, that there was *something* inside it. Because if there were standard *nothing* inside it, she wouldn't have a ball-configured area of complete silence in all bandwidths.

Whatever was out there, inside that ball, wasn't your usual conception of nothing. It read on her sensing screen, in this mode, as solid.

But it didn't have the mass or density one expected from a solid. What could scour an area of background radiation, foreground radiation, and normal particle decay?

Thinking about it raised hairs on her forearms. She pushed away from the k-band screen, which showed her a black ball in its center, and swivelled in her chair.

Across from her, Keebler was on his third protein bar, washing it down with a dextrose shake. He belched and slid his arm along a console he wasn't using, spilling empty wrappers to the deck.

"Well, little lady, ready for a bit o' spacewalkin'?" The scavenger was already suited up, his helmet hanging from his chair's arm.

So was she.

"As ready as you are, Captain Keebler." She couldn't put this off any longer. She mustn't seem overtly obstructive or recalcitrant. She needed to get through this whole trip without the scavenger finding any reason to ask for a reevaluation of her findings. And she needed to keep Keebler off the flight deck, where the two pilots and the AI pilot were still working on giving her the data readout she needed to put this ball on ice for the foreseeable.

She picked up her helmet reluctantly, flipped the self-test switch on its faceplate, and waited for the helmet's inboard AI to beep its readiness.

"You realized, Captain Keebler," she said carefully for the record, because everything said in here was being logged, "that none of scans are showing anything like normal readings inside that thing."

"Normal for empty's what you're lookin' fer, right? Well, it ain't empty. I know it ain't empty." Keebler's watery eyes gleamed.

"Normal for anything we know about. If it's not empty, then it ought to show something in one of our frequency ranges. It doesn't. Would you like to tell me why you're so sure it isn't empty?"

"I've had experience with it, is why."

The greed and the determination of this man were beginning to get to Lowe. She said, "What kind of experience?"

"You better come see fer yerself, D'rector. If I was t' tell ya, y' might not b'lieve me. And there's no need o' us gettin' on the wrong side o' each other over this."

Lowe's helmet beeped before she could retort that it was too late to worry about that. Saved by the beep, she said, "Suit up. Systems checks."

Once she'd settled the helmet over her head, Keebler

couldn't see her face because her visor was down, completing its self-test.

The inboard AI mated the suit to the helmet, integrated the electronics, checked the cooling, heating, and life-support systems, and read the results out in the left upper quadrant of her visor's heads-up display.

She ignored the process, waiting for the green light to proceed, or a warning or malfunction blinker to appear in its place.

When the green light came on, she said, "Suit freqs," to the AI, and then, "EVA-Alpha to Beta. Captain Keebler, can you hear me?"

"Sure can, D'rector." She could hear the triumphant humor in the bastard's voice. "Dual com constant," she told the AI. Then: "Let's get our tanks and get out there."

The airpacks by the two-stage lock weren't really tanks, but pack harnesses with air and manned maneuvering packages. She plugged her twelve-dins together, and the suit gave her another green: Everything was functioning.

"Shadow Beta's reads," she told the AI. Up came Keebler's life-support system. It, too, was perfect.

No excuse not to go out. And Keebler had heard her ask for a check of his systems, so he knew she was professionally concerned for his welfare.

She hit the lockplate and stepped into the cycler. Keebler followed and the inner lock shut. All she could hear was her own breathing, and Keebler's. His was deep and slow. Hers . . . well, dual com had its disadvantages.

She manually keyed in her optimizer package and the cuff of her suit pricked her wrist, sending stabilizing chemicals into her bloodstream. While it did, she wriggled her shoulders to make sure the jetpack in the MMU/life support was comfortably settled. It hooked to a harness that was integral to her suit, and if it were off center, you got really uncomfortable after a while, because the suit itself would grab you in all the wrong places when you keyed the MMU.

The outer lock opened, and the stars were only a polarized faceplate away.

Riva Lowe told her AI, "Neuron assist, voice command." She hated keypadding the MMU. A little disk came down out of the helmet and settled itself in front of her right eye. She could look through the monocle and see an unobstructed view, but the monocle was necessary to allow the neuron assist travel package to use her eyeball for targeting her destination.

It was almost like flying, as a bird might fly—effortlessly, naturally, thanks to the MMU monocle program. She glanced at her readout of Keebler's suit and saw that he was using a manual keypad control option. The older generation didn't adapt quickly; she could soar circles around the crusty old scavenger, double his efficiency at any extravehicular task, simply because she wasn't afraid to let her AI draw her intent from her muscles and their neural firings.

She said, no longer needing to cue the MMU directly at all, "Straight over there, Keebler. Stop six feet from the outer skin," and felt her jet pack kick in.

If the ball wasn't out there, looming closer and closer, she would have been enjoying herself. But it was, a silvery sphere that was nearly the size of the *Adamson,* blocking out more and more of the starfield, the closer to it she got.

Lowe was so surprised when the *Adamson* pilot contacted her on a privacy channel that she jumped at the beep and the appearance of a purple, strobing light.

She shifted to privacy manually, then said, "EVA-Alpha, no log. What's up, guys?" when she was sure that Keebler couldn't hear her.

"*Adamson* to EVA-Alpha," said the copilot's voice. "Director, we've got an emergency call from an Assistant Secretary Remson. He wants me to patch him through. Can you take it? He doesn't want to leave a recorded message and he says he can't wait."

Oh, no. Her saliva dried up. Her pulse thumped so that her optimization pack pricked her again. What could be this urgent? She said, "Patch him through purple, no log unless he asks for one. And fellas, don't monitor this one except as a bandwidth."

They'd only come on-line if there was an interrupt before the transmission ended.

"Roger, EVA-Alpha."

The ball before her ceased coming closer as her MMU took its cues from her intent and stopped her progress. She hung still in space and Keebler drifted past, his helmeted head turning her way questioningly. He gave an ancient handsignal: Was she in trouble?

She gave one back, ringing her gloved first finger and thumb: A-OK. She wasn't about to coddle him. Let him wonder. Let him wait.

But he kept jetting toward the ball.

And her com channel sputtered to life: "Riva, Remson here. You know your crazy Relic has broken into the docking area, gotten onto his ship, and is, in essence, holding it hostage. He's demanding to talk to somebody in authority and I'm too busy. So's Mickey. Get back here and clean up your own mess, ASAP. Remson, over."

"Come on, Remson, what can he do? Send some port cops in and put him in a padded cell."

"He can do what he just did. He can make waves. He can try to blast out of there. He can probably overload that fusion power plant of his. This is your mess, Director."

"I'll be in as soon as I can. Make sure the port people maintain the status quo. Ask Reice to pick a boarding team and meet me with it when I dock."

"Okay. It's your party. But he wants to negotiate."

"Then have Reice pick a negotiating team and a boarding team and meet me when I dock. As a matter of fact, tell him I hope you'll be among the negotiators." Remson would have to relay the message. "Meanwhile, I'm out here in a spacesuit. The sooner you go back to your luncheon or whatever, the sooner I can get out of it. EVA-Alpha, out."

Things never seemed to happen when you had time for them. She toggled back to the flight crew before she did anything else: "We're going to hurry this up. Be prepared for a little resistance from the scavenger. And get me a priority flight path back. We're going to break some speed limits."

Then: "Dual. Log." And: "EVA-Beta, I'm on my way."

Her suit took cues from her intent and she sped to Keebler's side.

When she'd braked, they were only an arm's length from the sphere. It started changing colors. Or it was reflecting her spacesuit, somehow catching errant light and rainbowing it . . .

But there wasn't anything to have caused the effect. Suddenly she could see her spacesuited form in its side. She reached out toward it.

She must have been closer than she thought . . .

"D'rector!" she heard in her com.

Her gloved fingers touched the sphere and, abruptly, she was somewhere else. The voice of Keebler chattering excitedly in her ears was very far away. She was a little girl, with her parents; she was cruising near Earth with a man who looked only vaguely familiar; she was old and somewhere she'd never been before, where a ringed planet hung in a lavender sky. And she was peacefully sleeping with someone by her bed, someone with huge eyes and an aura of wealth beyond material calculation, someone not human or even recognizably alien. . . .

"D'rector, see what I mean?"

She had no idea what Keebler had said, let alone what he'd meant.

But he was between her and the bulk of the sphere, gesticulating excitedly.

Well, she could review her log later.

"I'm still not convinced," she said through sticky lips. "You and I are going back to the ship. We'll look at our scans. We'll discuss this. I'm not sure that anything else I can do out here will help."

Keebler said, "Damn, I shoulda known," and started jetting away, following the curve of the sphere.

"Keebler, come back here!" she shouted. She wasn't going to go after him. She'd leave the scavenger out here with twelve hours' worth of life support and his foolish sphere, before she'd do that.

Her anger translated into a very speedy approach to the *Adamson*. Behind her, she could hear Keebler, swearing like a dockworker under his breath, as he followed.

She refused to answer any of his communications until they were both in the lock and it was cycling.

Then, to his insistent queries and demands for his rights, she said only, "We'll see what the scans say. We'll look at the AI readout." The inner lock safety light lit, it cycled open, and she stepped inside.

Lowe felt better almost immediately, as soon as Keebler had followed and the lock closed behind him.

While they racked their packs, she was carefully noncommittal to all his pleas.

Once she got her helmet off, she told him, "I'm going up on the flight deck. I'll be right back, Captain Keebler. Sit down and make yourself comfortable."

The scavenger squinted at her. "You're messin' with me, D'rector, ain'cha? This whole trip out here was just to satisfy some reg'lation. Y' never intended to let anythin' you saw out there make a bit o'diff'rence. An' don't think I don't know it."

"Captain Keebler," she said, putting her hand to her yet-spacesuited heart, "how could you suggest such a thing? I'm so busy that I had to take an emergency call while I was on the EVA with you. I took time to eyeball this artifact of yours in person precisely because I think it *is* important." Riva Lowe was prayerfully glad that this conversation was being recorded. "So important that I don't want to make an error in judgment, or be hurried into making one. Now you wait here. I'll be right back."

She left him and went forward.

When the flight deck lock closed behind her, she said to the two men who turned in their command chairs, "I've finished. That thing is weird. I touched it and I'm not sure what happened. I'm getting myself full med scans when I get home. That scavenger may need some male convincing.

One of you go back and tell him we're not towing it in with us. We're impounding it right here, under twenty-four-hour guard. I'll cut the orders now. And get us on that full-tilt flight path home."

The copilot stood up. "I'll see to him, Director. Sit here if you want."

They squeezed by each other in the narrow confines of the flight deck.

Once the lock had closed again, the pilot punched up the intercom so that they could hear what was going on back there.

And it did get heated, between the copilot and the scavenger, who was yelling at the copilot that he knew his rights.

The copilot's voice said, "You've got the right to sit quietly while you get a free ride home, buddy, or you've got the right to be restrained and dragged home forcibly. You've brought dangerous material into the Threshold spacedock area, and if you don't want to be arrested, here and now, you'll shut the fuck up so that I can get back to doing my job."

There was what might have been a brief scuffle, but by then Riva Lowe was already immersed in the report she had to write to impound the scavenger's find.

When she got to the part about touching it, she wrote, "Indeterminate temporal effects, which need further investigation."

And as she punched the keys, the tips of the fingers on her right hand tingled with tactile memory so that she put them to her lips and licked them, to see if she still had normal sensation in the skin there.

She did, but that was about all that was normal right now, so far as she was concerned.

That thing out there wasn't going one inch closer to Threshold. And she was going to get the full med scan she'd promised herself. As soon as she finished dealing with the Relic pilot who'd taken over his ship and was terrorizing the ConSec docking bay.

She was never going to hear the end of this from Reice,

who'd warned her not to turn the Relic loose. And Remson had let her know that Croft wasn't exactly thrilled with her, either.

She tried not to wonder how these two awful problems were going to affect her personally—her career, her reputation. But she couldn't help thinking about it.

And thinking about it made her hate the scavenger, the unidentifiable ball, and Joe South as well. If she could have justified it, she'd have let the scavenger go back out to his precious ball, and used her pulse beams to blow them both right out of her spacetime. And for all she cared, they could take Joe South with them.

But dreaming wouldn't make it so. She pushed the final entry key that would impound the ball and give three shifts of Customs agents overtime, keeping an eye on it.

Then she sat back. The pilot was just beginning his thrust sequence, and the copilot was coming forward, through the airlock.

"Everything's clear back there. Our passenger won't give you any more trouble, Director."

She gave the copilot his seat and went aft to find out if what he said was true.

The scavenger was sitting by one console, massive head on his gnarly fist, his ponytail askew. He was staring at a screen that showed a real-time view of the spherical object. He looked over his shoulder at her and said, "You win, D'rector. But it's only Round One. I brought that thing here so's I could crack it open, and I'm gonna. And not you nor the whole o' Threshold's po-lice is gonna stop me. It's just a matter of time."

"Perhaps."

"Y' can't keep me from comin' back here. You'll see."

"Perhaps." Lowe sat down at one of the stations and stared blindly at the terminal before her. This was going to be a long, unpleasant ride home. She could try not to listen to the scavenger, but she'd be better off to reason with him.

Unless she could find a way to place him in protective custody, or under house arrest on a technicality, in this mood he could cause her even more trouble than he had so far.

And she didn't need any more trouble. Not today.

"Stations," said the intercom. "Ready for burn. Counting . . ."

She canted her couch back and closed her eyes, as she strapped for the fastest ride home the pilots could deliver.

By the time she got there, she'd better have a plan of action in mind.

CHAPTER 12

Romeo and Juliet

Remson hated to do this to Secretary Croft, who was in the middle of the session debating a proposal to use Flangers instead of terrestrial primates for medical research.

Remson's personal opinion was that organs grown in vitro and DNA substitutes were plenty good for med research, but the researchers kept insisting that you needed complex, living systems if you were going to minimize undesirable side effects.

The Flangers that NAMECorp had brought in for the session were in the middle of the conference hall, and that made the debate emotional. It was harder to control tempers when living things were staring at the people deciding their fates.

Remson wouldn't have changed places with Croft for all the money in the Threshold Interstellar Bank. But troubleshooting was what Remson got paid for, and Croft needed to know what Remson had to tell him. And Mickey needed to know it now, before this meeting broke up for the night. And before Ayatollah Forat cornered the Secretary publicly to field his accusations.

Croft saw Remson waiting in the wings. The Secretary was a professional's professional. He leaned sideways, whispered in the ear of the dignitary next to him, and was out of his chair and striding toward Remson before the man in the chair next to his now-empty one could announce that the Secretary had passed him the moderator's job for the rest of the night.

"To what act of Providence do I owe your presence?" Croft asked gratefully, clapping Remson on the arm as he reached him.

Remson turned with his boss and the two of them walked behind the curtains, toward a side exit.

"Sir, I wish I had better news, but you'll understand my urgency . . ."

Croft shot a glance at him and kept walking, his sharp chin lowering just slightly, watching the toes of his shiny wingtips as they hit the floor. He didn't say a word, just waited.

"Sir, Ayatollah Forat's daughter, Dini, is missing, so her father claims. He's blaming Dodd, both for her purported tardiness last night, her general bad behavior since then, and now this. That is, he's blaming Dodd when he's not blaming the general corrupting influence of Threshold, with its 'sybaritic lifestyle.' "

"Where were the Medinan bodyguards, the purported 'sentient service staff' members whom he brought with him? Are you sure this isn't a stunt staged to cut our legs out from under us tomorrow, when those very subhumans come up for discussion? These people are virtual slavers. You can't trust them not to be concocting the whole thing to prove that the bodyguards are fallible subhumans, rather than what we're saying they are: a bioengineered species that's close enough to the template to deserve full human rights."

"Yes, sir," Remson sighed. "I thought of that, sir. They've got two bodyguards, an Ali-4 and an Ali-5, who are slated for destruction because of this mess. I assume we'd like to halt any such act until the Ali-4 and Ali-5 entities can be examined by an impartial panel, but . . ."

"But?"

"Well, sir, I wonder if we're not playing into their hands.

Their bodyguard class is still technically a class of support system, nothing more. If we interfere with the Medinans' replacement of what they insist are biological machines, then where are we?"

"In the soup, as my father used to say. What do you suggest, Remson?"

"I'd like to make a stab at finding the girl, sir. I'd like access to your modeler." Remson held his breath.

The modeler wasn't legal for government work. Its results wouldn't be admissible in any court as evidence, nor would its use be clearly within guidelines, even to find a missing person.

"If you do, I don't know about it. You realize that we haven't enough information on the Forat girl to do a successful model? So whatever you get is just for your own edification."

Nicely done, Remson thought admiringly. "Well, sir, the girl had brought a mocket—that's a pet indigenous to Medina—along, and maybe I could use the mocket to build a template, if the Medinans will let me have the mocket. Or maybe that's too risky—" He backed off, seeing Croft's face.

"I certainly wouldn't ask. Of course, if the thing got lost, or if it could be used to track the girl like a bloodhound . . ."

"Right, sir. I'll get right on it."

"See that you find her fast, if she's somewhere to be found, Vince."

"Yes, sir. I'll try, sir."

"And Vince—good work, so far. I'll try to stay clear of the old man. If that's not possible, at least I'm prepared. How's our Relic doing?"

"Waiting for his negotiating team, sir. I've got discharge papers, signed and sealed, if we'd like to employ them in any way."

"No, don't push that angle. If they're the originals, we wouldn't want to say how we came by them; if they're not, that's worse. Unless the Relic should kill himself or be killed during this interval, we won't be using those."

"Yes, sir. That's what I thought. But I had to check."

"Go work me a miracle, Vince." Again, the squeeze on Remson's arm.

Croft paused, and seemed surprised that he was standing before the exit. "Well, back into the fray. I'll probably be seeing our dear Ayatollah for drinks, now that I've had a chance to think things through, rather than attempt to avoid him."

To take the heat off me, and the attention, Remson realized.

He'd never worked for anyone remotely as capable as Michael Croft. He wanted to say that, but he couldn't find a way. He merely waited until his boss went through the door before he headed off to the Medinans' hotel, where, with luck, he could finagle the mocket that belonged to Dini Forat.

Vince Remson needed to find out who'd been helping that girl, because it sure wasn't Dodd. Some of what lay ahead was pure police work, some was databank searches, some was the sort of thing that Remson did best: the impossible.

Well, he was about to see if he could still earn his keep.

He delegated tasks from his car on the way to the Medinan hotel. Then it was time to knock on the suite's ornate door and ask to speak to whoever was in charge at the moment.

It was the first time he'd ever been in a position to relate directly to one of the Ali-class bodyguards, and it gave him the creeps. Or rather, the thought of them being considered disposable machines gave him the creeps.

The Ali who ushered him into the suite was designated Ali-7 and it was decidedly unhappy. Could machines perspire? There were beads of sweat on the Ali's lip. He knew it wasn't really a machine, just a vat-grown piece of genetic engineering, and that its hundred or so human parents shared the pride of the vat's produce with a team of bioengineers who'd taken a snip of DNA from here, and a bit from there, and added some source code that never occurred naturally in human beings.

So what was it?

Damned if he knew. Whatever it was, it was nervous, standing eye to eye with him. Remson was six foot two and stocky, pure Scandinavian peasant twenty generations back, and there were few men on Threshold of his displacement. There also were few with his combination of skills.

He evaluated the Ali and his experience told him he was looking at a well-trained fighting . . . being.

Not a machine. A being.

He said to the Ali, "I'm from the Secretary General's office." He flashed his ID. "I'd like to pick up some effects of the missing girl, to help me find her. Also, her mocket, who might be able to trace her like a bloodhound."

"Blood hound?"

"Scent its master."

"I can do that," said the Ali out of a broad, square face with wideset eyes and a hawk nose.

"Well, then you're welcome to come along, if you've got the time." Could the Ali help him? Would it?

It would, and it could, it seemed. The Ali came back with a woman's veil and the mocket, which looked like a little white dog at the moment, and put the creature down. He handed its leash to Remson.

"I have permission, sir, to aid you. My brothers' lives depend upon it." There was a very human gleam in Ali-7's eyes. His voice came from deep in his throat, a voice with a passable English accent.

Feeling heartened, Remson said, "Come on, then. Let's go."

He peered around. The suite seemed empty, but for Ali-7, but it was clear to Remson that he was supposed to surmise just that. Dini Forat could be locked in her room's closet, for all he knew, or might have been smuggled onto the Medinan ship in one of the oriental rugs that the Medinans had brought with them.

But out he went with Ali-7, wondering whether he dared have the Ali around when he used the modeler on the mocket. The big bodyguard moved with a grace that Remson envied, and a certainty only special kinds of men possessed.

Not men, he reminded himself. But the Ali-7 was more of a man, in Remson's terms, than most of the diplomats he'd been squiring around the conference.

Once they were out of the hotel and in Remson's long, low government car, he said, "Ali-7, tell me everything you can remember hearing about Dini Forat's disappearance, and I'll record it for our records. Even the smallest thing will help." He hit a toggler.

How smart were the bodyguards? The Medinans had avoided IQ tests, for the obvious reasons: You gave IQ tests to people.

Ali-7 absently lifted the little white mocket onto his lap and stroked the shivering pseudo-dog. It quieted immediately.

"The details, seen by Ali-4 and Ali-5, are as follows . . ."

Once the Ali started reeling off street names and club names and a detailed itinerary of Dini Forat's movements until she'd slipped out on Dodd, Remson knew he was on the right track.

When Ali-7 stopped for breath, Remson offered the bodyguard a drink from the car's bar. It was just habit.

Nobody could convince him that this wasn't a person, or at least a candidate for personhood. He wondered what would happen if he modeled an Ali. Then, because he was getting excited about the possibility, he said, "Can the mocket become any kind of dog? Can it be bigger? Can it have other attributes?"

The mocket was a Medinan life-form that molded itself into a pleasing image. It was some sort of chameleon life-form.

"You must show it a picture of what you want it to be. Also, it cannot be more than three times its current size."

"That's big enough. We'll show it a bloodhound—a talented sniffing dog—and see if it'll take that shape."

"Shall I continue?" the Ali wanted to know.

"I'm sorry, Ali-7, I cut you off. Surely. Tell me where Dini Forat was today."

"First she arose and left her bedroom for the bath. . . ."

The detailed account continued until they were nearly

back to Remson's office before he interrupted the Ali: "What did you say?"

"She called a number from a public booth: 0237-9047509."

"How can you know that?" Remson was so intrigued that he sat forward.

"I have Ali-5's word on it. He was surveilling her."

"Okay, that's good enough. Then what happened?"

"Mistress Dini went into a place where Ali-5 could not follow." The Ali shook its head ruefully. Its mouth tightened. Then it looked up. "We are not permitted into some places. It makes the job of protecting our charges exceedingly difficult."

"It's okay, fella," said Remson, as if it were one of his own men who'd been frustrated in the performance of his duties by red tape and protocol.

"When she did not come out, he went looking for a back entrance. We think now that Mistress Dini got into a car that came to the front during that time, but this is only supposition."

"Supposition?" The idea of putting this Ali-7 down like a dog, or pulling his plug like a piece of outboard equipment, was increasingly bothering Remson.

"Ali-5 and I went back to the place and questioned the staff—very politely."

"I'm sure. Tell me more."

By the time they parked under Remson's office complex, he wasn't sure he was going to need the modeler after all. He had a phone number; he had an approximate time of pickup from a vehicle at a specific location. Even a ConSec sergeant could get a plate number on the car, scrolling for general surveillance data. It would be easy to verify whether someone had entered the car, if the surveillance angle was right.

Remson was going to get a location and name on the phone number. Then he was going to take Ali-7 and the mocket out hunting with him.

After that, once he'd found the girl (if she was still on

Threshold and hadn't been smuggled out by an accomplice), he was going to talk to Croft about the Alis.

But first he needed to check with Security to see if anyone had called in a ransom for Dini Forat. If she hadn't run away purposefully, maybe they could just buy her back from a captor.

And he needed to double surveillance and security on outgoing flights, in case she was intending to slip away but hadn't done so yet.

"Come on, Ali-7, you're going to like the way we do police work on Threshold."

Remson held the door open for the Ali and the mocket he cradled so tenderly, which had belonged to his mistress.

Vince Remson knew then and there that he was going to run this Ali-7 through the modeler. He couldn't resist finding out whether the modeler thought it was dealing with a man. Vince Remson certainly did.

If the two of them could find the missing mullah's daughter together, it might help the Alis' case. At least, it might save the lives of Ali-4 and Ali-5.

CHAPTER 13

Do It Yourself

These scavengers were dangerous customers. Sling knew that all too well. He looked at the old guy with the yellowish white ponytail and smiled as if this Keebler were exactly the sort of client Sling specialized in servicing.

"What can I do for you, exactly, Captain Keebler?" Sling asked casually, but carefully, putting his rubber-soled boots up on the desk he'd made out of the wing flap of an antique spaceplane.

The fat old fart bared scummy teeth at him and settled into a slouch against the door that separated Sling's tiny office from the business end of his business: the shop, lab, and garage bay.

"Well, sonny, heard from folks that yer the best there is, with custom work."

"Sometimes folks exaggerate, Captain Keebler. Which folks did you mean?"

You couldn't be too careful. This old guy was too perfect to be for real. Maybe he wasn't a scavenger at all, but some kind of undercover cop trying to start up a sting operation. When you were as vulnerable to being caught on the fine point of the law as Sling often was, you went very slowly with people who just showed up on your doorstep.

Keebler named the two top men in the Salvagers' Local.

Sling had done work for both of them, some of which wasn't anywhere near legal.

"Well, what can I do for you, Captain Keebler?" Sling repeated the question, still not sure he really wanted to hear the answer.

"I need a special kind o' tool."

"Doesn't everybody?"

"One to get me inside somethin' that don't have no obvious entrance."

"Let me guess," Sling proposed. "You tried telling it 'Open, Sez Me' and it wouldn't, right?"

"Close enough, sonny."

"Name's Sling." Sling's feet came down off the desk. He picked up a corroded intake nozzle and tapped it against his palm. "And you've got to do better than that, if you're trying to tell me anything about your problem. If you're not ready to do that, there's no way I can help you." He dropped the nozzle on the desk.

"Got anythin' t' drink around here, Sling?"

"Sorry, fresh out." These scavengers usually had good reason to be nervous. Salvage rights weren't enforceable until you brought whatever you'd found into port and registered it. Sometimes what you'd found was nasty, therefore very valuable, therefore you didn't want to register it because the government would confiscate it and you wouldn't get diddly from them. There were whole classes of weaponry and fusionables and contraband (everything from drugs to explosives) on the Controlled Items list that would go—went—for a high price on the black market.

Sometimes that price could be your life, if you had what somebody wanted and he thought killing you would be cheaper than paying you for it.

So Sling tried to stay away from the scavengers. They were all mean. They were all crazy. They were all trouble. But Keebler was a well-connected scavenger; the union bosses whose names he'd dropped could make Sling's life a living hell if he didn't at least consider this old scumbag's problem.

So maybe, if Sling wanted to continue in the aftermarket business, he'd better be more polite: "Tell me what you need to get into and I'll tell you if I think I can help you, or who might be able to do the job if I can't."

"I need to get into somethin' nobody's ever gotten into before. Somethin' nobody's ever seen before. Somethin' real special." There was a glazed look in the scavenger's eye as he spoke. He came over to Sling's desk and leaned on it. "There's lots in it for y', sonny, iffen y' can gimme what I need."

Sling sat forward as well, leaning into a shower of garlicky breath without so much as a wince. "What do you mean?"

"I mean I got me an art-i-fact, is what. And I want a tunable AI, coupled with an electronic locksmith, so's I c'n open 'er up."

"How about a zero-point torch? Cut your way in?" A torch wouldn't have Sling's signature on it the way a custom black box would. He could sell this guy a torch and it'd be legal. What the scavenger did with the torch, that was up to him.

"Nope. Tried that. Do I look like some greenhorn to you?" The scavenger's scruffy eyebrows came together over his nose. "C'n y' do it, sonny? Or are y' just another pretty face?"

"I can do it, no sweat," flared Sling. "But how do I know you're not going to try robbing a bank with something like that? I got a legal shop here. I got records to keep. I got people to answer to."

"That's right, sonny. People t' answer to. Remember that."

"Lookit, you damn puddle of nuclear waste, you back the hell off." Sling came out of his chair. The old guy straightened up. But he didn't back off.

"Yer not legal enough t' mess with me about this, sonny. I been tol' that." He put huge hands on his love handles.

"Don't threaten me. You're not giving me squat to work with."

"You don't need to know but what I'm tellin' you. I said,

tunable. I want a EHF freq range—you ever heard of a bank vault locked up with a combination in the extra-high freqs?"

Whatever this was, the old guy was right—it wasn't bank robbery. It wasn't hijacking, either. "How can I do . . ." Sling closed his mouth. He probably could put together some kind of tunable EHF safecracker. It wasn't that hard. It was just weird. Nonstandard. Maybe not even illegal.

Maybe.

"So what's this box got to have, besides the EHF component?"

"A 'howdy-do, pleased t'meetcha, c'n I come in?' relay, coupled with a down-freq transponder so's I c'n talk to it if it c'n talk to me."

Talk to it? "Anything else? A nail file or a shoe-polisher, maybe? How small does this thing have to be?"

"I need t' be able to carry it out . . . EVA it."

"Okay, so it's got to be space-sealed. Smaller than you are. Anything else?"

"Yeah, one more thing. It's got t' remember how it got in, an' be able t' repeat or reverse the process."

"If you're talking expert program, old man, the price just doubled. You want an expert that can make sixty thousand or so decisions per second for something like this, and an AI like that costs." It was Sling's turn to put his hands on his hips. His gut knew this wasn't legal, somehow. The old guy was being too evasive.

"I don't need no expert program, just memory, sonny. Memory with repeat and reverse fer the winnin' sequences."

"Okay, now you tell me what it is you're trying to get into. Because if it's some government something, I can't have any part of it."

"This thing's not made in our damned spacetime, Mister Hotshit Aftermarket Cowboy. It's from somewhere else entirely. It's a gen-u-ine alien artifact, like I said, from a superior civ'lization, an' there's no law against it. Not yet."

This guy was crazy as a Loader on dope.

"You've convinced me, Captain Keebler." Sling wanted to

get rid of this scavenger, and there was only one way. "I figure that'll cost you about a quarter K-note, what with the self-contained power source and memory and all those presets." That should scare Keebler away. Sling mentally kicked himself for not trying money talk before. But before, he wouldn't have had any data on which to base a price.

"Half now, half later," said the scavenger brusquely, and held out his ham of a hand.

"Uh . . . yeah. That's fine with me. But payment in full on delivery." Sling tried not to wince under the pressure Keebler was applying to the fine bones of his hand. A quarter K-note? This must be some rich scavenger, or some seriously lucrative piece of space junk. Or something so illegal he'd be glad he'd recorded the scavenger's proposition. Just in case.

"When c'n that be?" The scavenger let his hand go.

"What? Delivery? Now you're in a hurry?" Sling rubbed one hand with the other to restore circulation. He bent over and looked at his calendar. "If I put everything else aside, I can have it for you by tomorrow night."

He'd get half the money before this crazy left today. And since he had nothing much to do, putting everything aside wasn't a real hardship.

If he didn't get busted for doing this, it was going to be a godsend. If he did get busted, he could try replaying the tape where he warned the scavenger that he didn't want anything to do with any illegal activity. So if it was a sting, he was probably in the clear.

When the scavenger gave him the down payment on a Space University Bank credit card, Sling was almost sure it wasn't a sting. Too upper-crusty for his image, by half, if that image had been constructed by the Interstellar Commerce Commission, the Contraband Enforcement Agency, or Customs.

When the smelly old eccentric lumbered out of his office, Sling was a comparatively rich man. Next time Captain Keebler showed up, there'd be something to drink around here.

Right now, Sling was going to have to hustle: he had to buy the components he needed to make the box, which, from what the old man had told him, didn't have a snowball's chance in hell of working.

No alien artifact was going to respond to the black box that Keebler had ordered. but Keebler had told Sling exactly what he wanted, and Sling would make him exactly that box.

The box would perform its functions, so Sling would earn his pay.

What in all of creation did that fool have out there, that he was trying to get into it without even an expert program to think the parameters through for him?

Sling stopped wondering about it and picked up the phone. He had to call around and see who had what he needed on the shelf. There wasn't time to order parts. With a quarter of a K-note riding on this fabrication order, he didn't want to be caught short, or come in late, or give Keebler any reason to leave him holding the bag—or, in this case, a black box virtually useless to anyone else and probably useless to Keebler himself.

CHAPTER 14

$$\triangledown$$

Caught in the Act

By the time Vince Remson assembled his ConSec backup team and had secured his clearances to enter the Cummings building, he'd had plenty of time to work up a head of steam over the possible repercussions of what he was about to do.

The sidewalk in front of the NAMECorp CEO's residence was crawling with officials. Richard Cummings, Jr.,'s son was in this up to his triply immune ears.

Every time Remson took three steps toward the building, somebody stopped him: a representative of NAMECorp; a nervous functionary from TTT (Threshold Trust Territory) Internal Security; one of the UNE people that were here to make sure that none of the rights of the Medinan girl were violated; and a worried staffer of his own with a communiqué from the Secretariat.

Remson kept telling everyone the same thing: He had a full understanding of what was at stake here. And he did.

The girl up there with Richard Cummings III wasn't going to be handed over to her own people for summary execution if Remson had anything to say about it. He had a medical team with an ambulance waiting to examine the girl. With any luck, she was still a virgin. If she wasn't, that still didn't mean that Remson was going to turn her over to the brutal justice of Medina. Doing so would make him an accessory to state-sanctioned assassination. He was determined to find a way around that possibility.

Finding a way around it involved the Cummings boy, who was also under a knee-jerk sentence of death already, according to Medinan representatives. But the kids had been tried and sentenced in absentia within minutes of the mullahs receiving Remson's report.

Nobody had expected the Medinans to play into the Secretariat's hands by going so far. But somehow, Remson was going to use the Medinan overreach to save the girl. You couldn't declare the son of NAMECorp's CEO, and NAMECorp itself, with all its star-flung outposts, the enemies of your state, its religious laws, and subject to death and destruction on sight, without somebody giving you an argument. Not in this day and age. And not on UNE and TTT turf.

So when one of Mickey Croft's personal security people came shouldering his way through the crowd of officials and police and vehicles to Remson, he assumed the man was delivering one more Medinan threat of reprisals and broken relations if both kids weren't immediately turned over to Medinan justice.

But the fellow said, "Hey, Vince. Got a message for you from Customs that Mickey said you'd want to hear. Director Lowe requests your presence on the negotiations team dealing with the Relic, ASAP."

"Damn the Relic," Remson nearly snarled, so unexpected was this additional complication; "and damn Riva Lowe, as well. I don't have time for her games."

The functionary put his hands in his pockets and looked at his feet, trying to stifle a grin. "You don't want me to tell her that, sir."

"You're right. Tell her to start without me. I'll be along as soon as I can."

The functionary turned to go.

"And tell Mickey thanks for the modeler—off the record."

The security man didn't look back as he raised a hand and

waved to indicate that he'd heard, understood, and would comply.

Remson took a deep breath and headed for the knot of people congregated before the Cummings Building. In their midst were Ali-7 and the mocket, now happily sniffing feet in its new shape of earth-type bloodhound.

Watching the mocket turn itself into something three times its size had been a real experience, enough to raise your short hairs. But by then, Remson had run the Ali through Croft's psychometric sampler-modeler, and his incredulity index was already redlined. There was nothing in the model of Ali-7 that differed in any way from a well-trained human commando—the sort of commando that Vince Remson had once been.

Well, Medina was far away and subject to UNE laws, if it wanted to trade with the rest of humanity. Once human and subhuman rights on Medina came under UNE scrutiny, lots of things were going to change. Things like treating women as little more than incubators with legs. Abortion was illegal on Medina. So was sex outside of wedlock, and wedlock was still a camel-trading affair.

Maybe Cummings, Jr., had enough camels to trade with Ayatollah Forat to save Cummings III's miserable life. Mickey's staff was trying to find the NAMECorp CEO right now.

But Medinan women hardly ever married infidels. . . .

So this conference could turn into everybody's worst nightmare, even without the Ali matter; even if Remson could bring himself to let what he'd learned about Ali-7 die with him.

But Remson couldn't—wouldn't—do that. Ali-4 and Ali-5 were going to die if Remson kept silent. So he wasn't about to do that. The least these fighting men of Medina deserved were real names. You had a right to die with a name, for heaven's sake. You had a right to walk around with your head high and some basic human dignity, no matter what you were trained to do.

The Ali-7 model had been more forthcoming than Ali-7 could bring himself to be, because Remson could filter out the cultural restraints of Medinan conditioning.

But the Ali-7 model wasn't admissible as evidence in court. Ali-7 was.

Remson cut through the crowd around the Ali and straight to the Medinan bodyguard. Ali-7 was still holding the bloodhound's leash.

"Is the mocket ready?"

Ali-7 looked at him with liquid eyes that held a degree of fellowship and trust in them that Remson hadn't seen since he'd left the Peacekeeping service. And also a brittleness that came from knowing you were walking into a situation that could kill you.

"The mocket is ready, Remson," the Ali told him. Ali-7 loved his life, however repugnant that life might be to an outsider. He pulled a corner of Dini Forat's veil out of his pocket and dangled it before the red-furred bloodhound's nose. The hound bayed.

Or at least the mocket gave as good an imitation of a baying hound as it could, having seen only one stock vid on bloodhound behavior.

Again, Remson recalled the cloud that the little white mocket had exuded before it tripled its size. All its hairs had stood on end. There'd been a smell that was sweet and fecund, and the air pressure in Mickey Croft's modeler room had seemed to change. Remson's ears had popped.

Maybe the mockets tapped Dirac's energy sea, like some sort of biological A-field transformer. Remson's atomic wristwatch, in exact sync with the clocks in the modeler room, had been two seconds slow thereafter to all the clocks outside, which might indicate A-field effects.

However the mocket had managed its transformation, it was a bloodhound now, and there wasn't any reason to delay putting it to good use.

Before the gathered representatives of the various interested parties, Remson said, "Okay, boy, find your mistress. Seek."

The bloodhound better be right. Otherwise, Remson's ass was in a concrete sling, all these people were here for nothing, and young Cummings was going to catch a different kind of hell for not answering his vidphone and probably aiding and abetting the interstellar transport of a minor.

Because Dini Forat *had* come back to the Cummings Building with young Rick. The information gathered by Ali-4 and Ali-5, and passed on to Remson by Ali-7, had checked out perfectly: Cummings had brought the girl here; Remson had the surveillance recordings to prove it.

As he and the Ali-7 let the bloodhound lead them into the Cummings Building's lobby and to the private penthouse elevator, Remson began praying that he hadn't made some awful mistake in judgment. His neck prickled as if he could feel the recorders trained on him. All on the record. All by the book.

If he was just flat wrong about the girl still being here, he couldn't even imagine what it would do to Secretary Croft's position vis-à-vis the Medinans in the hours and days to follow.

If he was wrong, he'd stopped all other avenues of search and let the girl get away clean. Or he'd been set up by the Medinans and fallen for some deadly bait, hook, line, and sinker.

The elevator closed behind them, cutting off the observer teams. Above his head, ceiling cameras rotated slightly, focusing on the Ali-7 and the bloodhound. Remson eyed the cameras and shook his head: *Don't talk.*

The mournful-looking Ali nodded imperceptibly. The bloodhound/mocket sat on its haunches and lolled its tongue.

Remson's ears reacted to the elevator's speed and he yawned to clear them.

Then the upward rush stopped, and the elevator door opened onto the penthouse floor.

The three of them stepped into the anteroom. The bloodhound strained toward the door into the suite and scratched at it with one paw. The Medinans held dogs to be unclean. Therefore, Dini Forat, avid vid fan, had made her mocket into the simulacrum of a vid star's little white dog. That should have told her parents something, if anybody'd given a damn.

The Ali wasn't armed. The Medinan bodyguard wouldn't take the zero-point stunner that Remson had offered. Ali-7's function was to protect his charge with his life, not to protect his own life, the Ali had reminded Remson placidly.

Remson wasn't going to argue with Ali-7. Yet. But something in him was so outraged at the Medinans that he had to remind himself that he was supposed to rescue the girl and her dumb boyfriend, not contrive their deaths.

If those kids died in some sort of scuffle up here, maybe it would be cleaner, but it wouldn't be better for the Ali.

If Dini Forat died, then Ali-7 died. It was that simple under Medinan law. If you were an Ali who failed in your duty, you died. When your charge died, you died.

Vince Remson reminded himself that everybody died, and pushed the doorbell like the civilized man he was. He could shoot his way in if the Cummings kid didn't have enough sense to open the door.

But the Cummings kid did open the door, smiling benignly, with a raccoon riding on his shoulder that had its tail wrapped around his neck.

Cummings III resembled his father, Cummings, Jr., whom Remson had seen numerous times and met once. Rick Cummings also looked like his dossier photos.

But there was something odd about the way Remson felt when he confronted the youngster. Why was Remson hesitating? Why did he feel this sense of wasted effort, of chagrin? Why didn't he just tell the kid to get out of the way and let him in?

The Cummings kid was saying, "Officer, there's been some terrible mistake. As you can see—"

The bloodhound, with a deep-throated howl, lunged past Cummings, dragging Ali-7 with it, into the suite.

The abrupt movement startled Cummings. The blond kid didn't get out the way fast enough. He collided with the Ali. His legs got caught in the bloodhound's leash. The raccoon fell from his shoulders as he stumbled.

Everybody went down in the melee except Remson.

Suddenly his head cleared. He saw a girl—Dini Forat, for

sure—standing right behind Cummings, her hand pressed to her mouth, her eyes huge over it.

Remson could have sworn she hadn't been there before.

"Dini Forat? I'm Assistant Secretary Remson, from—"

Remson also saw two more of the raccoons. One was struggling out of Dini Forat's grasp. The other was all humped up and hissing at the bloodhound.

"—from the Secretary General's office," Remson continued, struggling to get the words out. It was as if something was trying to stop him. "Don't be afraid, Ms. Forat. You're under our pro—"

The bloodhound was exuding another cloud of sweet-smelling miasma.

And it was changing shape.

While Remson watched, speechless, the mocket changed itself into an exact replica of the raccoons.

And Ali-7, who had it on a leash, pulled its choke chain tight so abruptly that the mocket nearly flew into his arms.

All of a sudden, the sense of restraint left Remson. Cold fury took its place, so that he nearly shouted at the Cummings kid on the floor: "Get up, you stupid bastard. Get your things. And the girl's. You're both coming with me."

The raccoons—the real ones, all but the mocket that Ali-7 held—were running madly around the room.

The Cummings kid scrambled up, his blond hair falling over his forehead. His face was reddening. He ignored Remson, saying, "Here boy. Here." He snapped his fingers.

One of the raccoons stopped in its tracks. Remson thought he saw it raise something to its mouth and bite on it: a beetle, with wildly waving legs.

Then he didn't see it.

Then Ali-7 and his mocket stepped between Remson and the Cummings kid, and he saw the raccoon eating the beetle again. And other beetles. There were bugs all over the room.

He looked closer. They weren't just any beetles. . . .

The Cummings kid yelled, "Don't you touch that!" as Remson shouldered by him to pick up one of the beetles.

"Leetles! Kid, you're in serious trouble!"

The Cummings scion ignored him. He turned on the Forat girl. "Now see what's happened. It's that damned mocket of yours! How am I going to get us out of—"

Dini Forat began to shake. She hugged herself and sat down there, in the middle of the room. Before Remson could stop her, she picked up a Leetle and popped it into her mouth.

At least she wasn't crying.

Ali-7 was stroking the raccoon on his shoulder, murmuring to it. The mocket/raccoon was munching a Leetle.

Ali-7 said, "Mistress Dini, come with us please. My friend Remson has promised me that I can be with you all the time, and that no harm will come to you. Up, now, please, Mistress."

The Forat girl chewed her Leetle placidly.

There were Leetles crawling over the rug, everywhere. The place was alive with them. And the raccoons were chasing them wildly.

Remson didn't get it. He didn't get it at all. "Excuse me, Ms. Forat. Ali, watch her. Cummings, let's have a little talk. Out here."

He had the stunner in his hand. He didn't remember how it had gotten there. Years of training couldn't be totally wiped away.

He put the stunner carefully in its belly holster and paced the rich young criminal as the kid walked into the hall. If he broke for the elevator, Remson was going to shoot him.

"Yeah?" Cummings's head was high but his chin was quivering.

"This place is crawling—literally—with contraband. We're in a heap of trouble, Ricky boy. And if you want out of it, you're going to do exactly what I say."

"I don't do what anyone says. When my father hears about this unauthorized search and seizure—"

"Stuff it, before you threaten a Territorial officer and things get worse. You better not have touched that girl in—"

Cummings looked at his feet.

"You're telling me you did?"

"We're in love," said Cummings, his glance meeting Remson's like a slap across the cheek. "There's nothing wrong with that."

"Then you'll marry her?"

"I—have every intention of doing just that."

"Oh, good. I'm sure your father will be thrilled."

"I don't think you know my father."

"I think I've got a smuggler on my hands. You and your girlfriend have got to do exactly what we tell you, to the letter."

"You stupid cop. We can't go anywhere with you." Young Cummings had his father's icy stare. "If Dini's folks get hold of us, we're both dead meat. If you know what's good for you, you'll pretend you didn't find us. I'm a smuggler; you're right. I'm going to smuggle Dini out of here, where it's safe. . . ."

"There's no place safe enough for you two. Didn't you see all those people down there? All those official vehicles? Now, we're going down there. And I'll have somebody come up here and fumigate this place. Those Leetles aren't going to officially exist—"

"No! You can't do that! The Brows will die. I can't let you— "

Remson realized that Cummings was high as a kite on Leetle. But that didn't mean an interrogation was invalid.

And there was something here he'd missed. . . .

"Brows? What's a 'Brows'?"

The kid's mouth closed into a tight, thin line.

Then it cycled for Remson: "The raccoons, right? You're going to tell me all about the Brows, hotshot. Right now. The whole truth. Hold anything back, and I won't promise that I can get you out of whatever you've gotten yourself into. . . ."

Cummings spilled his guts. This kid had not only smuggled in a controlled life-form, deflowered a Medinan maiden, and subsequently provided illegal drugs to her, but now it developed that he'd smuggled in a life-form previously undiscovered, as well.

Smuggling wasn't a minor offense. Smuggling in an unknown life-form, something that seemed to have psychological effects on third parties, something that made mockets take their shape . . . These kids were in so much trouble that letting the Medinans execute them might have been the kindest alternative.

But Remson couldn't do that. The Alis' lives were at stake. And maybe Croft could argue that Medinan justice would have to wait until the Threshold legal system finished with these two kids.

Given the mess at hand, and the Cummings family's clout, that could take twenty or thirty years.

"Let's go, Cummings. Get your lady friend and be ready to smile for the cameras. And count your blessings it's us, not the Medinan secret service, that found you."

Remson escorted the boy back into the room, where Dini Forat was standing stiffly beside Ali-7, on whose shoulder rode the mocket, still in the raccoonlike form of a Brow.

Ali-7 said, "Remson, what now?"

"Now we make everything come out all right," Remson said casually, giving the terrified girl his best smile.

And Dini Forat said, straightening up, "The Brows can do that."

Young Cummings said, "Dini, shut up!"

Ali-7 went for the kid's throat in a blur Remson was nearly too slow to intercept.

While he grappled with the Ali, the mocket scrambled onto Remson's shoulder. In a sudden burst of enlightenment, Vince Remson understood about the Brows.

"Ali, come on. You know we can't do it this way." Vince Remson was holding Ali-7's wrists in his hands, and young Cummings was backing out of harm's way.

The Ali was as strong as Remson, and struggling to break free.

"Ali, I'm counting on you to take both of them to the Secretariat and stay with them—you've got to protect the two of them now. I can't be with them all the time."

"That's right," Dini Forat said. "This is my husband, my beloved, Ali-7. You must protect him as you protect me."

The Ali slumped in Remson's hold.

Remson let him go. "Good. Now, can we lock this place up and close ranks against what's waiting out there."

"I want to make a call. I have a right to make a call," said Rick Cummings, already at the vidphone.

"Why not? We've got all day." Remson didn't, but he couldn't risk a procedural error. "Just make sure you tell your lawyer that this is protective custody, no charges have been filed by my office yet, and that everybody's concern is to get you to the Secretariat without the Medinans getting hold of you."

He didn't bother to tell the kid that there already was a battery of his father's lawyers downstairs. Somebody would patch him through to the waiting attorneys and those attorneys might have more luck talking sense into the idiot son of NAMECorp than Remson'd had.

With the mocket back on Ali-7's shoulder, Remson shepherded everybody out and closed the door, slapping a Secretariat lock on it, once Cummings had put down the phone and segregated the Brows from the Leetles, locking the Brows in his bedroom, because otherwise, "they'll eat all the Leetles, get sick and die, and there goes your evidence. You wouldn't want that that, would you?"

Remson wasn't sure whether the kid was just stupid, or good and stupid. If he'd been Cummings, he'd have let the Brows eat the Leetles and die, solving at least half of the problem.

But he wasn't Cummings, thank heaven.

And he was in a hurry: he had Riva Lowe waiting for him, once he got these juvenile offenders settled where no harm could come to them.

CHAPTER 15

Once a Pilot

The port police and Reice's ConSec sharpshooters were all over the docking bay like mold on old cheese.

In the situation van, pulled up parallel to the Relic ship just beyond the metal safety wall, Riva Lowe rested her forehead on her hand in frustration, hunched over the display console.

The screen directly in front of her showed her an overhead, ambient-light view of the entire scene, with the shooters' call signs indicated in red by their positions.

The screen to her right gave her a schematic of the Relic ship, with heat-signature readouts indicating Joe South, his operational fusion power plant, life-support system, and the seven operational consoles within the ship.

The screen to her left was pulling in a concurrent view, mirrored from the Relic ship's inboard sensors: she could see what the ship's AI was seeing; she could read the emanations right off *STARBIRD*'s screens, just the way Joe South did, even to the audio they were microwaving off the ship's windshields.

The last screen gave her combat readout, currently from Reice's helmet, where he was keeping track of his "boarding" force.

That one, she ignored. She'd determined that it would be

useless. She had no intention of forcibly boarding the Relic ship, or allowing anyone to try using the sharpshooters, no matter how many times she'd been told that the rubber bullets and tranquilizer loads wouldn't hurt the Relic pilot.

If the Relic pilot got frightened enough, and started playing with that power plant or his jump-capability, he could hurt her. Perhaps he could destroy the entire ConSec docking area. According to one expert program and three human specialists, he could even do some structural damage to Threshold if he engaged his spongejump function.

If she knew how dangerous the situation was, South knew it. Captain Joseph South wasn't stupid. She'd just finished listening to Consolidated Space Command's Lydia Jones tell her all about Joe South.

They'd been trying to dig up a living relative—or descendent—of the pilot, to tweak a hot spot in his psych profile. "No luck," Jones said from a tiny screen below and to the right of the schematic display.

"Well, does ConSpaceCom have any more bright ideas?"

"We'll get back to you," said the tiny woman's face.

"The hell you will." Riva Lowe was nearly out of time. She could tell by the way everybody was acting. "You people haven't exactly done your best on this thing. Why's that? Why the quick discharge and boot out the door?"

"Director Lowe, my orders where Relics are concerned are very specific. We can't have these people making sweeping claims as to what the service—a defunct service—owes them. Any of these two-bit pilots could decide that they own half of Threshold Bank's assets, if they compound their back pay for five hundred years. Plus there's their psych profile problems. Nobody's interested in these people. We have a surfeit of information from their native time frames; it was the Information Age, you'll remember. They're of no historical significance, their abilities are minimal, and their feelings of disenfranchisement lead to unpleasant interactions with modern society."

"So what are you saying?"

The miniature face blinked at her. "We have every right

to tell you that this man is no longer our concern. We have discharged him in good order. His back pay is being figured. We don't owe him a lifetime of rehabilitation. . . ."

"That's not the right answer," Riva Lowe said. "Call me back when you can tell me what I want to hear. Within fifteen minutes, or I'm going so far over your head, you'll never see the light of day again." She reached out to break the connection.

"Wait, Director." Jones's little face was pinched and drawn. "Look here. You can offer South whatever you wish, under your own authority. Just don't expect us to put him on our active duty list, as he'll probably demand, or to pension him for the rest of his life with expensive rehabilitation. He's really not our problem. We've the legal structure to support that determination. And no terrorist act by a single Relic can be allowed to interfere with that, no matter how high up my command tree you choose to climb."

Riva Lowe grunted. "Okay. I hear you. But you hear me! I'm going to do something about this pilot, and you're not going to remonstrate, officially. You're not going to give me a negative fitness report. You're going to support my decision, as long as it doesn't put him in a ConSpaceCom ship. Agreed?"

"Ah . . . agreed."

"What's his back pay?"

"For twenty years, with inflation, converted into our currency, about a third of a K-note."

"Let's make it 5 K-notes."

"Phew. Just arbitrarily?"

"The guy's been out there testing government equipment— United States government equipment—for five hundred frigging years. Don't you people have any—"

"Not in his biological time, he hasn't. He's been out eighteen months. Okay, Director." The woman looked down, and Riva heard the nearly inaudible tap of keys. "We'll pension him off that gross. But that's the best I can do."

"Great. I'll take it. This is logged and dated. Thanks for the help, Jones."

So much for military assistance. But she'd done better for South than he'd have done on his own. He wouldn't starve, although he couldn't live in luxury for the rest of his life.

She hoped he gave a damn. Lowe stared at the little screen, then sat back and stared at the larger ones. Where was Remson? Her negotiating team had broken for lunch, waiting for the representative from the General Secretary's office. Lowe wasn't hungry.

She looked at her watch. Twenty minutes until they came back. If she was going to try anything decidedly nonstandard, this was the time to do it.

Just as she was punching orders into her keypad, Reice called in: "Come on, Riva, let's go in and get the bastard. What if he decides he's never going to talk to us, just blow us all to perdition?"

Reice's face blossomed where his team readouts were: he was looking into his own scanner so that she could see his face.

"Reice, when I want your advice, I'll ask for it." Now was her chance. "But I think I'm going to be able to get in there. And I need you to go along with my idea if I can. . . ."

"*In there?* You must be out of your—"

Lowe stabbed a button so that Reice could see her face, as well. "Did you hear me, Lieutenant?"

"Riva . . ." Reice's face worked. "If you'll take me in with you, I could live with it."

She might as well go in with a pulse rifle already blasting. "You can blow up the ship if I don't come out, Reice," she teased. "Think of it, all that nice flash and bang. . . ."

"Come on, this is serious."

"I've waited for the Secretary's negotiator as long as I can. We're scaring the life out of that Relic, holding him incommunicado like this. His ship's systems are picking up our invasive scans, you can bet."

"*We're* holding *him* incommunicado? If I didn't know better, I'd think you had a personal interest in this pilot. But since you don't take a personal interest in men—"

"Cut it, Reice. There're men, and then there's you."

Lord, this was all on the record. Why were they behaving like this? Why was she letting Reice get to her?

Still bristling, she continued, "Lieutenant, I'm putting you on notice that I may well enter the Relic ship within the next few minutes, and that I'll expect the required long-range support up to the ship's air lock, but that I'm going inside alone and I'm walking up to the ship alone."

She hadn't known that she'd decided to actually do that until the words came out of her mouth.

Reice knew that tone. "Director, it's your decision. ConSec can only disagree with your judgment, not your right to implement it. Reice out."

My, my, the lieutenant was testy.

But then, so was she.

Well, having declared herself on this probably suicidal course, she must proceed, or look like a total idiot.

Finishing the sequence that would allow her to hail *STARBIRD* on its standard com frequency, she felt as if someone else was in charge of her body.

If Remson showed up now, he'd probably give her a way to back down without looking quite so foolish.

Thinking of the possibility, she found herself hurrying, not dawdling.

She really did want to take care of this Relic situation, the way she'd promised Mickey Croft she would.

The screen cleared and she was looking at somebody who didn't have a soul in the world who cared about him. South was bleary-eyed and his face was puffy from sleep and bristly with beard. Depilatories weren't big in the early twenty-first century, she supposed.

"*STARBIRD*, this is Emergency Command. I'd like to come over there and talk to you, face-to-face. Just me. No large boarding party. Unarmed." She raised her hands to where he could see them, as if that would prove something. He was in his aft redundant control module. She could see that from her schematic. But she didn't expect to see a pillow behind his head. . . .

"Yo, Emergency Command. You mean your own self, lady?"

"I'm Director Lowe, the person in charge here." Hadn't she told him that? Hadn't they told him that? Hadn't anybody told him . . . but no, her orders had been specific. "I'm sorry I took so long, but I had to familiarize myself with the specifics of your case."

"Now I'm a 'case'?" The pilot's eyes narrowed. They seemed to be nearly all pupil.

"Now you are, since you've taken over that ship."

"My ship. I just want to take my ship and leave, lady. My mission's in interrupt. I need to return to my home base—the Earth's U.S. space station."

Had South lost what was left of his marbles? Was the stress too much? Was she too late?

"Your ship's safer here. Your mission's accomplished, Commander, as of your docking in this bay. You'd really better let me come talk to you in person. This is a very complicated mess you're in, and I want to help you get out of it."

"Yeah, I bet. Well, I want to continue to Earth, I told you. And I don't need a passenger. We're not set up for passengers. This is a testbed."

"I know that, Commander. Now—"

"If you know that, you ought to know to call me just plain old 'captain.' "

"Sorry. Captain." Riva Lowe's mouth was getting dry. Her eyeballs were beginning to tingle as they strained to read microdefinition from the pixels of her viewing screen, some hint of what was behind the pilot's facade. "May I have permission to come aboard your ship? I have some good news. I've made some progress on your behalf. I really want to sit down with you, face-to-face, and work things out."

"Come aboard my ship? Yeah, okay. If you put it like that . . ." He leaned sideways, out of her view. Then he was back. "Door's open, ma'am. Don't let the mess bother you. . . ." And his screen blanked.

She blinked at the empty viewscreen. Just like that. Come aboard his ship . . .

The phrase gnawing at her, she prepared to do just that.

Now that she was making progress, she had to follow up before Remson or someone else who could stop her appeared and spoiled everything.

She didn't understand why she felt so elated as she grabbed her briefcase, put it down—must go empty-handed—did the same with a handheld vidphone, and then ran out of the trailer, pinning a microtransceiver to her collar.

To hell with the video record. She spoke into the transceiver as she ran down the steps of the trailer and over to the kiosk: "Reice, he's letting me aboard. Don't do anything to get me killed, and I'll spot you a dinner."

Reice's voice came up from her blouse's collar. "On Spoke Nine, in Gravity Point Ten."

"Fine. We'll have spaghetti." What an infuriating man. But she knew it was Reice's way of apologizing, and saying he trusted her, after all.

The kiosk guards got out of her way when she said, "Get out of sight and put those rifles *down*."

Then she was all by herself, walking up the apron to the Relic ship in a wash of painfully bright floods.

The air lock below the red arrow on the black hull of *STARBIRD* wasn't open, she noticed as she got close. Had the pilot changed his mind?

Or was South going to do his worst, now that he had a human he could take with him if he blew the power plant?

You could never tell what people would do under stress. She'd overseen enough busts of contraband runners to know that.

She walked stolidly onward, feeling every footfall against the composite apron jar her spine. A part of her was relieved to have gotten this far. A part of her was afraid she wouldn't get much farther.

After all this, if South didn't let her come aboard, she'd look unbearably foolish.

Her hands were empty, held conspicuously out from her sides. She kept walking. She couldn't possibly present a threatening picture to anyone remotely sane.

But then, she'd seen South's profile. There was some

question as to whether he met the standard of sanity as Threshold defined it.

She was less than five feet from the ancient air lock, looking for a button to push to open it from outside, when it gave a great, gusty sigh and ratcheted open.

Now was the last moment at which she could break and run. She thought of Reice and his sharpshooters, watching her every move. She thought of the negotiating team, still on their lunch break. If this didn't work, she'd be in line for a strong reprimand. If she was in any condition to receive one.

She climbed up into the ship and the past surrounded her.

The air lock shut behind her with a clang. She was in a dark closet. She reached out her hands and touched the inner lock. A red light came on. Then it turned green.

She saw a lit arrow and she pushed it.

The inner lock split and drew back, revealing the pilot, just zipping his coveralls.

He held out his hand and she took it. "Joe South," he said.

"Riva Lowe," she said.

South's face was tired and there was a mixture of hope and suspicion on it, but beneath that was an almost puppylike pleasure at seeing another human being who wasn't overtly threatening.

He dropped his gaze and his head. "Welcome aboard. Birdy, shut things up tight again."

He was talking to the ship, she realized. The lock at her back snapped shut. The lights flickered, then came back on. She smelled canned air and South's nervousness.

He rubbed the back of his neck and gestured forward: "Flight deck. I don't suppose there's room for us to talk up there." He indicated the area they were standing in: "Here's no place to sit, either. You want to come back to my bunk?"

"That will be fine," she said, acutely aware that this was the same man she'd seen pacing the interrogation cell in the station house.

"I better go first. Watch your step."

The ship was tiny inside. It must be mostly drives and electronics. She saw racks of equipment that she couldn't really recognize. She saw two antiquated space suits. She heard him say, "Careful, now," and saw that the bulkhead bore the legend *Step up*.

She did, and followed him down a dimly lit corridor, which veered sharply and ended in a small cabin.

Here was the pillow she'd seen. A bunk/cubbyhole studded with a redundant control system and some sort of physiology support package took up most of the space. There was a shelf with compartments that must be the galley. A door at the rear said HEAD.

"You can sit." He motioned to the bunk. "I'll stand."

Lowe said, "Thank you," and sat primly. Craning her neck, she could see that the bunk had a transparent seal that would come down in certain circumstances to isolate it from the rest of the ship. She searched her historical knowledge but couldn't remember what it might be: an early sleeper for jump, or just a secondary survival system if the main life support went down.

South was watching her. "Different, huh?"

"Different, yes."

"Everything's different . . ." He bit his lip and rubbed his jaw, then leaned against the galley shelf. They were so close she could have reached out and touched his chest.

"I'm sorry," she blurted, "that you've had such a hard time." 'Time' probably wasn't the best choice of words, either. "We'll get this sorted out. That's why I'm here."

"And you've got the rank to do that. It's good to talk to somebody who does. I'm sorry, really I am . . . but I couldn't get anybody to listen to me."

"I know. You Relics are a real problem." That sounded awful. "Sit beside me." She patted the bunk.

He shook his head. "Birdy'll get all worked up, the way I'm torqued."

She had no idea what he meant. "We can solve this if you'll come to my office. Let everyone see that you're reasonable."

"I need to stay with my ship. I was out there. It doesn't make any sense to me. I just want to get on with my mission."

"Please, Captain South, believe me, you'll not be welcome on Earth. Earth is very restricted. Earth animals and plants are very precious, now. Only a few people live there, park rangers and behaviorists and ecologists. . . . There's no society there that resembles your old one even as much as Threshold."

"What about the Earth station?"

"Consolidated Space Command is nothing like the service you still feel allegiance toward, Captain. If you'll let me," she took a deep breath, "we'll find a way through all this red tape and get you everything possible in the way of support . . ."

"I don't want support. I want to finish my—"

"Mission. Yes, I know."

"I want to do my job. I told that lady from Reintegration or Vet Admin or whatever: I'm retrainable."

"I'm sure you are. Just let me help you. I'll get you a job, one you'll enjoy."

"Flying."

Why was she doing this? "Flying. I promise. With my Customs service. We'll train you. We'll get you through reorientation. Just don't be in such a hurry. There's too much you don't understand."

"Like how come somebody tried to get me to sign discharge papers and then stole them? Like how come I'm getting the boot as if I were some—"

"We know what happened. We'll get you the money that's really coming to you." He wouldn't understand how much more she'd already negotiated for him than he would have gotten without her. "You'll have a kind of pension, or at least a trust fund." If he was working for her, she could help him.

"Why are you doing this?"

"Ah—somebody had to take a hand. We have some delicate problems on Threshold right now, and no one wants you to

become another of those. So your case was delegated to me
. . . It's too complicated to explain."

"What's going to happen to Birdy?"

"To—"

"Sorry. *STARBIRD*. You going to put her in some kind
of museum? Cause she's still functional. This ship's as good
as— "

"Captain South, this ship is an . . . antique. No one's
going to fly it anywhere. And we don't have those sorts of
museums. I imagine she'll be decommissioned and her parts
recycled." She was bluffing. She had no idea what Con-
SpaceCom would do with this old wreck.

"I thought there's no Space Command, really, to decom-
mission her."

"That's . . . a fair assumption."

"Then if nobody wants her, can I buy her? With this
money you say I've got? Get a pilot's license, after some
more training? And do whatever I want that doesn't hurt
anybody—" He held both hands palms up to her. "—as
long as I don't try to go near Earth?"

Riva Lowe felt like crying. There was a lump in her throat
and she tried to clear it. She looked at her hands in her lap,
and folded them. The desperation in the pilot's voice was so
controlled, so deep, and there was so much loneliness in
him.

She should have realized that the primitive AI on this ship
was the only friend that Captain Joseph South had in the
universe.

Lowe said, "I don't see why something like that can't be
arranged. After all, the ship has no weaponry. And you
could always park it at one of the spacedock mobile parks
and live on it. . . . I'll see what I can do."

"You're not just telling me all this? To get me to come
with you?"

She looked up at the pilot again and now she saw the
coiled energy, the aggression held in abeyance, that she'd
seen when he was pacing like a caged animal.

"I am the Director of Threshold Customs, Captain. I'll

excuse your question by making allowances for your igno-
rance. This is an official negotiation." She touched the
transceiver on her collar. "I'm keeping a record of the terms
we settle on."

"So am I," said South, without indicating any recording
source. His jaw had a sharp line to it; his mouth was taut at
its corners.

"In that case, will you come with me now, to my office,
so that we can get started on clearing your ship and yourself
for Threshold entry, and helping you claim what's yours?"

"There's somethin' I'm not getting here."

There was something Riva Lowe didn't understand, herself. She couldn't take her eyes off the pilot as he rubbed
the back of his neck again and looked at her askance, as if
he'd tasted something surprising, but not necessarily sour.

"How about I stay here, and you come back with some
documentation that even somebody like me can see proves
that you'll be able to do what you say you want to do?"

"I can't work that way. You need to come with me as a
sign of good faith."

South crossed his arms and shook his head. "Can't leave
Birdy alone. Not if there's one fucking chance in a million
that I'll come back and find her disassembled. I haven't
even dumped my trip log yet. I gotta do that. Old X-3 was
one hell of a flyby."

"X-3?"

"My target solar system. I've got all the data still on
board."

"Right. Well, we'll find someone who knows what X-3
converts to in modern terms, and then we'll be able to judge
whether the data's been superseded by later exploration. But
you will have to come with me."

"I told you I—"

Remson's voice came out of her collar and South jumped.
So did she.

"Director Lowe, I'll guarantee the ship's safety as sacro-
sanct. He can lock it up. Now will you both please come out
of there so that I can leave?"

"Hello, Assistant Secretary Remson," she said to the transceiver, watching South's neck muscles cord and his chest, under folded arms, heave.

"We were just coming. Aren't we, Captain?"

"I guess," said South doubtfully.

When she started to get up, South held out a hand to her. She didn't at first realize what he was doing. But the ancient test pilot was helping her up.

Chivalry was long dead in modern times. Riva Lowe blushed, took the outstretched hand belatedly, and decided that she had no right to be insulted.

The man was from the Stone Age, after all. Well, the Information Age, which was close enough.

The Relic led the way out of the ship, as if she couldn't find the air lock on her own.

In it, he said only, "I'd kind of like you to go out first. If they're going to shoot me, you might as well be clear."

So South knew about the sharpshooters all around, and was trusting her anyway.

Riva Lowe said, "Don't worry. We're civilized. No one's going to shoot you." Not even Reice.

"You're the first person who's bothered to help me, so I'll take your word for it." South's voice was grim and his words were clipped short as he waited for the outer lock to open.

It didn't.

"Come on, Birdy, don't be a mother hen," South said finally from the dark.

The outer lock drew back and she blinked in the light of the floods.

"Take my hand, Captain," Riva Lowe said and stepped down that long way onto the apron.

She could see Reice and his soldiers, and Remson and the negotiation team, waiting for them.

She'd better come up with a plan to justify doing everything for South that she'd promised, and fast. Maybe she could send South out with the scavenger, the next time the old fool insisted on looking at his ball. It would give South some flight time, and pin back the scavenger's wings. If she could find a way to tie the two men together, it would keep both of them out of serious trouble, and nothing terrible would come of it.

So she'd tell Remson, anyhow. You had to have time to look for logical flaws, and none of them had time to do much more than keep the lid on things, lately.

Joe South said, "Lady, I sure hope you were telling me the truth," as they approached the kiosk and Reice's ConSec sharpshooters spread out, guns trained on the Relic pilot who wasn't from so far in the past that he didn't know when he was about to be arrested.

"You can depend on it," she said, and fingered her transceiver, telling Reice to back off and get her car. "I'm taking South to my office. You can follow along with some of your boys if you've got nothing better to do."

Vince Remson waited only long enough to congratulate her, say she should call him later, and shake South's hand.

"I'm Remson. I guaranteed your ship during negotiations. If you need me, here's my card."

South took the card and looked at the big man hurrying away. Then he looked at Reice's sharpshooters, still alert to any false move, and back to Lowe.

"*STARBIRD*'ll be here when I get back? Nobody'll try to stop me?"

Again, she saw the tension ripple over the test pilot.

"Nobody will try to stop you. Welcome to Threshold, Captain South, if a little belatedly."

There was a reasonable chance that, with Remson behind her, she could deliver at least half of what she'd promised to South.

CHAPTER 16

$\triangledown$

Where You're Standing

Young Dodd was nearly in tears when he scuttled over to Croft's seat on the dais with a piece of hard copy in his hand. The symposium was in full swing, and too many in the packed hall noted Dodd darting out from behind the star-spangled curtains.

When he'd read Remson's tersely declarative message twice, Michael Croft handed it back to Dodd, said "Thank you. No reply," and rubbed his eyes.

Croft could still see the words of Remson's message as if they were printed on the insides of his eyelids: *Have both kids in protective custody, your offices. Informing parents officially. Possible contraband/controlled substance violations require investigation. File data available. Type: ROMEO&JULIET to review. Do not, repeat, do not allow parents immunity defense. VR.*

Remson was stoked. Dodd was paralyzed with guilt. Rumors of smuggled Olympian life-forms and—worse—sex and drug scandals were running through the conference like dysentery.

Mickey Croft opened his eyes and his audience was still

before him. Among the humans were representatives of the bioengineered subraces: the camel-lipped from desert worlds, the lizard-green from swamp planets, the larva-pale tunnel dwellers from mining complexes deep within the crust of spheres too rich to be ignored but too inhospitable to respond to terraforming.

Michael Croft could have been born a sub if his luck had been bad. So could any of the rest of the human elite. Replicating robots and expert systems couldn't take the place of human colonizers, and the subs were genetically tailored to flourish where the standard human template would fail.

They had rights and their rights must be protected, no matter the tendency of mankind to abuse other species. The framers of the UNE Constitution had wisely prepared to protect the rights of all species, and Mickey Croft was dedicated to those principles. But that didn't mean you neglected human rights. Human rights violations were as much a part of Croft's purview as the protection of subhuman and alien rights.

Someday perhaps a species would come along who would treat humanity as it had treated all less aggressive species. If that day came, Croft wanted to be sure that humankind's record was as presentable as possible. If ever humans were faced with a stronger, smarter, more deadly and less beneficent race than itself, who considered humans no better than subhuman or lesser alien forms, mankind had better have a clear conscience.

People must do better among the stars than they'd done on Earth, or one of Croft's descendants would curse him for causing the cycle to repeat. It was cheaper, in the long run, to treat all life-forms fairly and keep their populations high than to begin reparation and repopulation projects. The fate of the Earth and its denizens demonstrated that.

But Croft couldn't seem to instill his zeal for long-range thinking in his fellow UNE members. It might be human to mistreat everyone you could get away with mistreating, to cheat and steal and oppress whenever and whomever possible, but it wasn't laudable. Or acceptable.

This conference had been the first major attempt to regularize interstellar rights that had seemed to have the tiniest hope of success.

Now it was about to blow up in Mickey Croft's face, due to a couple of horny teenagers from powerful families.

Croft couldn't keep his mind on the speech of the camel-lipped Epsilonian at the end of the dais. When this session was over, the audience was going to be allowed to ask questions. The answers to those questions would be beamcast to the ends of creation.

Croft found himself praying that Remson really had managed to keep the lid on things.

It was Croft's only hope.

But as he watched, with the Epsilonian's voice lisping in his ears, he saw three people in NAMECorp uniforms escort a tall blond man in a business suit into the conference hall.

Well, somebody had found Cummings, Jr.

Croft wanted to rub his eyes again. But he'd done that once already. He shifted in his seat, ostensibly to look at the Epsilonian speaker. Beyond the woman from Commerce beside him was a lesser Medinan mullah.

The mullah glared at him and made a motion: he drew his leveled hand across his throat.

Oh, good. So the Medinans were simply awaiting their moment.

Between the Epsilonian speaker and the mullah's chance to talk were only two other functionaries. Croft considered recessing the conference unilaterally.

But there were too many professional reporters and diplomats in this handpicked audience. That would never do.

He faced front once more and stared ahead blindly, focusing on the panorama of flags that hung at the back of the hall. He felt as if the fifth-force generators had failed and, weightless, he was drifting toward the ceiling. But there was nothing wrong with the artificial gravity around here.

The Epsilonian ended his speech with an impassioned plea for full human status for his "brother workers in the wastelands of creation. All of us share with the rest of our honored United Nations of Earth brotherhood a common heritage. We should have equal status. We demand equal rights. We will sit in our seats at your table and acquit ourselves as men have always acquitted themselves: as best as humanly possible."

An Epsilonian in the audience stood up, clapping his broad hands loudly. Others followed suit. Somebody shouted "Bravo!"

Croft nearly kissed the humpbacked, camel-lipped Epsilonian, so glad was he for the time-out called on Armageddon.

But in the tumultuous standing ovation, as he himself stood, the mullah reached behind the woman from Commerce and poked Croft in the ribs.

Croft craned his neck, his brow raised in an interrogatory.

The mullah nearly shouted, "If you proceed on this course, my orders are clear."

"What course?" Mickey Croft shouted back.

"Our princess shall be returned to us!"

"In due time, of course, my good man. We're—"

The mullah looked away, out at the throng.

No good. Croft considered prayer, then bribery, then capitulation. The diplomat in Croft counseled him to do whatever he must that could possibly save the conference at this stage.

He looked out over the crowd of faces. They were taking their seats. The applause for the Epsilonian was dying away.

And in the last row sat Richard Cummings, Jr: "King Richard the Second," as he was known.

Cummings was a more threatening presence than even the Medinan. If Croft had been lucky, Cummings would have been on the other side of the galaxy, so far away that word would only now be reaching him.

But Cummings had, in all probability, been on his Earthly preserve, counting plovers' eggs or hunting from his own herd of white-tailed deer.

Michael Croft hated Richard Cummings with every fiber of his being, and Cummings returned the sentiment. There were the rules by which everyone else played, and there were Cummings's rules. The publicly flashy environmentalist was privately a trophy-hunter, a taxidermist, a gourmet specializing in the flesh of Earth's endangered species.

It was enough to sicken any honorable man.

It could be, Croft told himself, that the Cummings boy and the Forat girl deserved one another.

But he could never be sure of that. One didn't indict the children of evildoers, or tar whole bloodlines with the same brush. That was where prejudice and intolerance began.

Sitting before his microphone, Croft took time during the introductory remarks of the next speaker to type in the code that would bring up the text of Remson's report on the dais-mounted display terminal/communicator/translator system with which each speaker's place was equipped.

When he'd finished reading it, Croft was stunned, and the moment for the Medinan mullah's speech was at hand.

The mullah stood up, took his mike in hand, and straightened his voluminous tribal robe.

"Colleagues," he began, "we of Medina had come here in good faith to take part in this historic conference and to undertake our customary pilgrimage. But as you may know, the UNE has decreed that we may not set foot upon the Earth in all our multitude of pilgrims.

"The hajj is a pilgrimage to Mecca made by people of my religion. The UNE has interrupted and interfered with this sacred duty."

The mullah glared around at the audience.

There was a rustle as people shifted in their seats.

"This affront we were willing to sustain. We were even willing to take part in our most sacred rites via satellite, milling with the Earthly faithful only by vid and in spirit. All of this, we granted the UNE to show our good faith and our spirit of compromise."

Mickey Croft wondered whether he should try to stop the mullah. He wished that Forat himself was here. Forat had been scheduled to be here, but had sent this man at the last moment, claiming illness.

A terrible suspicion started forming in Croft's mind, and that suspicion was accompanied by a tightening of his stomach that made his whole body seem unwieldy and brought a sick, sweet taste to his mouth.

The mullah continued, "But now the affronts have become too execrable for us to sustain. The infidels who pull the strings of the UNE have no honorable ends in their minds. They wish only to impose their will on other peoples, as they choose. Look around you, and you will see here the puppets of UNE imperialism! We of Medina urge you in attendance who are still your own masters to sever all—"

From the back of the room, a voice interrupted, booming: "What about your Medinan 'sentient service personnel,' mullah? Your slaves that you breed and slaughter as you please? Are you going to give them the chance to decide whether they're puppets or their own masters?"

The speaker was Richard Cummings. On his feet, face white, Cummings continued: "You're not pure enough to be talking about 'honorable ends,' not when you've got chameleon species you're using for questionable purposes, as well as slaves. And not when you're imposing barbaric punishments on your own women, without even bothering to declare them as subhuman, though you're treating them that way. You want to talk about rights, mullah? Let's talk about human rights. Women's rights. When's the last time any of the rest of you ordered your own daughter's assassination—head chopped off, if I'm not mistaken—for consorting with a foreigner?"

The mullah actually threw down his microphone. The sound was deafening. Gathering up his robes, he stalked off the podium and stomped out of the hall without another word.

Among the audience, assorted others stood to leave with him.

Croft took his own microphone in hand. "Order! Order. If NAMECorp's representative would like to be heard, he knows the procedure. Everyone, stay in your seats. I have something to say."

And most would stay. This was a conference in mid-abort, but something could still be salvaged. Mickey Croft was an expert at salvaging what he could.

Out there, in the audience, were reporters, and reporters could carry a lot of weight, if the words they used were the words you needed them to use.

"We are calling a special session to debate the rights of such creatures as the Medinan sentient service personnel. During that session, we'll also discuss the procedures for transporting newly discovered life-forms of indeterminate nature. And life-forms which fit the 'chameleon' description that the gentleman from NAMECorp has brought to our attention. Now, although it is somewhat difficult to hold an open discussion on the question of potential Medinan abuses without Medinan representatives present, we'll take some questions on related issues for, say, a half hour. Then we'll recess. Hopefully, this afternoon, the Medinans will return and we can continue with their participation. One way or the other, I want to assure all of you that, on Threshold, no rights of any person will be violated. Ever. No matter what local customs may be elsewhere, or what pleas of diplomatic immunity may be tendered: on Threshold, we consider justice to be an inviolable right of all life-forms."

The audience erupted into cheers and shouts as Croft sat down.

He was in no hurry to choose a reporter to begin the question-and-answer. The conference might be well and truly aborted, but that didn't mean he would concede the fact.

Let the Medinans walk out and stay out. Let their revolutionary fervor slip its bonds. Let there be riots in the street. All well and good, if that was what was necessary to bring this matter under the conference's scrutiny.

According to what Croft had read in Vince Remson's report, not only were the futures of the Cummings and Forat children at stake, but the very lives of the Medinan bodyguards known as Ali-4, Ali-5, and Ali-7 were on the line.

As he recognized the first questioner, Croft summoned Dodd with a handsignal. When the youngster came over, bent low to avoid being too obvious, Croft told him to catch Cummings, Jr., and tell him that Croft wanted to see the NAMECorp CEO privately this very day.

"Let him pick the time and place, Dodd. But don't let him off the hook. Do this, and I'll forgive you for the mix-up about the Forat girl."

"You will?" Dodd's fat face became radiant.

"I will."

Dodd went hurrying out with a newfound determination.

Croft wished he could find some similar light at the end of his own dark tunnel. He'd entirely missed the first question.

Mercifully, the woman from Commerce was answering it. It seemed to have something to do with new standards for importing previously undiscovered life-forms.

Let her chew on that one. Croft stabbed at the terminal before him. In just a few seconds, he'd called for a full-scale meeting of his staff, in his most private office, posthaste.

Now all he had to do was get out of here so that he could attend it.

CHAPTER 17

Favor in Return

South stared unabashedly around the Customs Director's half-cylindrical blue office, grateful that the floor beneath his feet was flat. Riva Lowe didn't seem to give a damn about South's mission to X-3, but she wanted to help him. *Was* helping him. Even if she was evasive about her reasons, only an idiot looked a gift horse in the mouth.

Some guy named Remson had guaranteed *STARBIRD*'s security, even given South his card.

Now here he was in the heart of Threshold's politico-military complex, by the looks of it, with this lady who specialized in hacking through red tape with a half-smile on her lips and a tongue like a machete.

South ought to be thanking his lucky stars. But he wasn't. He didn't understand a damned thing that was happening to him. He didn't even understand why, at what Lowe had shown him was the central Stalk, or hub, of Threshold, he was experiencing normal gravity.

"Artificial," Lowe said when he asked, with that half-smile that was beginning to drive him crazy—the sort of smile you give to an idiot or a kid because you're simplifying down to his level.

But she leaned back in her weirdass chair and somehow a schematic of Threshold appeared behind her, on what he now realized was a large-format display screen.

He looked at the complex of toruses and dodecahedrons and balls and frisbees, all strung on the Stalk or connected to it by tubes and cylinders and strutwork, and he blinked.

The schematic was color-coded: blue for government and administration; red for industrial; yellow for residential; orange for agricultural; purple for commercial/recreational; green for academic/scientific.

"We're still growing," she told him, and tapped her chair's arm. The schematic was replaced by a view of Threshold from somewhere inside, out toward the stars. "What you'd see if we had a window in here." Again, she nearly smiled.

He said, "Ma'am, I don't know how I can thank you for what you did for me and Birdy. . . ."

"I do." She sat forward, and suddenly everything that had been bothering South—the ultramodern surroundings, the obvious power wielded so offhandedly by this hundred-pound woman, his sense of helplessness in a situation he didn't understand—everything receded.

Here was the catch. He could feel it. Whatever she'd been planning, whatever she had up her sleeve, was about to hit the table.

All the adrenaline Joe South hadn't been able to metabolize during the long siege shipboard rushed through him. He was dizzy. He was infinitely tired. He was wide awake and trembling like a leaf, waiting for her to tell him what she had in mind.

Like the good test pilot that he was, he automatically sucked in his gut, tensing his solar plexus, and pressed his hands together in his lap, performing an isometric stress-relieving exercise.

It helped enough that when she opened her mouth to speak, the meaning of her words penetrated his over-amped psyche.

"I want you to take a passenger out to Threshold's Number Seven spacedock for me. It'll be good practice for you, using our docking bays and our traffic control procedures."

The screen behind her changed again, into a split image of Spacedock Seven and a routing diagram of how to get there from *STARBIRD*'s current berth in the ConSec docking bay.

He heard himself say, "I'm going to need a copy of that, and an etiquette manual or a flight sectional or whatever you've got for flight rules around here."

He didn't bother mentioning the temperature malfunction he'd had with *STARBIRD*'s fusion power plant. Birdy and he would find a way to take care of that. The last thing he needed was to accidentally discourage her from giving him a mission—any mission. Because a mission meant they trusted you. You weren't some crazy if you had a mission. You weren't some criminal, either.

"Here you go." Hard copy came out of a slot in her desk. She reached across to give it to him.

His hands were still trembling when he took it. South hoped she'd put that down to eagerness.

He said, "So this is it? I can go?"

"Not so fast, Captain," she said. She hadn't straightened up. Riva Lowe had both elbows on her desk and she was leaning toward him. "You'll need to sign some more papers, first. We want you gainfully employed as a Customs agent. You'll need background on the passenger, and the mission."

Papers. He didn't want to sign anything else. He was hardly listening. Instead, he kept trying not to look at her, the way her breasts nearly grazed the desktop.

"Wait a minute. I can take my own ship, right?" he asked.

"Right," she affirmed. "We'll get you trained on something better later, but for now, this way will be best. We want this passenger satisfied that his needs are being attended to, but we don't want him out at this site alone, or capable of doing any damage to the artifact there, or trying any intimidation tactics on the agent who escorts—"

"Artifact."

"I'll put together a briefing for you. Don't worry. You'll have more trouble with the scavenger—the salvage expert whom you're ferrying out there—than with any other part of this. Just don't let him out of the ship—"

"Out of the ship? Lady—Director Lowe—nobody goes out of my ship except under—"

"Exactly. That's why this is a perfect start for you."

Another document came out of her desk's slot, and when she handed this one to him, their fingertips brushed.

Damn, he'd been away from society too long. You didn't mess with your boss, no matter how pretty she was. And you didn't ask too many questions when somebody was doing you a favor.

"That'll give you some official clout with the scavenger, if you have to use it." Again, she nearly smiled at him.

But not quite.

It was at that moment that South realized Riva Lowe wasn't a bit more relaxed now than when she'd come walking into his ship like salvation.

Was she scared of him? "Ma'am, I really want you to know that, after all you've done, you can count on me. For anything you need. Whatever I can do . . ." He spread his hands. He was still holding the last document she'd given him.

"Good. Here's the scavenger's address."

Yet another piece of printout came his way. And a little card with a magnetic strip on the back. "Take public transportation until you know your way around. Use the card when it's Customs expense or when you need to identify yourself." She sat back.

"Is that it?" Maybe he could get out of here without signing anything. He stood up, suddenly anxious to leave before she changed her mind. He had a mission, after all.

"Not yet, Captain. We've got to go over the matter of passing title to your ship. Are you sure you want it, given that it'll take a good bit of your money?"

He didn't understand the money stuff here yet. But he had what he needed. "I liked what you said—I own the ship, I can live on it in some sort of trailer-park situation. Then I don't need so much cash, right? You'll be paying me something. . . ."

"Ah—" She seemed slightly disappointed. "All right. We'll

do that. Keep in mind, when you buy things, that your salary's still minimal. Try not to spend more than you earn, and you'll be fine. If you get into trouble with the currency, just remember that you're grossing a third K-note a year, before taxes. . . ."

He didn't care. He signed the papers she handed him: *STARBIRD* was his!

"When do I have to pick up this salvage guy, and is he going to be glad to see me?"

"Call him and arrange a time as soon as you think you can handle it. I'd like him out there with you as soon as possible. I know your ship's slow by our standards, but don't mention that to him. He should consider himself lucky to have somebody bothering to take him at all. He's not to go out there in his own ship—or any way but with you. So he may be testy at first. He's a little . . . crusty. Don't take any guff from him. Remember, you're a Customs agent. There must have been Customs agents in your—days."

"Yeah." He looked away from her. Was this some kind of trick? Was she just trying to get him out of the way? He had no business having any kind of reaction to somebody like her, let alone the reaction his body was considering.

He took all the papers that she'd given him and held them before him in both hands. "When I get back, we'll start in Customs school, and some kind of pilotry course, right?"

"When you get back, we'll have to. Your license to operate is inherent in your credentials, but you'd never pass a flight test at your current familiarity level."

She was one hell of a bureaucrat. And she was as out of reach as his hometown was.

He stared into Riva Lowe's exotic eyes for one painful moment, then dropped his own. "You got any more papers for me to sign?" He shifted from foot to foot.

"Right here—"

Beep. Beep. Beep.

"Stand by, South."

She took a handset out of a desk drawer and swivelled her chair around. A small viewscreen blossomed on the back wall. He couldn't see what was on it; her chair was in the way.

He couldn't really make out what she was saying, either. It wasn't his business to try.

He was already wondering about getting that temperature malfunction checked out. If it were just a bad sensor, it wasn't going to be much of a problem. . . .

He wandered around the room, looking at pictures on the walls of places he'd never dreamed of, and reading citations for services that didn't exist in his time.

Then she said, "South, something's come up. I've got to go. You've trusted me this far. Trust me a little farther. You've got my word and Remson's, as well, that we'll work things out for you. When you get back, make an appointment to see me."

When he turned to look at her, Riva Lowe was standing, holding her hand out for him to shake in farewell.

And the next thing he knew, he was in the outer office, and somebody at a desk outside was directing him out of the building.

When he got downstairs, he needed to find a public tubeway. Then he could get started on his mission.

He took a wrong turn somewhere and ended up in the Customs garage. The garage was the most familiar thing he'd seen since he left the ConSec docking area and Birdy's care.

There was a guard in a little glassed-in kiosk and he asked the guy what the best way to get to Loader Level was. "I gotta find this aftermarket shop . . ."

The guard tipped his hat. "Okay, hotshot. Don't try your cover out on me. You want to just gimme your card and we'll get you set up?"

Thinking that there was no harm in trying, South handed his new credentials to the guard, who slipped the card into a viewer. "You'd want a pretty beat-up taxi with a human, then, huh?"

"You bet," said South, having no idea why he'd want that, or exactly what he was going to do with a human when he got one.

But the guard handed back his credentials card and punched some buttons. Then he leaned out of his window and said, "You guys have all the fun. Bet you're going to load up your per diem on this one, eh? I got you a real scuzzy taxi-driver, one of the best we've got around here."

"Thanks," said South when the guy paused for his approval.

"Ain't seen you around, so that means you've been out in the boonies for quite a while. We don't get many of your kind in here." The guard had a conspiratorial tone in his voice and an admiring look on his face. "You need any special sort a' orientation, you feel free to ask for me. That's Bubba Ryan, in Technical Services. We're the ones who really know what it takes to shake up the underside."

"I'll do that."

"And if you want any afterhours, you just holler."

"Like I said . . ."

Up to the barrier at the kiosk came an electric car with fenders of different colors, dents all over it, and a driver with pink paint covering one side of his face and what looked like a toilet-plunger dangling from his left ear.

"He'll take good care o' you, sir," said Bubba Ryan with a wave as he slid back into his kiosk and raised the barrier.

A human driver. Made sense now. South got in the back of the taxi and said, "I need to go to an aftermarket shop in the Loader zone run by a guy named Sling. I'm not sure just where it's—"

"I been there. No problem," said the driver, and gunned the car's motor. Music in a foreign language, polyphonic and strident in 7/4 time, filled the vehicle.

Fine. South didn't want to talk, either. If he said anything wrong, he'd probably lose his ride.

He had no idea whether he had to pay this guy, or not. He decided he'd assume it was on the house, and sat in the back reading his papers until the car stopped and the rear door was opened remotely by the driver in the front.

The guy didn't ask for money, and South didn't volunteer any.

But when he was out of the car, he realized he wasn't in

front of anything remotely resembling what he remembered as Sling's aftermarket shop.

South said, "Wait a minute. This isn't where I'm supposed to be . . ."

And, over the music, the driver snarled, "Asshole! It's right up the street there. You want to look where you're going?" and pulled away in a whine of ill-tuned motor.

South shrugged off the critique. He didn't know what he was doing. Somebody was bound to notice.

He craned his neck. Overhead, you could see the strutwork of the module. No pretty false ceilings down here. The street was full of rubbish—food and drink containers, twisted hunks of metal, wires and cables and chipboards—and the lights overhead were mimicking daytime.

Of the half-dozen people he passed on the way to Sling's door, no one gave him more than a sidelong glance.

When he knocked and no one answered, he thought maybe he shouldn't have come. He was taking an awful lot on faith, leaving Birdy to fight her own battles just because Riva Lowe had told him everything would be all right.

And he hadn't mentioned coming down here to Lowe, though she'd certainly be able to find him—or find out he'd come here—if the Customs people behaved anywhere near like MPs. It'd be logged that he'd taken a car with a driver down here.

Well, she hadn't told him not to come.

And it was seeming like a waste of time. Maybe he could call that Bubba guy and get some "technical services" for *STARBIRD* right out in the open, since she was sort of a commandeered Customs vehicle.

But his gut told him not to draw attention to the fact that his ship might have a mechanical problem. And he didn't want just anybody messing around with her.

He knocked again, got no response, and was about to leave when he saw the little button you were supposed to press for entry.

He pressed it, and the outer door drew back.

How could he have forgotten that?

But he'd been pretty drunk the last time he was here. He'd been more than pretty drunk, and Sling had led the way.

In the vestibule, the outer door closed behind him as if he'd entered an air lock. He searched for another depressible switch, and found one.

This time, the door didn't open. Instead, a voice came from a speaker grill above the door: "Yeah, who is it? I'm busy."

"Sling? It's me—Joe South. I need something."

"Crap. Hold on." Sling grunted and then the speaker chirped off.

The door opened and South stepped inside.

The shop smelled of torches, tortured metal, and hot insulation. So did Sling, when he came ambling out of the lab room. "Hey, there. Long time no see. Not that we were seein' much the last time. What's up? I'm on a tight schedule."

"I've got a delicate problem with an . . . antique piece of equipment." It hurt to talk about *STARBIRD* that way. "I want somebody I can trust to look at it while I stand there."

"Oh, boy. I knew you were . . . never mind. What's the problem, and what's the equipment?"

"Possible faulty heat sensor; possible overheating for real in a fusion power plant . . ." As he explained just what he needed, he saw Sling's eyes widen.

"You got one of those things and it's in working order? Man, you're curiouser and curiouser, you know? Can this wait until I get my rush job done? I'm getting lots of money for doing almost nothing, but the package is taking some time to put together. . . ."

"I need to take somebody for a ride, and I need this problem not to be a problem."

"You going to pay me for this, or am I doing it because I like you?" Sling pulled a rag out of his back pocket and wiped his hands.

"I can pay you for it. And for a little extra help, maybe, too."

"Come on back. We'll talk while I work." Sling led the

way, stuffing the antistatic rag into his coveralls' rear pocket as he went.

Sling stopped before an assembly bench that was clean and white and dust-free, spread with micro parts and tools to work on them. He put on magnifying goggles and said, "Let's hear the rest."

"I got to take a guy out to look at something. The guy's a salvage specialist. I need the—"

Sling looked up at him, the goggles making him seem like a giant fly with a human mouth. That mouth curled. "I knew you were heat the minute I looked at you. Keebler sent you to check up on me, right?"

"Keebler?" That was the name on his orders. "No way. But I've been looking for him. What's he like?"

"Pain in the butt. Crazy-ass. Throws his weight around. Just your average bucket of trouble. You're beginning to seem like his only son."

"Come on, Sling. You volunteered to do whatever I needed done. Now all of a sudden you don't like the company I'm keeping. Sounds to me like you can't deliver. If the project's too tough for you, recommend somebody who's got a real working knowledge of vintage spacecraft. . . ."

Long shots don't always work.

This one did. Sling pulled off his goggles, rubbed his hand over his mouth, and said, "Whatever you're into, don't get me busted, okay?"

"Promise."

"Let's see, we'll need . . ." Sling circled around the lab, picking up test kits and equipment and putting everything into a satchel. When he'd filled the satchel, he said, "You going to give me a taste up front?"

"Taste?"

"Pay me something in advance. So that I can at least prove I was hired for whatever this is, on the up-and-up, if the cops come to get you while I'm working on the . . . antique. By the way, where is it?"

South already had both of his credit cards in his hand. One had a low limit, he knew. The other was government.

He shrugged and handed both of them to Sling. "Whichever of these'll take your fee, charge the whole thing now."

"Worble eggs! This is a fucking Customs—"

"I just got that card."

"Oh, man, if this is forged, you've got more balls than your average crazy. If it's not . . ." His eyes narrowed. "Better not be stolen. Tell me it's not stolen."

"It's not stolen."

"Okay. Nine C's okay with you?" Sling took the Customs card into his office, lugging the satchel, which was so heavy it threw his gait off; the aftermarketeer nearly limped.

"Fine." What difference did price make, when you didn't understand the currency? Even if he could have evaluated the price, fixing *STARBIRD* was South's first priority. When your life hangs in the balance, there's no such thing as too expensive.

Sling ran the card through the slot and it came out the other side. "Okay, it's not stolen. Print here."

South stuck his thumb in the square of the receipt as if he'd been doing it all his life.

"Let's go. Where'd you say we were going?"

"The ConSec docking bay." South headed for the door.

"Aw, crap, South."

South turned around. Sling hadn't moved, except to put down the satchel. He had his hands on his hips. In one of them was the crumpled receipt.

"You're telling me you're a cop? For real? Customs? Is this a bust? Because if it is—"

"Why would it be?"

"Uh—then I'm just helping the law, right? About the scavenger? About Keebler?"

"That'll do."

"Promise."

"I really just want you to fix my ship. Then, if you can tell me anything about this Keebler, or help me get in touch with him, that's great. I'll appreciate it."

Sling twirled his braid's tip in his fingers. Then in an absent, habitual motion, he put the very end of the braid in his mouth and sucked on it.

South waited, wishing he understood the protocols around here a little better. He'd been honest with Sling. Sling had just taken everything South had said and turned it around, preferring to believe the opposite.

Sling's cheek quivered with the motion of his tongue as, inside his mouth, it twirled the braid's tip.

Eventually, after a long measuring interval during which South didn't flinch, Sling took the braid out of his mouth and said, "Okay, I'm helping Customs on this one. But just take it from me up front, that black box that Keebler's ordered won't work. I'm building him exactly what he asked for, which isn't illegal; but it won't work. And whatever he's doing besides that, I don't know squat about."

"Good enough. Now can we go fix my ship?"

"Yes, sir." Sling hoisted the satchel.

"After that," South said, sensing his advantage and pressing it, "you and I'll get a drink and figure out how you can help me connect with this Keebler. If he's going out to that parking site, he's going with me, on my terms. Or he's not going."

"I knew I shouldn't have gotten involved in this," Sling said. "But there was nothing I could do. At least you're on the right side of the law. Maybe you guys can keep Keebler off my back when he realizes this box won't work . . ."

"Maybe. But my ship better work."

"That's no problem, South. I can fix a cold fusion plant in my sleep. My granddaddy taught me all about 'em. I'll give you a torque boost while I'm at it—on the house."

So maybe it was fixing the ship in the ConSec bay that made Sling so nervous.

Or maybe it was South who was nervous, letting somebody whose credentials he couldn't evaluate mess around with *STARBIRD*.

But Birdy seemed to think that Sling was doing a decent job.

And since Sling agreed with Birdy, that it was just a faulty sensor, and the power plant's readings spec'd out nominal when they fired her up and monitored the numbers, South relaxed.

Now he didn't care if he got the salvage expert, Keebler, to come along without bitching about *STARBIRD*'s space-worthiness.

If the scavenger was going out to that spacedock, according to Riva Lowe, he was going out as South's passenger.

It shouldn't be too hard to convince some marginally legal player where his best interests lay. It sure wasn't hard to get Sling's cooperation once South had flashed his Customs card.

But if it all came to nothing, Birdy was happy again, and so was South. They could break for the unknown with *STARBIRD*'s optimized power plant, and never look back.

If worse came to worse and this place just kept getting more unbearable, that was exactly what Joe South was going to do.

It was nice of Riva Lowe to have faith in him, and to give him a mission.

But nobody seemed to understand how hard it was to come home and have home not be there anymore. Or to listen to people tell you that the Earth—the place that had borne and bred you—wasn't somewhere you were welcome. The whole Earth, off-limits.

And Sling thought it was weird that South had *STARBIRD*'s original milspec operating manual. . . .

When it was time to leave with Sling, South almost couldn't bring himself to go. But the salvage expert named Keebler was waiting out there, somewhere. The least South owed Lowe and her Customs service was to give the mission a try.

There'd always be time to chuck everything and run like hell. It just wasn't Joe South's idea of something to be proud of. And he was proud of his performance so far, even though all he'd done was keep his temper and tough things out.

If Riva Lowe had any idea what kind of man it took to grit your teeth and look Threshold in the face, she'd have been thinking of him as more than a charity case.

But maybe he should be glad she was thinking of him any way at all, South told himself as, after locking up his ship, he followed Sling out of the docking bay.

It wasn't until he actually met the hoary old scavenger and started hearing about the "gen-u-ine ball from a superior civ'lization" that South began to feel his memories stirring.

But he couldn't be worried about his dreams. Or about aliens. There were aliens all over Threshold: green-skinned ones and hairy-lipped ones and human ones, as well.

But every time he looked up from his drink and saw that scavenger sitting in Sling's office, sucking on his yellow teeth, South would remember the aliens in his dreams.

Which was just what he didn't need, since nobody on Threshold gave a damn about his dreams or his spotty memory or anything to do with his exploratory flyby of X-3 . . . not even enough to download his trip log.

So the scavenger probably wouldn't care, either. All the scavenger cared about was his black box and his chances of getting into the artifact at the spacedock.

He reached out a gnarly hand and patted South's shoulder. "Don't worry, sonny. Y'll be rich 'n famous along wit' me. An' y' tell yer Customs office that I'm real grateful they come to their senses about this. Real grateful."

Over the scavenger's head, South could see Sling roll his eyes.

But Sling hadn't seen what South had seen. Sling had never been on an x-mission. He'd never jumped out of spongespace into uncharted realms. And he'd never had dreams with sad-eyed aliens in them, under lavender skies with a ringed planet just setting in the purple haze.

CHAPTER 18

Justice of the Peace

"Comments, anyone? Before we adjourn and I bring the kids in to face the music?"

Mickey Croft was nearly through with his staff meeting, and facing a camel-trading session with Cummings, Jr., after he'd walked the two children through a disciplinary session meant to protect them from the harsher discipline of their families.

Hopefully, all damages were subject to limitation. Everything could be mediated, that was Croft's credo.

This conference was testing that credo, and Mickey's faith in himself.

Not only had the Medinans walked out, they were threatening to disrupt the remaining activities, planning demonstrations in the street, and whipping themselves into a fervor of religious zeal that might actually erupt into violence.

If Croft had even guessed that the hajji—pilgrims—could be organized to support political ends during the conference, he'd have set the conference for a different date.

It was an oversight that might haunt him for the rest of his days.

Vince Remson, his resident expert on fundamentalist cultures, said, "Sir, I'd like to ask for increased security, not only for the two children, but for all the conference members. And I think a curfew is in order, for visitors of all sorts, so that we're not accused of persecuting the faithful. And let's provide busses to the Meccan viewstation, so that those that want to take part in the religious ceremonies are not obstructed, and must make a choice: either attend their ceremony, or Forat's demonstrations. I think that should take care of at least half of the pilgrims—those who aren't here specifically in the service of the Medinans."

"Yeah, but how do we know," said the ConSpaceCom general in attendance, "that the Medinans haven't orchestrated this whole thing—every misstep, even the girl's purported love affair?"

The ConSpaceCom general was a paranoid by profession, but Croft was in no mood to look on the dark side of things.

"Because, General," he told the heavy-set, bull-necked officer, "they'd never sacrifice a woman of such stature, or embarrass their chief mullah. Right, Remson?"

"Right," said Remson. "And, if I may say so, they'd never have put themselves in a position where the sentient service personnel issue came under such hot debate. The possible destruction of the Alis, due to their failure to prevent the girl's escape, has brought them unwanted scrutiny. I modelled Ali-7, with Mickey's permission, and I'm absolutely convinced that we're dealing with human—not subhuman —rights violations of the highest order. Not that I can prove it yet. But I will, given time. And if we treat the issue as a subhuman rights question, we'll have the support of all the subs gathered here. The Epsilonians, for one example, will rush to the defense of any subhuman culture that's being so overtly exploited. They need an extreme case to buttress their own. We'll be able to ram through an execution prohibition, at least; probably property and reproductive rights as well."

"Good," Croft said. "Now, if we can keep the principals alive, as well as the peripherals, we'll really have done something." Croft looked down his long glass conference table. Riva Lowe was sitting at the far end of it.

"Riva, you've been unusually silent today. What about

the contraband issues: the Leetle smuggling; the status of this new life-form of Cummings, the Olympian Brow; and the misrepresentation or underrepresentation of the mocket?"

"Um, Director Croft, we'll need some time on the Brow question: NAMECorp has its own standards on worlds it's administering—worlds like Olympus that haven't yet applied for territorial status. But I'm not sure that that can protect the Brows, since the Brows need to eat contraband—Leetles—to survive, and Cummings the Third knew that. Also, if Remson is right and the Brows can affect human behavior, they ought to be prohibited out of hand. The simplest rationale is to prohibit the importation or transportation of the Brow species on the basis that it needs to eat quantities of an already proscribed life-form in order to survive; we won't give Leetle breeding rights to any prospective owners or breeders of Brows. Therefore, it would cause undue hardship to the Brows to export them from Olympus, where Leetles occur naturally and can't be proscribed, according to the Indigenous Species Protection Act."

"And the legal position of Cummings, who used the Brows as an aid to smuggling?"

"Sir, I'll do whatever you want on that. It's so complex an issue that NAMECorp can tie us up in court for years if we overextend ourselves. We've got young Cummings on Leetle smuggling, and the girl on Leetle possession, and I think that's enough to allow us to interpose ourselves between them and the Medinans. I don't see the percentage in looking for more sweeping charges at the moment, when we have cloudy issues, at best, which will surely come into dispute."

"All right. Anyone else?" Croft looked down one side of the table and up the other. The ten department heads were sheafing papers, closing briefcases, preparing to leave.

He saw Remson pass a note to the ConSpaceCom general, but was content to let Remson handle the worst-case sort of planning that had to be done with that agency.

If ConSpaceCom entered the picture, it would mean that ConSec, as well as diplomacy, had failed in keeping Threshold orderly and secure and the application of superior force was then the only option.

Michael Croft detested force and single, last-ditch options. The idea that Threshold and the Territories must act aggressively upon the fundamentalist leader and his rabble was abhorrent.

Therefore, Croft would proceed as if the option did not exist. If it must exist, Remson would oversee its application. That was Remson's job.

"Dismissed, everyone. Good luck. And see you at the banquet this evening, bright-eyed and smiling and to all appearances unconcerned that anything will come of these disruptions."

Face was everything. Croft mustn't end up with egg on his.

Young Dodd was waiting with the two teenagers in an anteroom. Once his staffers had all filed out, Croft slid down in his chair, taking a moment to relax and loosen his tie and summon strength for what was to come.

These children couldn't possibly know what their puppy love might cost the civilized universe.

But Croft remembered when he was young and nothing mattered in the way that love mattered.

One grew out of it. Or one grew into an understanding of love as a deeper matter than a reproductive urge coupled with feelings of insecurity and a genetic recognition of some other party as a likely co-parent.

But you couldn't tell that to these two kids. They'd risked everything, even their lives, for one another in full understanding of what was at stake.

If it weren't so toweringly stupid, it would be touching. But Croft couldn't afford to be touched. He also couldn't afford to be angry, which he would dearly love to be.

Anger he must save for Cummings, Jr., who deserved it in any case and should have raised his son with a higher regard for the law, if not a greater sense of personal responsibility.

"Dodd," said Croft into his intercom, "bring them in."

The two children came in the far door arm in arm. The

girl's eyes were wide and young Cummings's were sullen, even from this distance.

"Sit down, both of you."

They sat where Dodd positioned them, at the far end of the long conference table.

Croft, watching Dini Forat, remembered the effect she'd first had on him, and his attitude toward young Cummings softened slightly. These children were only that—children.

But they were child smugglers and child fornicators. Worse, they were children rebelling against the customs of generations.

"Both of you know why you're here. I'll not belabor your errors. You know they may still be deadly. I'd like to know what each of you would like to do, given your current situations. You first, Ms. Forat."

The girl stood up to address him. Her boyfriend jerked her arm so that she sat back down.

"Sir," she said. "Rick and I want you to marry us. Right now. Right here. Then my father will see that he cannot do this to us, that our love is true and strong and he should be ashamed of himself."

Croft's eyebrow raised despite his determination not to be surprised by whatever the children said or did.

"Indeed. And you, Mr. Cummings? Do you concur?"

"Yes, Secretary General, I certainly do." Cummings laced his fingers together on the table in a passable imitation of his father's negotiating behavior. "If you'll marry us, and drop all other charges, we'll leave immediately for Pegasus's Nostril, NAMECorp's habitat around the planet Olympus. We'll take the Brows back with us—it was a mistake to bring them. We'll take just enough Leetles to make sure the Brows don't die on the trip. That way, everybody's happy." With a half-smirk and a toss of his head, young Cummings sat back in his chair.

"I wouldn't say everybody's happy, Mr. Cummings. Not at all." But it wasn't a bad proposition, coming from a teenage boy.

"If we drop the smuggling charges and the contraband charges against you two, I'm not sure we can hold off your father, Ms. Forat, long enough to get you both out of here in one piece. And there remains the execution order that Medina has issued on both your heads, wherever you may be. You'd be living in constant fear of Medinan agents. There must be some way to appeal to your father's reason."

"Trust me," said Dini Forat bitterly. Her voice shook. "My father will relent only when it is politically embarrassing to continue. Let us do this thing, Secretary Croft. It is the best—the only—way. And we will not be separated. If anyone tries to separate us, we will fight."

"It's suicide, the way it is," Cummings III said quietly. "The Medinans will kill us—hunt us down, find us and kill us. You surely can't stand by and let them murder citizens of—"

"I know my duties, Mr. Cummings. All right, it's not a bad plan. I'll consider it. I'm seeing your father next, Cummings. Try to keep in mind that whatever I work out with him is ultimately in your best interest."

"To hell with my father," Cummings snarled, and then said: "I'm sorry, sir. We're grateful for all you've done."

"Won't you marry us right now?" Dini Forat was on her feet. "It will show my father that we are not to be trifled with . . ."

"Perhaps tomorrow, Ms. Forat."

"Tomorrow will be too late," she said, before Cummings could stop her.

"I certainly hope not. As a matter of fact, Ms. Forat, I trust not. Dodd, escort them back safely."

The Cummings boy had Dini Forat under his arm as Dodd led them out the door.

Now all Croft had to do was find the energy to make the boy's father see the wisdom of buying off the Ayatollah Forat with whatever the Medinan wanted most.

Since Cummings, Jr., was a skinflint and a tyrant, Croft had his work cut out for him. But with lives hanging in the balance, he would summon the energy, somehow, to prevail over the injured pride of both parents.

He must.

CHAPTER 19

A Better Place

Dini Forat cuddled her mocket, once again small, fluffy, and white, in her lap and stared out the window of the Cummings limo as the car sped toward the building owned by her beloved's father.

Beside her, Rick was stiff and tense as his father lectured them both.

There was nothing to do, Dini understood, but to be silent and appear to obey.

The elder Cummings was saying: "Rick, I don't know what I'm going to do with you. To get you two out on bail, I had to promise Mickey Croft the moon."

Dini looked away from the glory of Threshold, staring at Rick's father in horror. "The moon! Surely you did not pay an entire—"

"A figure of speech, Ms. Forat," said Rick's father. When the elder Cummings looked at her, Dini felt disquieted. There was a marked similarity in the looks of father and son. Would Rick resemble this forbidding, gruff, icy-eyed person when he was old?

Richard Cummings, Jr., had a face full of lines, tanned like old leather. His pale eyes stared out of it, swimming in startlingly bright whites, as if out of a ceremonial mask. His teeth, too, were white. There were more wrinkles around his eyes than even around her own father's and, from the sockets they described, his nose jutted like a ship's prow or a cannon on a battlement.

His was a mean face, an arrogant and unforgiving face, a face as devoid of sensitivity as her own father's. She hoped against hope that her husband-to-be would not earn for himself such a face.

The father's stare took her measure, then something in it changed. "A figure of speech, but a prophetic one. Whatever I promised Secretary Croft is only a pittance compared to what I'm going to have to use to bribe your father to call off his dogs and make this marriage official—sanctioned by Medina. Can you give me one reason I ought to do that, Ms. Forat? Pay a king's ransom for a bride I'm not at all sure is suitable for my son, when I can just sit back and wait and end up with my choice of debutantes from good families whose cultural base is more . . . appropriate to my family's needs?"

Dini Forat said, without thinking, in a hurt and angry voice, "Because my father will kill Rick, as well as myself, if you do not find a way to placate him."

And Rick, speaking for the first time since his father had come to secure their release into his custody, said, "You mean, more appropriate to your dynasty's needs, you bastard. Don't pick on her. Whatever it costs, we can afford it. And I'm going to marry Dini, one way or the other." Rick crossed his arms, jabbing Dini in the breast as he did so.

Dini's mocket growled at Rick.

"We?" said his father in a dangerous voice. "And what's this 'one way or the other' crap? You're going to do exactly as I say, until the hearing. Both of you. You're not going to leave this level—not going to leave the building except under armed guard and stringent precautions."

The car slowed, passing through a tunnel-like lock. Dini craned her neck and, sure enough, she could see the star-spattered sky through the ceiling above them.

"You're worried that we might jump bail? I should have

known." Rick Cummings skewered his father with a disparaging glare. "All you care about is món—"

"I'm worried that, as Ms. Forat suggested, someone might try to kill you both before I can talk some sense into Ayatollah Forat. I know you couldn't have heard, but Dini's father and I had a rather unpleasant initial encounter. It's not going to be easy to come to terms. You'll both want to understand that whatever this costs is going to come out of—"

"My hide," Rick finished his father's sentence wearily. "What else is new? Thanks for the bail money, Dad-O. But we don't need any more lectures. I'd rather have stayed at Croft's under house arrest than listen to you—"

"If you'd listened to me . . ." Richard Cummings began, raising his voice.

Dini clapped her hands over her ears. Her mocket began to whine and jumped off her lap to cower on the floor.

Rick put his arms around her. "Now look what you've done. Why don't you go back to whatever rented wife you've got this week, and whatever safari we dragged you away from? That's what's really eating you, isn't it? We took up some of your precious time."

"That's about enough out of you, young man."

Rick subsided, stiff and staring straight ahead.

The elder Cummings rubbed his face with his palm as if he were some animal cleaning itself. Then he began again, in a much quieter tone: "Stay out of trouble. Stay with my people. We've all got to pull together to get through this."

Dini reached down to lift the quivering mocket back onto her lap. Then she risked a look at Rick's father.

For a moment, she thought she saw real concern in those pale eyes. He smiled at her tentatively. The smile was forced and false.

But she smiled back, smoothing the mocket onto her lap.

"What about my Brows?" Rick wanted to know as the car pulled up before the Cummings Building.

"Your . . . Oh, the new species." Humor tugged at the father's mouth.

Or perhaps it was pride. Dini couldn't be sure. She was

having trouble holding the mocket, who wanted to crawl back down onto the floor.

"That's right. The undiscovered species. Worth a fortune, admit it. Can't you bring yourself to even admit how great they are? How much they're going to be—"

"Not since you brought them in here, to everyone's attention. We're going to send them back to Olympus, with just enough Leetles to keep them alive. Croft's idea."

"My idea," Rick flared.

"Oh, and was it your idea to slap them with a permanent export ban? We'll never be able to use them off-planet, you idiot!" This time, it was the father who looked away, out the window as the car pulled to a halt before the building bearing his name. "Get out, both of you. Don't fool with the Brows, no matter how proud of yourselves you are. They're under a Secretariat seal until we can ship them home. And don't eat their Leetles. They've got just enough Leetles in there to get them through the spongejump—"

"They're in *there*?" In Rick's voice, surprise was mixed with grudging admiration.

"They're ours, son. In a way, they're yours. Of course they're in there. I said this whole thing's cost me. They're probably tearing up my den right now. I'll take any damage they do out of your—"

"Hide. Yes indeed, I'm well aware of that. Well, here's where we get off." Rick leaned around Dini and pushed open the door.

She knew her beloved well enough to notice the strange expression on his face, but not well enough to identify it. On someone else, she would have thought the look to be mischievous.

Gathering up her mocket, she got out of the car. Rick said a few words to his father that she didn't catch, and followed.

Then the car pulled away, leaving them on the doorstep of the Cummings building, where three uniformed NAMECorp security men were waiting for them.

She started to say something, but Rick hushed her, "Not now. Wait until we get upstairs."

So she cuddled her mocket, who was panting happily now and wagging its stubby tail, as the guards escorted them up to the penthouse.

Inside, there were no signs of the mess the Brows had made. No sign of the Leetle infestation that, really, had caused all the trouble.

She put the mocket down and it ran, yapping, down a hallway.

"It's scented the Brows," Rick said authoritatively. Then he turned. "Okay, fellows. Sweep this place and get out. You can protect us well enough from the foyer if you're any good at your job."

The security men eyed one another. Their leader gave a signal and they split up to examine all the rooms for signs of Dini's father's henchmen.

She looked wistfully after her mocket. There were Leetles in there with the Brows.

Leetles made everything all right. Brows made everything more than all right.

Dini didn't feel anywhere near all right. She turned to ask her beloved, "Couldn't we just—?"

"Shut up! Not yet. Wait until the bug sweep's done."

At first she thought he meant a sweep for Leetles, then she realized what he did mean: Rick was afraid there might be hidden listening devices in the apartment.

"But who . . ." Then she did shut her mouth. Any number of parties might be interested in hearing what she and Rick had to say: her father, his father, Mickey Croft's office . . .

The security men frightened Dini's mocket. It came barreling out of the hall and leapt into her arms. "There, there, Pepi," she crooned to it. The mocket looked just like the dog of her favorite vid star. She'd even named it after the star's dog. Medinans, of course, couldn't have dogs. Dogs were unclean. But a mocket was a mocket, whatever shape it took.

The guards consulted briefly with Rick and they left, shaking their heads.

When the door closed behind them, Rick said, "All clear. We can talk. But let's hurry. We don't have much time."

"Time?"

"We're getting out of here."

Dini nearly dropped her mocket on its head as she let it go. It yapped once, shook itself, and again raced down the hall toward the room where the Brows were being kept.

"But we can't! You heard your father . . ."

"I heard him. And I understood him. You didn't." Rick took her hands in his. "Dini, we're taking the Brows and the Leetles and your mocket and we're getting out of here. I've ordered my ship readied. By the time we get there, the security men will have bribed the right people, and we'll be able to sneak away."

"Away?" Dini was aghast. "But where will we go?"

"Home. To Pegasus's Nostril. My father's company owns the habitat. We'll honeymoon on Olympus. The Brows are going home, and we're going to take them."

"But that's jumping bail!"

"It's only money. I have to give my father the leverage he needs with your father."

"Are you sure?"

Rick Cummings pulled her against him. "Of course I'm sure. Now, let's go see our Brows. A couple of Leetles, and you'll feel better. You let one Brow ride on your shoulder, the way I taught you. The other one will look just like the mocket to anybody but us. We'll get into a van that'll be downstairs, and go straight to the dock.

"We'll be loaded into the cargo area of my ship, and I'll have different identification. So will you. The Brows will make sure we look like the people on our papers, and sound right too. Don't worry!"

She broke away from him. "How can I not?"

"Because I'm your husband—or will be."

"Oh, if only Secretary Croft would have married us!"

Rick Cummings spun her around. "But he didn't, did he? I've been planning this ever since Dad showed up to get us out of Croft's clutches. Even before. I know my father. I know how he thinks, the way his mind works. On the

Nostril, we'll be married in the grandest style. And no Medinan thugs are going to find us, or terrorize us, or stop us. I promise." He gave her a little push. "Now, are you coming, or not?"

"What choice have I?" If she'd refused to go with Rick, things would have been even worse for her. She would be alone, a violated woman helpless before Medinan justice. And she loved Rick. She was sure she loved him.

The mocket was whining at the study door.

Rick Cummings said, "Come on. Let's go get the Brows." As he hurried down the hall, he didn't even look back to see if she would follow.

But she did. And when the door opened, revealing the Brows who sat up on their hind legs in delight and made little chittering noises, Dini knew everything would be all right.

When one Brow came scampering over with a Leetle for her, she knelt down to take it. "Oh, thank you," she crooned to the Brow. Its tiny black fingers curled around one of hers. With her other hand, she carefully took the proffered Leetle and popped it into her mouth.

Dini closed her eyes in delight. Leetles were bad for most people, but most people didn't have Brows. Leetles made communicating with the Brows much easier. And Leetles made all the anxiety inside you melt away as if it were snow on a mountain peak in summer. Anxiety was fear of the future, and the Brows helped you mold your future.

She looked up at Rick, who had one Brow on his shoulder and the second in his arms. He was beaming.

"Ready for our great escape?"

Of course she was.

Dini picked up her Brow and it scrambled up to perch on her shoulder. Its tail curled around the back of her neck and the tip of it beat against her breastbone.

"Come on, Pepi; come on." She called her mocket, and it came up, wagging its tail.

"Here, take the Leetle feeder cage." Rick handed her the cage, which let the Brows get at only a certain number of

Leetles per day. It had been very generous of her Brow to offer her that Leetle.

But she'd really needed it.

Out they went, down the stairs: Rick, his two Brows; herself, her mocket on its leash, a Brow balanced on her shoulder; the cage of Leetles, in her hand.

And as Rick had predicted, a small van was waiting. They all climbed in the back. The driver shut the door, got in front, and swivelled his seat to hand Rick some documents. "Okay, sir?"

Rick looked the documents over. "Perfect. Just perfect." He handed a set of documents to Dini. "You're a NAMECorp employee, Dini. How does it feel?"

She looked at the papers, which said she was a female exobiologist named Mackenzie, and a qualified pilot as well.

"How will we ever pull this off?"

"The Brows," said Rick confidently. "Just be brave, and show your Brow how you want people to react to you, and everything will be fine."

And everything was fine, all the way to the dock, where they went aboard a ship of some kind through a cargo-loading hatch that fit the back of the van like a glove.

She never saw the outside of the ship.

Inside, she'd never encountered a ship this small, or this complicated-looking. She put the cage of Leetles down where Rick told her to, and the Brow jumped off her shoulder.

Her mocket tugged on its leash. Once Rick had said farewell to the NAMECorp men and closed the ship up tight, she let the mocket go.

It wanted to explore with the Brows, who were climbing over and under everything.

"Dini, come sit up here with me," her beloved called.

She did, and sat for the first time in the cockpit of a starship.

She could hardly believe it was a starship, it seemed so tiny. But despite the small control area, and the even smaller viewscreens, the ship had a galley and two cabins and a lounge and a cargo bay.

Rick was caressing the control panel, a look of total concentration on his face.

Finally he sat back. "Here we go, Dini. Next stop, freedom!"

"Next stop, home for you," she told the Brow who'd put one little black hand on her thigh and was now trying to crawl into her lap.

She shooed it.

"Let him up here. I might have to talk to the traffic controller, and if I do, he'll be handy to have around."

But, evidently, Rick did not have to talk personally to anyone.

Everything seemed to be handled by the ship's artificial intelligence.

Lights lit. A roar began. Numbers flickered on controls she didn't understand.

And in the rear, somewhere, a vibration and then a roar began.

Belts came out of the seat and she was secured in a harness.

"Just sit back, enjoy the ride," Rick crowed. "We'll be out of pursuit range in less than four hours."

They weren't out of pursuit range yet.

But soon enough.

The ship started moving.

"What's that, Rick?" Her hands were at her throat. One Brow was perched on the headrest of her acceleration couch.

"The power plant, silly. We're beginning to move. Easing out of the slip. The next thing you feel will be thruster burn. . . ."

Rick Cummings kept up a general description of what was happening until, triumphant, he said, "We're on our own. Course laid in."

And she felt the acceleration rip through her as her beloved aimed their vessel at the stars—at freedom, safety, and a whole new life, beyond the reach of her father's domineering hand.

CHAPTER 20

Second Thoughts

Riva Lowe slipped into Mickey Croft's modeling chamber, feeling like a criminal skulking around in the dark.

Inside, she felt her way as her eyes adjusted to the dim, multicolored illumination of ready lights and standby modes on consoles.

Lowe sat at the padded control console and powered up the main screen. A tiny point of light appeared at its center and blossomed before her.

The modeler was ready to go.

She had no business being here right now, let alone using her precious modeler time for what she wanted to use it for. But it was her modeler time, that she'd wheedled out of Mickey. She could use it for whatever she pleased.

She leaned her forehead on her hand. She should never have decided to review the scavenger's log, that was the problem.

She should have gone back to her apartment and gotten some much-needed sleep. People who are overtired make mistakes, and she was as prone to error as anyone else in the advanced stages of sleep deprivation.

Riva Lowe had no idea when she'd slept last. She was so tired she couldn't remember exactly how old she was—what the number attached to her last birthday had been.

She'd better pull out of it. She'd better get herself together. It didn't matter how old she was, but it mattered that she couldn't decide whether she was thirty-eight or thirty-nine. One was supposed to know these things. She could figure it out, but she wasn't sure she wanted to do that.

When she'd looked at the scavenger's log, she'd had the damnedest reaction to the footage of the ball. She'd felt . . . disturbed by it. She'd been especially disturbed by the image of her finger touching the ball. Every time she ran it, she saw again the strange vistas that she'd imagined when she touched it. An EVA can skew you, sometimes. A bad oxygen mix, a tiny mistake by the in-suit chemical optimizer.

Maybe that was what had happened. When she'd run the log in her office, Riva Lowe had been so tired that she'd nearly dozed off, waiting for the data to come up. Once she'd started to view it, she'd been wide-awake.

Viewing that log was like reliving the experience. More vivid, even. Perhaps she'd been underestimating how violently she'd reacted to the whole interval. Every time she heard Keebler's chatter, it set her teeth on edge.

But she'd repeatedly run the log sequence during which she'd touched the ball. Over and over. When she looked at her housekeeping system, the system said that she'd run that log twelve times.

It was almost addictive, to run the tape and watch the vista in her mind's eye. The lavender sky. The ringed planet in the mist. The big-eyed . . . She stopped thinking about it. So she was having some weird psychological aftereffects from the EVA. Happened to the overworked and overachieving sort of civil servant now and again.

She'd apply for a few days leave. And she'd give it to herself. As soon as this was over.

Sure she would.

The modeler before her waited patiently. She'd told herself that she'd come here to model the scavenger, Keebler, because the tape chatter had been disturbing. Because she needed to define action parameters for the scavenger so that she could efficiently predict his behavior.

Now that she was here she knew that she'd been fooling herself. The person she really wanted to model was Joe South.

What a scandalous waste of the government's time and Mickey's money. What a foolish, adolescent, thing to do.

She wasn't going to do it. She was a trusted professional. If Mickey ever found out she'd used her modeling time on a Relic, his estimation of her would take a nosedive.

If she let herself do it, so would her own.

So she set up parameters for modeling the scavenger.

She had plenty of file data on Keebler. She had speech patterns and behavior matrices. She had whole reaction grids because of the time they'd spent together on the ship.

She fed the data into the modeler and waited.

When the modeler had digested the physical and behavioral information on Keebler, it blinked READY.

Lowe pressed a key to continue, and above the modeler console, a holographic image of the scavenger from the neck up appeared.

She put her finger on the joystick and rotated the head three hundred and sixty degrees.

Then she pressed the initializing function, and the modeler's AI brought Keebler to life.

No longer was she looking at the holographic ghost of a face. She could see Keebler's head in all its greasy glory, complete to enlarged pores and crow's-feet.

The image was so good, it was spooky. She rubbed her arms. She was almost hesitant to talk to this thing. If it really had been the actual disembodied head of Keebler up there, she would have felt no more hesitancy.

She said, "Keebler, tell me about the ball."

"It's gonna make me rich 'n' famous," leered the head.

"How can you know that?" she asked, overcoming her reluctance to be brusque by reminding herself that this wasn't Keebler, that Keebler would never know she'd asked these questions or what answer, if any, his simulacrum gave her.

The modeled head of Keebler said, "I seen inside it. I seen . . . what to do."

"And what's that?"

"Open her up. It's waitin' fer it."

"It's waiting for what?"

"It's waitin' fer me to open her up. Then I'll be rich 'n' famous."

Riva Lowe leaned so far back in her chair, arms dangling,

that her fingertips brushed the floor. Of course, the model wasn't a panacea. It could only draw likely responses from the base she'd given it. It couldn't tell her what it didn't know.

"So what else can you tell me about the ball, Keebler?"

"Only that, when I get her opened up, it's a whole new world fer me. I'm gonna be rich—"

With an irritated snort, Riva Lowe hit the program's interrupt key.

Keebler was frozen, mouth open, beady eyes narrowed with greed.

This was no good. Or she was too tired to make anything of what she was seeing. She ended the sequence and the head of Keebler disappeared.

Then, furtively, she took the data on Joe South from her breast pocket and put it into the modeler's slot.

When she'd processed the image, it stared at her with more than human eyes.

"Hi," she said, and felt ridiculous.

"Hi," it said back.

"What are you going to do next?" she asked it, because the insipid question was the only one she could think of, now that she had a model to question.

"I have a mission," it told her.

She knew that.

"And then?"

"Try to get another one."

This, too, was useless. She was too tired. She asked the modeler to save the image. She had plenty of time left on Mickey's clock. She could come back after she got some sleep.

Carefully, she returned the modeler to its standby mode and left, making sure the room was exactly as it had been, and that all its locks engaged as she thumbprinted out.

She'd had the strangest urge to tell the model of South how uneasy she felt about the ball that Keebler had at spacedock. But what good was telling the model?

By the time she'd reached her apartment, she was determined to tell South about this odd feeling.

South should have a chance to view her log of the EVA with Keebler. She shouldn't send him into this without a proper briefing. Even though she couldn't evaluate the data yet, he had a right to be aware of it.

Or so she told herself, when she wasn't telling herself that she was just making up an excuse to call the Relic pilot in the middle of the night.

She put the apartment on a cleaning cycle, took a shower, and argued with herself: She'd go straight to bed; she could call South in the morning.

If she insisted on briefing him right now, he'd think she was as crazy as a Relic. Or else he'd think she was a lonely woman pulling rank to get some company on a lonely night.

She could have gone to one of Mickey's banquets, hobbed and nobbed her way through a full-dress crowd of heavyweights. But she was so busy, and so tired. . . .

She was so disturbed by that EVA log.

She was disturbed because she was tired. She was tired because she was disturbed.

She got out of the shower bag and the bathroom dried her with solicitous, warm breath.

Somehow, she found herself sitting by the vidphone on her bed, in her white robe, waiting for her paging system to find South and connect them.

When it couldn't, she realized that South might already have left for spacedock with the scavenger. She verified that this was the case and then sat back, disappointed and yet relieved.

She'd probably dreamed up this whole mini-crisis, complete with weird intuitions, to justify calling the Relic pilot in for briefing at this ungodly hour. If she'd found him, she would surely have given him her home number.

Since STARBIRD, South, and his passenger had already left, according to Traffic Control, she wasn't in danger of making a fool of herself. At least, not tonight.

She snapped off the vidphone, then got into her bed, still in her robe, and tried to go to sleep. But she couldn't.

When the phone rang, she was so sure it was some sort of trouble about Keebler, South, and that accursed ball that her heart raced.

Very unprofessional.

So she tried to sound as if she weren't in bed, and she

tried to seem like the good professional she was: "Riva Lowe here."

"Director, this is Dodd from Secretary Croft's office. The Secretary asked me to call to inform you that Ms. Forat and Cummings III are not in their quarters, and we'd like your service to keep a collective eye out for them."

Dodd was such a little twit. He delivered his bombshell with about as much urgency as he'd have displayed telling her that the vegetable for tomorrow's luncheon menu would have to be changed.

"Whoa, Dodd. What's this 'quarters' stuff? I thought they were in custody."

"Cummings, Junior, arranged with Mickey for the kids' bail on the drug charges. His lawyers are making a case that we don't have one—a case, that is. Technicalities, you know. So Mickey let them go over to the Cummings Building."

"And they're not there?"

"Not at the moment. No one's really too upset yet. They're probably just out painting the town. But do alert your people. If they should try to leave, they're to be detained and this office alerted. We'll return them to the Cummings Building. Very gently. Very politely."

Painting the town. Where did Croft get these guys? All passive voice and passive aggression. "If these kids aren't in the father's apartment, if they've snuck off somewhere and are out dancing and drinking, you'd better make sure that some very polite and very gentle Medinan hitmen don't get them before we do, Dodd. Now get off this line. I've got calls to make."

It wasn't Dodd's fault that he was a born bureaucrat. It wasn't Lowe's fault that, when she gave the alert, nobody came up with anything resembling a sighting of the two adolescents.

She instituted full security screening everywhere and started to get dressed. Sleep just wasn't in the cards tonight.

Lowe was going back to the office, just in case the kids tried to get off Threshold in the next few hours. When you needed to handle something very delicately, it was best to handle it yourself.

As for her feelings about Joe South and the scavenger's ball . . . both of those would have to wait.

CHAPTER 21

$$\triangledown$$

A Reason to Quit

Reice always got the nasty jobs, the dangerous jobs, the jobs that the brass would have done themselves if they had the stones. It was almost enough to make him want to quit the service.

You couldn't leave the task of finding the mullah's daughter and the NAMECorp heir to just anybody, he consoled himself. This was sensitive. That's why you needed somebody like him.

"Find those kids before the mullahs do," were his orders. Remson the Great had come down from Blue Mid to brief him personally at ConSec HQ in Blue South. "Medinan law dictates the death penalty. Nobody wants a spark that could ignite full-scale violence among our visiting pilgrims, not with the conference still going on."

Vince Remson had always been a master of understatement. It was Remson's way of emphasizing things. When Remson would get to the heart of his matter, the part a ConSec commander would yell at full voice, Remson would nearly be whispering.

So when Remson murmured, "Threshold won't support violent demonstrations in its streets," Reice knew what he was hearing.

Either ConSec found those kids before the Medinan hitmen did, or all hell was going to break loose.

Half of Consolidated Security was out looking for the lovers. Reice's commander had broken out six standard search teams for street work. Remson had augmented that with a dozen of his information jocks who were straddling hot computer terminals round the clock. If the kids were on Threshold, somebody would turn them up in short order. On the Stalk, you used services, and services were computerized. You went places, and to get there you went through locks and tubes and doorways. You were seen by human and electronic eyes when you did.

That was the problem: The Medinans couldn't be allowed to see the kids first.

Even Consolidated Space Command was lending a hand, supplementing the on-Threshold search with its remote sensing capabilities throughout the inner solar system. If Cummings, Jr., tried to smuggle the kids to his estate on Earth, ConSpaceCom would catch them—coming or going. Consolidated Space Command had more hardware in the inner system than it knew what to do with, hardware that made the protection of Earth's sanctity a certainty.

No one had turned up those damn kids. Not hide nor hair. Not even a false alarm. If they didn't try to leave Threshold to get to Earth, and they didn't try to sneak into this or that private club for a good time, and they didn't try to use their credit cards, they could hold out, wherever they were, for a long time. It was movement that got you nailed.

So maybe conventional wisdom was right: maybe the kids weren't moving. Maybe they were simply somewhere else on Threshold under NAMECorp security. NAMECorp security was the best money could buy. So good that nobody could get hold of Cummings, Jr., for comment. Not even Remson.

But if none of those suppositions were true, then Reice had his work cut out for him.

Remson had given him carte blanche, which was always nice.

With it, Reice was doing the impossible: trying to comb the missing kids out of the Stalk's innumerable nooks and crannies, using his connections and his wits. And that entailed putting together a surveillance net that included not only the Customs facilities, but the distance between Threshold and the jump belt: the outer solar system.

Space was a big place. Nobody these days needed to be reminded how big. You could mine it and you could launch marker buoys until you died of old age. You could send out multiband electronic snooper packages and you could scatter lidars and synthetic aperture image-return spacecraft, and it was all about as effective as sending out notes in bottles if you were trapped on a desert island on Earth in the old days.

Space was just too damned big.

So you watched the sensible routes and you let the rest go.

Reice had decided to try some less sensible routes today. He was following his instinct as he called in his flight plan.

You couldn't do anything until you checked in with ConSec headquarters, even with carte blanche.

When he got to Blue South, there were uniforms and civilians everywhere. People had to elbow each other out of the way to turn around. The ConSec HQ looked like somebody'd said there were two tickets for an all-expenses-paid trip to Io hidden somewhere on the premises.

The confusion was a result of the all-out search coupled with the beefed-up security, but it bothered Reice as he threaded his way through the melee of personnel until he realized that there was method in the apparent madness.

Men and women in street clothes were huddled before the commander's office, and Reice recognized them as an infiltration team when he got close enough to cut through to his boss's door.

Mickey Croft's people weren't missing a trick. Half of these folks in slightly antiquated clothing were wearing the collarless shirts of Medinan pilgrims; some of the women had scarves around their necks, which would double for veils when they got out on the streets. Each person was being issued a lapel transceiver disguised as a button or a flower or a Medinan-style ornament.

They'd fan out among the pilgrims and take a pulse on the demonstrations that the Medinans were planning. They also might be able to identify the hitfolk and the Ali-class bodyguards among the less dangerous element.

Reice said, generally, "Remember, guys, there's no such thing as a noncombatant in civil disobedience."

Somebody groaned and made an obscene gesture. Somebody told him to come out on the streets and see if he still felt that way. A woman said, "Reice, how's the hunt for the kids?"

As he brushed past the ConSec undercover staff, he tossed back, "My chances of finding the kids are about as good as yours of arresting the crazies looking to murder them."

And that was true enough to make everybody feel bad. You could arrest a perpetrator only in the act or in the process of planning a conspiracy.

It was one of those times when law and order was at the mercy of lawlessness and disorder. You had to wait until somebody did something wrong. You couldn't arrest somebody for wanting to do something wrong.

Reice pushed through into the commander's office and there, looking as if he'd been vat-grown in place, was his boss, in the middle of an electronic horseshoe. The ledge of the command center was strewn with empty drink containers and food wrappers.

The Old Man looked twice as harried as usual, today.

When he saw Reice, he leaned back with a sour look on his face, elbows splayed on the terminal bumpers around him: "So, hot stuff. Got any more bright ideas?"

"What was my last one?" Reice knew how to play the Old Man.

"Having those Space Command idiots turn on all their toys in case Sir Richard the Second tried to trundle his kids off to Earth."

"No luck there. Well, I'm going out the other way, today."

"What do you mean, the *other* way?"

"Spacedocks and such. And on out." Reice tried to make it sound casual, as if it weren't the only remaining logical possibility, and therefore, the truth. Because they'd missed the boat. All of them. They'd never thought, beyond having Customs raise security at the port, to check what was going out-system.

"You're not telling me you're going to troll for those kids in patrol cruisers?" The crotchety, overworked commander leaned forward. "You do recall just how big an area we're talking about, Reice? And how few people we've got. . . ."

"Yes, sir. I'm just going to take the Blue Tick out and have a look at some likely sites. Maybe ask for a few data pulls while I'm out there. Who knows, maybe I'll come up with something."

He wasn't about to proclaim that he knew the answer, that he'd realized that all of them had screwed up.

You didn't walk into the Old Man's office and say it was too late to close the barn door. You let events do that.

"All right, Reice, you've got Remson's approval. And mine. Go waste some time and money."

"Yes, sir. Thank you, sir," he said and got out of there before the Old Man thought to ask him why he was taking this tack.

He wasn't sure why, yet. He just had a suspicion.

As he took the priority tube down to the ConSec docking bay, he busied himself figuring out how to ask the questions he wanted and get the answers he needed without incidentally indicting anyone else's performance.

You had to be careful, when you smelled a screwup of royal proportions.

The *Blue Tick* was ready and prepped, in the pursuit craft bay. All he had to do was log his purported itinerary and go aboard.

Inside her, he started up his emergency-priority departure module and let the ship clear its own way through traffic and red tape.

There were times when he loved his job, and this was one of those times.

While the ship was clearing her flight patterns and sliding out of her slip and into the police emergency tube that would convey her out of Threshold Terminal, Reice started a search program running.

The program would collate every departure for eight hours prior to the search programs run by everybody else. And it would flag every NAMECorp vessel to have logged out of the Stalk's docking facilities, no matter the ship's purpose, in that time frame.

If Reice was right, those kids couldn't be found because they weren't around. And if they weren't around, then they'd gotten out somehow.

And if they hadn't gone to Earth, as ConSpaceCom swore, then they'd gone the other way.

As Reice's hot little pursuit cruiser picked up speed in the tube that would spit her out of the Blue South police exit, he waited for verification.

Getting it might take awhile. Getting Riva Lowe to release Customs data to him, en masse, wasn't the problem. Getting to her to get the data was the problem.

Reice knew that nobody in her office was going to do what Reice wanted done without a personal okay from the boss.

And he wasn't going to ask for it himself: she wasn't going to be thrilled when she saw the request come up. It would look, at first glance, as if he were trying to lay the error-chain at her doorstep.

Which Reice wasn't. Not even after the fiasco over the Relic pilot, no matter how bad it had been, would he go looking for some way to blame Customs for losing the kids.

But the kids were lost. It was just that nobody else was willing to admit it yet. And to find them, you had to admit that what you were doing wasn't working.

Since Reice wasn't doing anything else—had been relieved of all other duties to concentrate on this one—he had a cleaner plate than most.

He leaned back in his seat when the warning light lit and

closed his eyes as soon as he'd strapped in. He loved the feel of complete and constant interaction with a ship as good as this one was.

He settled his head into the headrest, which electronically fed him data, much in the way an EVA helmet did, and closed his eyes. The mnemonic/electroencephalographic transducer in the headrest beat the hell out of an EVA helmet. Using it was like being at one with the ship.

The AI expert program did most of the work, but it had to be targeted. It had to know what you wanted it to do. And no matter how big a place space was, it seemed a lot smaller when you could look at it through the relayed integrated data systems that a ship like this could access.

So Reice started searching, grid square by grid square, all the space around him as he instituted his own search pattern that should eventually bring him to the spacedock area.

He was looking for anything anomalous, because the kids' ship might be using some sort of masking device.

But only a little while after the *Blue Tick* had reached cruising speed, his data request from Customs came through.

And then he knew exactly where he was going.

NAMECorp had a freighter that had left less than an hour before the Customs alert. That freighter had a pickup at Spacedock One in three hours. After that, it was scheduled into a jump lane.

If Reice could catch it before it jumped, he could board it and search it.

And if he did that, he was nearly sure that he was going to find two fugitive teenagers aboard.

If he could catch it before it made its spacedock to take on additional cargo, he was completely sure he'd find them.

So he reached up and let his hand trail with easy familiarity across the control panel above his head. Then he went back to work.

Given the *Blue Tick*'s top speed, and the freighter's innocuous progress, he might just do it.

But the only way to ensure that he didn't have a real problem on his hands was to preserve the element of surprise.

So he didn't alert anyone, not even ConSec HQ, that he thought he'd found the kids.

He just broke every traffic regulation in the book, and worked on bending the laws of physics.

He had to get there in time. And he'd always said that the laws of physics were different for pursuit craft.

Blue Tick was flashing all her lights; every warning meter she had was alive. Cowboying around like this, you never knew when you were about to punch right through the envelope into disaster. But you had to try, every once in a while, to do the job your way, because otherwise it wouldn't get done.

And if those kids figured out he was coming after them, with the lead they had, he might not be able to catch them before they jumped for Pegasus's Nostril, the freighter's logged destination.

Or, worse, for parts unknown.

CHAPTER 22

Enough Rope

Vince Remson was almost out of ideas. And that scared him. Sitting with Mickey on the rooftop of the Secretariat, looking down at the gathered throng of fundamentalist crazies out front, Remson couldn't understand how Croft could be so calm.

"They're exercising their right of free assembly," said Mickey Croft between two bites of a scone loaded with marmalade. "Don't worry so much, Vince. Eat your breakfast. Who knows when we'll have time for another decent meal, instead of all this ethnic slop we've been swallowing at the receptions." Croft took another bite and swallowed it with a swig of breakfast tea.

There was nothing wrong with Croft's appetite. To look at the impeccable diplomat, you'd have thought there was no crowd of fist-waving demonstrators chanting slogans outside his door.

So maybe Remson was overreacting. No, overreacting would have been sending in riot police with pressure hoses and rubber bats.

"I don't know how you can eat like that, Mickey," said Remson, picking a raisin out of his scone and putting it in his mouth to see if he could jumpstart his salivary glands.

"You should have seen me last night, when the Ho delegation decided that I was the one to get the honoree's portion: stewed eye of worble, including the socket, served from the entire head that they brought with them for the purpose." Croft shuddered and his mouth collapsed into a prune of distaste. "Tasted like a rubber glove with lemon sauce and a filling of worms."

"I'm glad I missed it. Are you ready to hear the upshot of the Ali situation?"

"That's why you're here, dear boy—to brief me."

"I just wondered if you wanted to finish eating first."

"If I could eat only when the news was good or nonexistent, I'd have starved to death by now. Tell me about the Ali situation." Croft put both elbows on the white tablecloth. "I'm all ears."

Sometimes Croft seemed rather overendowed in the ear department, but Remson hardly ever thought of Mickey in terms of physical pluses and minuses. Still, the turn of phrase made him stifle a grin.

And that relaxed him somewhat. "Sir, we're reasonably sure that at least one of the top mullahs—perhaps even Beni Forat himself—will attend the session on the 'sentient service personnel' matter. It's our position that, since the Alis meet the standards of human as described in the UNE Code, Title—"

"Spare me the specifics, unless the citations aren't going to come up on my terminal at my seat when I need them, the way I've come to expect when you're running the show."

"Oh, you'll have all the data, sir."

"Good, then you can call me Mickey again and we can stop pretending that this is really much different than any other crisis."

"If you say so . . . Mickey. The data will support a claim of full human citizenship: They've been psychologically conditioned and bred for generations to perform the bodyguard tasks without question, but they're as human under a microscope as any of the rest of us."

"Slave mentality? Are you sure the Alis want this review, Vince?"

"I'm sure they don't, as a class. But nobody wants to die, not really. And at least three of them will die over this Forat girl mess. Even without 'decommissioning deaths' through error, they're expected to die when their masters die as a matter of course."

"Are you going too fast with this, Vince?"

"For the Alis themselves? Probably. If they get their freedom, they'll have the freedom to starve and the freedom to fail and the freedom to make errors, just like the rest of us. They have a decision-free system, presently. They won't like having to make so many choices at first. But it's unacceptable to condone by implication the perpetuation of human slavery just because the slaves, on the whole, are comfortable being slaves."

"Can I quote you on that, Vince?"

Remson nearly blushed. "Sorry, sir. These men are perfectly capable of picking their own wives, of siring female children as well as males, of seeking gainful employment in a number of areas on Medina and in security forces and armies off-planet. So I don't see that we can do anything else but petition for status on their behalf."

"Oh dear, Vince, you are a crusader. You realize that crusaders make enemies?"

"As long as one of those enemies isn't you, Mickey, I can live with it," Remson said very softly, watching the other man.

"Not me. I agree with you. You have this Ali-7 person at hand?"

"Yes, sir. That's . . . probably part of the reason that the crowd's down there." Part of the reason that Remson felt so bad about the crowd being there. "Ali-7's a strong individual. I've offered him a job with my service, so he knows he has some kind of future and we're not just going to do this and then let him be shipped back to Medina for whatever consequences may follow."

"A job? Vince, are you sure that's wise?"

"No, Mickey. I'm not sure. But it didn't make any sense, otherwise: he needs some incentive, a way out, at least. I

don't know that he'll take the job. He may go back with the
Medinans if the guarantees are sufficient. Remember, as I
told you, the bodyguard class has been conditioned to do
that job for generations. They'd be as lost without the
Medinans as the Medinans would be without them. And the
Medinan culture itself is too different from ours to allow
Alis to be comfortable here."

"That's an understatement." Croft picked up his scone
again, looked at it critically, and put it back on the plate.
"Well, crusader, let's get to it. You realize that this has as
much chance of igniting this situation as any other of our
. . . problems."

"As the Forat girl's elopement. Yeah, that's possible. But
it may draw enough attention away from that to allow Beni
Forat to come to an accommodation with Cummings, out of
the spotlight."

"Since you've thought this through, I have no further
objections."

Croft stood up.

So did Remson. "I wish I could use the modeler data. It's
unequivocal."

"What," said Croft as he led the way to the elevator, "did
the modeled Ali say about your plan?"

"Well, it's just a model, of course. . . ." Remson closed
his eyes for a moment, remembering. "It cried, sir. It cried
big tears."

"Heavens, no wonder you're so sure it's human," said
Croft in a hushed voice as the elevator opened to take them
downstairs.

Below, they took an understreet tube to the conference
hall. There was another crowd outside it.

In the meeting room were only a few people. One of
them was Beni Forat. Another, in the gallery, was Richard
the Second.

Remson's jaws began to ache as he left Mickey to his
duties and went to find Ali-7.

When he entered the room where his people were keeping the Medinan bodyguard, the Ali looked up at him with
those trusting, limpid eyes and said, "Now, Remson?"

"Now, Ali." He nearly cried himself. This bodyguard had more courage than Remson would have had, were their roles reversed.

Vince had explained to the Ali why he should have full human status, and they'd discussed it in terms of acting for the sake of generations to come. Terms the Ali could understand.

Now there was no last minute doubt in the bodyguard's eyes, just trust and commitment and a sadness that proved he understood that, from here, there was no going back.

"Then let's do it." Ali-7 got up, smoothed his tan shirt and pants, and walked toward the door through which Remson had come.

Two of Vince's boys got up to follow. He forestalled them with a handsign. Ali-7 deserved all the respect that Remson could give him.

He was walking into a room where one side would say he was a human being and the other side would argue that he was not, that he was barely equivalent to an animal, and had no more rights than a machine would have.

And if Remson's side won the day, all the Alis would be totally disenfranchised from that moment on. If Remson and Mickey didn't win, Ali-7 and his cohorts, Ali-4 and Ali-5, faced immediate execution and all of their ilk would bear the brunt of Medinan fury and resentment.

The Medinans were very vengeful. And they didn't like to be embarrassed.

Vince Remson wouldn't have changed places with Ali-7 for anything in the world.

The Ali looked back: "Something wrong, Remson? Are you coming?"

"Nothing's wrong. I'm coming." Vince Remson had started this. He had to finish it.

In the small meeting room, Beni Forat glared at the Ali with knives in his eyes all through the UNE experts' testimony.

Ali-7 sat off to one side, an exhibit, not a player in this drama. The Flangers had shown as much animation as the Ali did.

Remson began to lose heart. Didn't the Ali realize he should let a little emotion show, at least indicate that he was following the proceedings with concern and interest?

The Flangers, the big chimp-faced marsupials, had sat like stones, and in the end the ruling had gone against them: They would be the next race on whom mankind performed medical experiments.

If the Ali didn't do something, he might be the test case that kept the Medinan bodyguard class enslaved for eternity.

Once a ruling was made, there was a precedent. If the precedent was in the Medinans' favor, it was going to be twice as hard for the Alis to make another try for human status.

Remson found that his fists ached, so tightly were they balled in his lap.

Three human experts spoke in the Alis' favor; three AI expert systems displayed data that showed the Alis response curve in all measurable areas: physical, mental, emotional.

In all of those, the Alis' curves and the human standard curves were comparable. The IQ tests hadn't gone as well, because the Alis were untutored except in basic skills necessary to performing their functions.

When the human experts and their AIs had finished, the Medinans began their arguments:

"Please dim the lights for my visual presentation," said Beni Forat, striding to the podium in a swirl of robes.

When Remson realized what the mullah was planning, he squeezed his eyes shut.

But he couldn't keep them shut. Neither could Ali-7.

Behind the mullah, vid began to roll: pictures of Alis throwing themselves onto their masters to protect them with their bodies; pictures of Alis performing ritual suicide beside masters who'd died of old age. Pictures of "malfunctioning Alis": men run amok. Pictures of purported genetic bioengineering that produced the first Alis (Artificial Living Individuals).

When the propaganda vid was done, Remson was shaking with rage.

The lights came up.

In their brightness stood Ali-7. And he was weeping.

The Ali took one step toward the Medinan. Security people rushed in.

The Ali raised one hand. It said, "Father Forat, we wish only to serve you. But to serve you as men. Are we not men? Do we not feel as men? Die as men? Suffer as men? Love as men? Often we have asked ourselves such questions. And now, someone has said, 'Perhaps, yes. Perhaps you are men.' And in my heart, I know it is true. We are still your children. We are still your servants. Only let us serve you as men, and die as men, with as much dignity as a man when he dies, no more. It would make us so proud if you would say we were men."

Remson wiped his own eyes.

He couldn't see Beni Forat clearly. But he thought he heard someone in a row behind him whisper, "Look at it. It's crying."

And then Remson knew it was going to be all right. The UNE couldn't walk away from such eloquence. They were going to win this one for the Ali and all the rest of the Alis, no matter what Beni Forat had up his sleeve.

When Beni Forat began demanding that the UNE and the Ali himself prove that the Medinan bodyguards had souls, because souls were what differentiated men from beasts, Remson was sure.

You might be able to exhort your followers to murder other men by saying those soulless unbelievers weren't men at all, but these weren't Forat's followers.

And if there was a person in this room possessed of a soul, it was the mild-mannered, self-effacing bodyguard with the tears of anguish on his face.

CHAPTER 23

$$\triangledown$$

Right Place,
Wrong Time

Even with all the extras South had wormed out of Sling during *STARBIRD*'s retrofit, the X-99A was still a one-man testbed. There was no way his passenger, Keebler, could be anywhere near comfortable anyplace on board.

Maybe that wasn't such a bad thing, South kept telling himself, whenever Keebler started getting on his nerves. Which was about every ten minutes.

"Can't y' get any more speed outta this bucket o' bolts, sonny?" Keebler demanded, sticking his head over South's seatback, his huge bulk wedging itself into the tight confines of the flight deck.

"Nope," Joe South lied. "Sorry." Sling had given him a torque boost; he just wasn't anxious to try it with a passenger aboard, even Keebler. And part of his mission was to keep Keebler out of trouble for as long as possible. So far as South was concerned, this was a shakedown cruise for the retrofit that Sling had done, and he wasn't going to be hurried through it. He was keeping an eye on his power plant's temperature. When he was content that it was functioning A-OK, then maybe he'd push the envelope a little.

But not without his suit sealed tight and not with this fool on his back.

South was wearing one of his Extravehicular Mobility Units, visor up; Keebler was squeezed into the spare suit. Otherwise, they couldn't have talked to each other at all.

Sling had flat told Keebler that there was no way to make Keebler's contemporary suit electronics and South's ancient ones talk to one another. South could have kissed the aftermarketeer.

Then Keebler had balked—righteously enough—about not having personal life support. It was against the law, it turned out, not to equip a passenger with a helmet and a spacesuit. But giving Keebler one of *STARBIRD*'s suits meant that South couldn't get away from Keebler just by slapping his visor down, playing dumb, and shrugging his shoulders once or twice during the trip: incommunicado just wouldn't wash; he had to listen to the crazy old fart.

And so did Birdy. South had designated Keebler's suit as Input B and told Birdy to ignore any commands coming from it, but that didn't mean he wasn't keeping a running record of what went on in here.

If the scavenger named Keebler got any crazy ideas about clubbing South senseless and taking over the ship, Birdy had her orders: Blow the atmosphere, disconnect the flight deck manual controls and the bunk system as well, and return to the Threshold docking bay after using the in-suit physiology package to sedate the scavenger.

More prepared for trouble than that, South couldn't be. But there was all kinds of trouble.

Keebler had this knack for rubbing you the wrong way, especially when you were a teeny bit sensitive about being a few hundred years behind the times.

"By the time we get to Spacedock Seven, sonny, I'll have died o' old age and that there ball will've taken so many meteorite hits, it'll be worthless."

"Don't call me 'sonny,' " South said for the umpteenth time and slapped his visor down. It wasn't just a nonverbal punctuation, something he did for emphasis. He was going to lose his temper if he wasn't careful. With his visor down, his suit's AI kicked in: the physiology package clucked and went to work on his blood chemistries. About the time that the scummy taste in his mouth cleared up, the cooling package had his body temperature back down where it should be.

No use getting all hot and bothered about the scavenger. That wasn't why South was here.

In the suit, it was easy to screen out Keebler's annoying chatter: he just dumped the com channel and brought up Birdy's instead. He had a ship to fly.

Birdy was having a ball. The X in X-99A stood for exploration as well as experimental, and to Birdy, everything man-made out here was worth cataloguing.

His sector map was getting a serious update. On his visor, South pulled down a quadranted display with a central punch window so that he could watch his flight deck in real-time; while in the lower left he could see the Threshold complex and every ship and unmanned spacecraft they'd passed on the way out here.

And one of them was right on their tail, he noticed.

"Birdy, can we identify that vehicle?"

Birdy said no, almost wistfully.

South wondered how come, and then put it down to the incompatibility of *STARBIRD*'s equipment with so much of this modern stuff. But they had Sling's general hailing frequency package, and South knew from experience that if one of their ships wanted to talk to you, it could.

"How about giving me a comparison of our vector and its?" Anything was better than talking to Keebler. And if Director Lowe had put a tail on him, somebody to make sure he was doing his job correctly, South's feelings were going to be hurt. More than hurt. If she could spare a ship to shadow him, that ship could have taken Keebler on this joyride, so what did she need him for?

He was beginning to get uncomfortable enough to start sweating again when Birdy put up the two plots and they weren't the same at all.

"Where's it going, Birdy?"

"Spacedock One," said Birdy, as if she'd been doing it all her life.

"Let's see all the spacedocks, with my ETA at Seven."

Smooth as silk, up came the data he'd asked for. Whatever the quality of the tinkering that Sling had done, the astrogation data he'd fed into Birdy was turning out to be real helpful.

"Okay, back to regular rearward scan."

There was more traffic back there now. There was probably lots of traffic out here, all the time.

South was feeling somewhat better, enough better to try toggling his suit system through some forward scans to see if he could migrate Birdy's data upgrades into it.

Sure thing, he could get Spacedock One through Seven, clearly annotated, on his suit's heads-up display without Birdy's help.

Terrific. Sling was probably worth however much South had paid him.

He started using his synthetic apertures to give him closeups of the various spacedocks and their traffic. He and his suit system and Birdy were going to be negotiating some pretty tight—

Keebler's hand came down on his shoulder and South actually jumped. His gloved hand caught the old guy's arm and he nearly pulled Keebler into his lap.

His visor came up because South voice-commanded it just before he started half-yelling: "You crazy old son of a bitch. What do you think you're—"

"Sonny," said the flabby face of the scavenger, contorted with pain. "I didn't know whether you'd had a heart attack in there or what. Y' wanna let go o' me?"

"Yeah, yeah. Don't do that again." He pushed as he let go and the scavenger retreated.

But not far. "Y' know, sonny, we're about t' make hist'ry. You should be treatin' me with a li'l more respeck. When y' get out there an' y' see that ball, an' y' start seein' other things . . . other places . . . well, then y'll understand."

"Other things? Other places?" South had had just about enough of this fool. He didn't need this kind of talk to spook him. He rotated his command couch a quarter-turn so that he could face his antagonist. "I don't know what you heard, buddy, but you're not going to scare me with your 'superior alien civilization' bullshit! I'm just hauling your ass there to cover—" Then he remembered that he hadn't told anybody about his dreams. Nobody'd even bothered to take South's data dump on his X-3 flyby. And he was obviously overreacting.

South shut his mouth.

The scavenger was looking at him oddly from out of that huge, broad face that seemed to be squeezed into its helmet. "That's okay, sonny. I know what's it's like t' know nobody's takin' you serious."

"I'm seriously not letting you out of this ship when we get out there," South snapped back, embarrassed and angry. His suit was whirring at him to seal it so that it could do its work on him. He ignored it. "Even if you could maneuver in that suit without a training session, it's so small on you it might not be airtight. If you've strained something to just the edge of survivability, and it rips out there . . ." He made an imaginary checkmark on a nonexistent clipboard. "One less scavenger."

"Lookit, son—Captain South. I got this box, see, that yer friend made fer me. You got any objections to flyin' close up—say fifty yards 'r better—parkin', and then lettin' me see if this box does what it's supposed t' do?"

"What's it supposed to do?" South asked innocently.

"Open 'er up. If she opens, maybe we can fly right into her, if you've got the balls."

"Last time I looked, I had no complaints." That lady director had told him this guy was crazy, and was a handful to boot. "There's not enough room to fly into that thing from what I was told— Never mind. We'll see when we get there, okay?"

"Okay. Good enough, fer now. You cooperate with me, sonny, and I'm gonna cut y' in on the biggest find of the cent'ry."

"I thought I was that, for about three minutes," South said bitterly, and rotated his chair around. He had to keep an eye on his instruments somehow, and if he couldn't use his voice, that meant the flight panels.

Birdy shouldn't have to do all this on her own.

"Yeah, I figured y' fer a Relic the first time I saw you."

"The hell you did." They were coming into what Birdy thought was the outer com range of the spacedocks. She was sending a standard encoded beacon that was supposed to get them a clearance.

Sling had explained the procedures. They were all AI functions, nothing he had to worry about unless he wanted to do something that wasn't preplanned and precleared with Spacedock Flight Control and the Stalk's Port Authority.

South was beginning to feel extraneous, watching Birdy flash go-codes at him as she got them.

"I did *so*," said the querulous voice of the scavenger, and South, for the first time, realized the old guy was probably as lonely as he was. Out beachcombing the sea of space, just about, for years at a time: it could make you a little garrulous, a little abrasive, when you came back.

"What's it like," South said to change the subject, "scavenging a white hole?"

"Y'know, back when you were in school, the universe was a whole different place. Now it's . . . gettin' crowded. A man's gotta hump some to find any peace an' quiet. White holes is nice. Y' find yerself one, if nobody else's claimed it, and whatever comes out's yours. All y' got t' worry about is the spacetime displacement and the stresses."

"Huh?"

"Y' don't wanna fall in. Y' c'n fall in a hole, even if it's white. Y' get in, y'll never live t' get out. Not in anywhere near the shape or form or time y' started."

"I'll remember that." Time you started? "So if the stresses are so intense, how do you protect yourself?"

"You're from before zero-point power plants and asymptotic rectifiers. There's an energy sea, underlying everything we know about. Think of a sea sponge: what you can see's spacetime like what we walk around in; what you can't see's filled with your energy sea that keeps it all from collapsing. Y' can get around lots o' problems, like time lag in communicatin' and travelin', by knowin' how t' git in an' out o' the energy sea where y' want. That's how come the kind of spacetime kamikaze job you had don't exist no more. That's how come this kind of ship is obsolete."

"Has this lecture got a point, or are you just tweaking my knowledge base?" South bristled whenever somebody talked about *STARBIRD* being obsolete. "We're getting you out here in one piece, me and my obsolete ship. I don't see that you'd save all that much time in—"

"Jesus!" said the scavenger.

"What the—?"

Something flashed by them so fast and so close that Birdy had to veer the X-99A sharply to avoid a possible collision. South could still see it in his forward real-time viewscreen. He began pulling up magnified views of the speeding spacecraft.

"It's that ship that wouldn't talk to us," he said to Birdy through gritted teeth, forgetting all about Keebler.

But Keebler thought South was talking to him.

"Somebody's lookin' for a speedin' ticket, or lookin' to outrun the guy tryin' to give 'im one. Betcha there's a pursuit ship back there, sonny. Better stay on your present course."

South said, "Rear scan for pursuit."

Birdy wasn't made to do that. He wasn't made to do that. But up flashed the rear scan with a fast-moving blip coming their way, on exactly the same heading as the one disappearing ahead.

"You're right, Keebler." South hunched forward and then sat back, saying, "They're going to a different spacedock than we are. We can get across to where we need to be before the pursuit ship crosses our path." He used his armchair handpad to key in some micro changes.

Then he asked Birdy for a close-up of Spacedock Seven.

And there it was, up ahead, centered in *STARBIRD*'s large forward viewer on high magnification.

South stopped breathing. He just stared. All this time, the artifact had been a tiny blip with a set of coordinates beside it. He'd never expected it to be anything like . . . this.

Even in the viewscreen, it was weird. His eyes seemed to tickle when they fixed on it.

It was silver. Then it was gold. Then it was red, and pink, and at last it was lavender, and violet.

The colors raced across it and South wanted desperately to close his eyes. But what difference would that make?

The ball looked, from this distance, exactly like the planet he hadn't visited, but remembered as if he had. His X-3 flyby memories unfurled their wings and began flapping around his face, so that he actually brushed at his eyes with his hands.

Then the shifting colors stopped. The ball was silver, like a three-quarter moon seen from a Kansas field.

And he heard himself say in a choked voice, "Did you see the way that thing changed colors?"

"I didn't see nothing strange. Just m' ball, sonny. Just m' ball, lookin' like it always does."

South couldn't believe that Keebler would deny something that obvious. Maybe he hadn't seen it. Craning his neck, South twisted in his seat to look at the old guy.

"Like I was tellin' y', sonny, there's lots o' things in the universe that we can't usually see, because we're stuck on the outside o' that sea sponge, livin' on a surface that's just plain outta sight of most o' creation. Iffen we were to keep on expanding until we was everywhere, we wouldn't be so damned sure about what we think we know, because we'd find out we don't know squat, the way we did when we first got outta the inner system and realized that complex gravity wells had skewed all our science 'cause we'd been livin' our whole evolution inside a special case."

"What the fuck does that mean?"

"Means that there," Keebler's sinewy chin jutted, "is a gen-u-ine alien artifact from a superior civ'lization, sonny. Gonna change ever'thin'. Gonna make me—an' you—rich 'n' famous. And y' know damn well I ain't lyin', don't y', Cap'n Explorer?''

"Go get stuffed. I don't want to see or hear a word from you until I've parked beside that thing." And South slapped his visor down.

Better than earmuffs. Better than nothing. For some reason, Joe South remembered a soapstone carving his father had gotten in Indochina—three seated monkeys, joined at the hips, one with hands over its eyes, another covering its ears, the third holding its hands to its mouth: See no evil, hear no evil, speak no evil.

Seemed like a real good piece of advice, just then. He was going to fly his ship, stay out of the way of cops chasing speeders, and generally watch where the hell he and Birdy were going.

If he hadn't promised Riva Lowe that he wouldn't let the scavenger out of the ship, he'd have let the old fool EVA and left him out there with the black box Sling was so sure wouldn't work.

That box better not work. The very thought of opening that ball was sending chills throughout South's body that neither his suit's climate-control system or his physiology kit could defeat.

For a reason he didn't understand, or didn't want to look at too closely, Joe South decided this was as good a time as any to test out Sling's torque-boost.

If Birdy and he had extra power, with all these other ships out here, maybe they should know about it. And pretty soon, he'd be in slow zones.

So while he had the chance, he might as well try it. The worst that could happen was a quick and clean death as *STARBIRD* came apart under the strain.

He and Birdy watched together, once he asked for the power, as *STARBIRD* passed her old redline and the indicator kept climbing.

When they were still alive and going twice as fast as he'd have figured X-99A could survive, Birdy and he fixed a new redline based on engine temperature and pressure. But he was only guessing.

He'd run out of space, not power.

Spacedock Seven's slow zone, and the artifact parked there, were directly ahead.

If, when this mission was over, Joe South still couldn't get comfortable with Threshold society, Sling had made a suicide option into a real option.

Now, if he wanted, he and Birdy could decide that it was Earth or bust, or break for parts unknown, and give anybody chasing them a run for their money.

STARBIRD was one hell of a machine, in anybody's spacetime, thanks to Sling. If Keebler hadn't been around, South would have been crowing out loud and dancing around, congratulating every part of the ship he could reach.

But Keebler was around, and Birdy was running a damage assessment program, just to be sure that *STARBIRD* was as good as she felt.

If any little thing at all was wrong, maybe another trip to see Sling would fix it. But nothing Birdy could test was reading as if it were damaged. South hadn't really been worried about that—not at this point. When you bought it in an x-craft, it was always quick, and fiery, and unequivocal.

What he was worried about was that ball of Keebler's. They were headed right toward it and he was going to have to park beside it and sit there while Keebler did what Keebler wanted to do, no matter how weird that ball made Joe South feel.

It's a bitch to walk into one of your dreams with your eyes open and have to pretend that you're not worried. At least when you're asleep, you can look forward to waking up.

CHAPTER 24

$$\triangledown$$

Escape Vector

Dini Forat was worried about the female Brow. The Brow was running around the freighter's cabin crazily, throwing things.

Rick had sent her back to comfort it, but it couldn't be comforted.

As a matter of fact, her presence seemed to make things worse.

She thought calm, happy thoughts at it. But it just jumped around more. Why wouldn't it listen to her?

"Come on. Come here." She knelt down and held out her hand.

The Brow humped up its back and hissed at her. The other two, who'd been curled up together in a corner, both got to their feet.

The one that had hissed started walking toward her sideways, its back arched, its tail lashing.

For the first time ever when with a Brow, Dini was afraid. She'd closed the door when she'd come in here, because the agitated Brow had been throwing things around the cabin.

Trying to appear confident, she got up and backed toward the door.

The female Brow kept coming toward her, hissing as it came.

The two Brows in back were now slinking up behind the female, their bellies low to the deck and their snouts extended. Their noses seemed longer and more squared off. She could see their nostrils quivering.

She backed away and nearly stumbled over an overturned water bowl. The female Brow jumped into the air and landed only a foot in front of her.

Then it sat up on its hind legs and seemed to reach toward her with its little black hands.

She was afraid to take it. There were claws at the ends of those fingers. She'd never been afraid of those claws before.

"Rick," she called, forgetting for a moment that he couldn't hear her with the door closed unless she manually engaged the intercom by the door.

So she added, "I'm going to see Rick," in what she hoped was a soothing tone. "He'll know what's wrong with all of you. Is it that you don't like space travel? I don't really like it either, but it's safe. My father says it's safe." She closed her mouth and chewed on her lip.

Her father would never speak to her again. But at least he wouldn't have her killed.

She looked down at the female Brow, still on its hind legs with its arms upstretched like a baby.

Dini could almost hear it saying, *Pick me up.*

It was a wonderful creature. If it was frightened, that was her fault. It was feeling her fright. Rick would be furious if he knew she was so afraid that the Brows were upset. She was furious with herself.

"I'm sorry," she said, as she reached down, very slowly, to pick up the Brow. "It's me, isn't it? You're upset because I'm upset. Well, we mustn't be," she crooned softly now to the animal as she lifted it in her arms. "No, we mustn't be."

It scrambled so desperately for her shoulder that its hind claws raked her chest. She was sure she was bleeding, but there was no time to check.

The Brow was on her shoulder. Its tail was wrapped around her throat so tightly that she grabbed the tail with one hand.

Then she walked carefully to the door, not looking back, saying, "You two stay here and I'm going to take her up front with me so that she'll calm down. . . ."

When she opened the door, the other two Brows streaked by her and out.

"Oh, no!" She stepped into the corridor, the one Brow still on her shoulder. "Rick! They got out! They're loose."

She thought she heard him call her from the flight deck. That was where the Brows must have gone.

They must have gone there, because there wasn't any other place they could have gone: every other bulkhead was shut tight.

She balanced the Brow carefully as she went forward. As she ducked her head to get through into the little control room, the Brow sprang from her shoulder into her empty chair.

Rick had called this craft a "dual-place with single pilot capability." But since that pilot could be an AI pilot and didn't have to be her husband, she'd never given it a second thought.

Now Rick had two Brows in his lap and they were jumping around frantically, onto the control panels, and off again.

"Dini, help get them off me! What are you doing, letting them loose like this? Did they get at those Leetles?"

Dini reached down and grabbed for one of the Brows clambering over Rick.

She caught it and it nearly bit her. It actually opened its jaws and then it stopped. Its intelligent, dark eyes blinked, and it reached for her like a baby.

"Oh, sweetie . . ." She picked up the second Brow and cuddled it. "It's just frightened."

It was a good thing that her mocket was safe in their bunkroom. She had one Brow in her arms and was trying to convince the one on her acceleration couch to let her sit there when Rick finally convinced the third Brow to climb off his lap and up on his headrest.

"Uh-oh," said Rick.

"What?" She'd just reclaimed her seat. She had a lap full of Brow and both arms full of Brow. "What's uh-oh?"

"Oh, they punched some buttons, some presets, that's all. We're a little off course. It's nothing," said Rick, still trying to maneuver himself free of the Brow who, perched above his head on the seatback, was pulling at his hair.

"Ow! Dini, we can't have them up here. We've got to take them back, now. And we've got to figure out what's wrong with them. . . ."

"But you said they punched some buttons!"

"The AI will take care of it. Come on, let's get them back where they belong."

"Easier said than done," she warned. "They know what we're talking about."

Her Brows didn't want to go anywhere. The one on her lap was standing on its hind legs, as if it wanted to look out of the forward viewscreen. Its tiny hands were digging into the bumper. Except for the ringed, lashing tail, which was so bushy at the moment, it looked like a person in a fur suit.

The one in her arms was trying to burrow into her armpit. It was making pathetic little noises.

"Come on, Dini! I can't have them up here!" Rick was standing, now, holding his squirming Brow with both hands.

"Well, fine," she said. "You take that one back, then come up here again and we'll each take one of these. We can't get the three of them back there if they don't want to go, and you know it!"

What she said was true, but she was surprised at her own vehemence. The Brows didn't want to go. They wanted to stay. She could feel it, and she could feel their distress. She'd never realized that the Brows could broadcast their feelings so strongly.

She couldn't bring herself to grab them by the scruffs of their necks, the way Rick had his, and drag them off to that windowless prison when, up here, they had company and they could see what was going on.

She knew the Brows wanted to stay with her. She just knew they felt better now. They wanted to look out the window. . . .

"They just want to look out the window, Rick. . . ."

"Dini! Damn you, all right!"

Rick stamped away with his Brow under his arm. She could hear it mewling in a soft, almost human voice.

Her male Brow was still standing on his hind legs, looking out the windscreen at the stars. Then he scrambled up on the console and the female Brow took her head out of Dini's armpit for just a moment and peered up into her eyes.

The ship seemed to veer slightly.

When Dini looked up again, the male Brow was climbing carefully down into her lap again.

When he got there, he circled around and she stroked his fur. It came out in clumps. It stuck to her hand. She sneezed and rubbed her eyes.

And when she looked up again, the male Brow was once more trying to stand on his hind legs and look where they were going.

But now the view wasn't of a starscape, but of a spacedock. Or at least she thought it was a spacedock.

She almost called Rick, but she remembered the AI pilot. It would know what to do.

By the spacedock was a big metal ball with multicolored lights running across it.

The standing Brow, seeing the spectacle, started to purr. The female Brow pulled her head out of Dini's armpit long enough to make a noise, which the male answered.

"Ssh," Dini told the female Brow, who was shivering. "It's all right. It's all right. We won't let anything happen to you. Just because he's brave enough to look out the window doesn't mean you have to look. . . ."

Then Dini herself looked up, past the male Brow, and saw something she didn't understand.

The ball was growing at an alarming rate, and changing colors too rapidly for the effect to be simply reflections from their approaching ship.

And between them and the ball, space itself was growing agitated.

Dini had never seen such a thing before. Space was always clear. This was like a dust devil. Then it was like a tornado, a video she'd once seen of what it would be like if you looked down its funnel.

The tornado was between them and the spacedock. She couldn't see the dock at all anymore. She couldn't see the colored ball. She could only see the spinning strangeness in front of her.

She screamed, "Rick! Rick!"

The male Brow, frightened by what it saw or her scream, jumped off her legs onto the floor and started growling. In her arms, the female Brow answered and it was suddenly scrabbling to get free of her.

"All right! Go! I'm not holding you!"

She put up both hands and then someone grabbed them.

She nearly died of fright.

"Oh! Rick, you scared me. It was so strange."

"What? I had a bitch of a time getting that Brow to let me go. We've got to—"

He glanced at the windscreen, which was black and opaque. "Good. You turned that viewscreen off. Let's get these two into the back—"

"I didn't."

"You didn't what?"

"Turn it off. The wind—viewscreen. I didn't know you could. . . ."

"You didn't turn it off? Then the AI did. That's fine." He was reaching for one Brow. It didn't fight or hiss. It came tractably into his arms. "Whatever was wrong, it's over now," he said. He held the Brow out to Dini: "See? Calm as can be."

She reached down and the female Brow took her finger in its hand. "Come on." She patted her lap. "Come on. Up!"

The Brow jumped into her lap. It still was covered with loose hair. She lifted it and got out of her seat to follow Rick aft.

"Now, Dini, when I open this door, let's just put them in quickly, in case the whole thing starts up again," said her beloved as they stood before the Brows' cabin.

"All right," said Dini, "but I don't see why this one has to go in there. She's so scared. When the ball started changing colors and then the whole starfield spun like that, she just shivered."

"Starscape? Spun? Ball? What are you talking about?" Rick, still holding one Brow, froze with the door open.

The Brow jumped out of his arms. Hers wiggled, and she let it go in the doorway. "Go on, go in there."

Rick grabbed her roughly. "What did you say?"

"Close the door or they'll get out again."

"To hell with them. . . . Never mind." And Rick nearly ran up the corridor, forgetting to lock the Brows inside.

Dini's feelings were hurt, and the female Brow was sitting in the door's track. "Fine. Run about if you must," she said, and went forward, leaving the Brows free to come and go as they pleased.

When she got to the flight deck, Rick was sitting in his padded chair with an arm crooked over his eyes. The chair was canted back and he didn't acknowledge her, although he surely had heard her come up—at least felt her leg brush his arm as she took her place.

So she didn't say anything either. Let him be that way. What did she care? She had given up everything for him, and now he was treating her as if she were some sort of inferior person.

She settled back, prepared for a long silence.

Almost immediately, he said from under his arm, "Do you know what that spinning you saw was?"

"No. I said I didn't."

"That was a spongehole."

"A what?"

"A spongehole. Either the Brows touched off an emergency punch-out sequence, or there was some kind of disturbance in the continuum. Whatever, we're in it and we're lost in it, out of communication, until we come out of it. Wherever that will be."

"I don't understand."

Rick's couch shot upright: "Here. Here's what happened."

He stared to replay the sequence of events that had begun when the dust devil appeared in their path and blocked out the colored ball.

"I saw that. I called you. You were too busy with the Brow."

"You saw it. And you just *sat* there?"

Dini crossed her arms. Her mouth was dry. She crossed her legs as well. "I called you, I said. What was I supposed to do? You have an AI pilot. Why didn't it do something?"

"I don't know. Maybe the Brows programmed a workable sequence, somehow. Maybe . . . I don't know. I don't know." He rubbed his face with his hand and succeeded only in moving the Brow hair on it into his nose. He sneezed.

"Is it bad?" she said finally, when Rick continued to stare at his controls. She didn't know anything about controls such as these. She didn't know anything about spongespace or star travel, really. She wasn't supposed to know these things. Just because her fake papers said she was a licensed pilot, that didn't mean that the knowledge had somehow seeped into her. Rick was being so unfair.

"Bad? What's bad? Who knows. If we destroyed any property back there with that unauthorized punch, my father will have to pay for it and we'll catch hell. If we ever find any place civilized enough to have a NAMECorp base."

"What do you mean, Rick?" Her voice sounded squeaky and very young.

"We don't know where we *are*, Dini. We don't know where we're going. It's not just you that doesn't know. It's not just me. The AI doesn't know. The jump was not in a standard lane. It's not an explored route. We're going . . . somewhere."

"Somewhere nobody's ever *been*?" Her squeak trebled.

Rick looked over at her then. "Now don't panic. Don't cry. We have lots of food, and maybe, if we're out long enough, we can coax the remaining Leetles to breed so the Brows will have food. . . ."

"You can't mean this. You're trying to scare me. . . ."

His voice softened but the look on his face was a stiff look she'd never seen before. He cocked his head. "I'm not trying to scare you, but I'm a little scared myself. We'll come out somewhere, and then we'll see where we are."

"That's all, really? We'll just see where we are, and everything will be fine? We'll jump back in and go on to Pegasus's Nostril and get married the way we planned, right?"

Rick didn't answer. He seemed about to yawn, but he didn't do that either. He simply stared at the control panel in front of him.

"Right?" she insisted.

"Right," he eventually agreed.

A great weight lifted from Dini Forat's chest that she hadn't known was there until it was gone. "Good. That's good. Now, since we're agreed on what we'll do, I feel better."

"Me too," said Rick unenthusiastically, perhaps sarcastically.

Again, she felt angry. "If you're so smart, what were we doing headed toward that colored ball in the first place? We might have collided with it."

"I didn't know anything about that colored ball being there until I saw the sequence. It shouldn't have been there. But there's a reasonable explanation. I told you, it must have been the Brows, jumping around on the astronics console."

"Then they're psychic. They were upset before anything happened." For some strange reason, this made her feel better. "The Brows are much happier now, and you know it! The female was purring."

"That's all the assurance I need."

"You're so snide."

"Dini . . . I don't want to fight with you, but you don't know what you're talking about."

"If you're so smart, why can't you get us back home, now?" Her voice was thick and it shook.

Her beloved didn't answer. He just reclined his couch and put both hands over his eyes.

Then one of the Brows came forward again and sat up at her side, putting its adorable head in her lap. Its fingers tugged on her suit.

She had a feeling that the Brow was really trying to tell her that everything would be all right. In its eyes she thought she saw a glint of satisfaction, almost pride, as if it had done all this on purpose and it was happy about wherever it was they were going. It certainly wasn't worried anymore. Rick was being such a brat. . . .

And then she realized that her poor little mocket had been locked up all this time.

She'd go feed Pepi and play with the Brows, who were feeling ever so much better.

The one who'd come to get her scampered down the corridor, then turned and looked back to see if she was following, as if asking her to come and play.

Everything was going to be fine. The Brows were happy. Only Rick was unhappy, because he was a man like any other man and he couldn't bear to admit to a mistake.

The Brow cavorting in her path stopped and reached up to her. She lifted it. It nuzzled her ear. "You wouldn't hurt us, would you? You wouldn't lure us into some awful fate? You're trying to tell me everything will be fine and not to worry, aren't you?"

The Brow actually licked the tip of her nose and began to whistle its happiest sound.

Whether or not she could convince Rick of the fact, Dini was sure that the Brows thought that something wonderful was going to happen.

Let her beloved think dark thoughts of being forever lost in space. When the Brows were this happy, nothing could be terribly wrong.

Nothing.

CHAPTER 25

▽

What You See . . .

"Damn! Did you see that, Keebler?" South tried to rub his eyes and hit his hand on his visor.

"What? I didn't see nothin'."

South toggled a switch and Birdy replayed on the console's viewscreens what South had been watching on his helmet's heads-up display.

In magnified, living color; in multispectral imagery and with three levels of resolution, South watched again as the speeding NAMECorp freighter veered sharply across *STAR-BIRD*'s bow a second time, heading straight for the ball on a collision course.

The ball's colors coruscated brilliantly for approximately one minute and thirty seconds while the freighter approached. Then the ball disappeared to visual scanners, occluded by a spacetime perturbation that swallowed the big ship whole. Then, in its turn, the perturbation disappeared.

"See *that*, Keebler?" South said as his visor retracted.

"Must be a glitch in your sensor array."

"Glitch my ass," South said, and asked Birdy for infrared and every other damn thing she had: electro-optical, lidar, anything. . . .

In every available search mode, viewed any which way he could, utilizing all signature readers, the speeding freighter was swallowed up by a virtual hole in spacetime. South had seen holes like that before, twice in his life. Both times, he'd pushed an experimental button that punched the hole, into which he and *STARBIRD* flew.

"I dunno what's so excitin' about a spongehole, Cap'n. They're all over the place."

"Here? This close to a spacedock? Even I know that's not safe. And did you see the way that ball was lit up? Looked like Christmas . . ." Did they still have Christmas in the twenty-fifth century? He'd heard the scavenger call on Jesus, so at least some of these folk were Christian. . . .

"Safe, schmafe, when somebody's a-chasin' yer ass. . . . Here comes that cop we was expectin', hot on their trail."

In the single monitor that was left displaying real-time, you could see the closing patrol cruiser.

South would never forget what one of those looked like. And then he magnified the image, dumping the replay to bring it into focus across the boards.

"The *Blue Tick*." South toggled on his hailing frequency and let Birdy do the rest.

Pretty soon a voice he'd never mistake said, "South, is that you?"

"Yep. Reice, if you're after that freighter—"

"I was but I can't scope it at all now. You see it?"

"That's why I'm calling. It disappeared into a spongehole, right in front of me. My telemetry says the hole's between that . . . artifact and *STARBIRD*, so maybe somebody ought to alert the Spacedock Seven people and—"

"What are you talking about, you crazy Relic? Holes don't open up all by themselves. And they sure as hell don't open up around here. And nobody'd try to open one with a freighter like that, even if it were equipped to do exotic entries. Conditions aren't exactly primo for spongejumping. . . ." Reice trailed off.

Keebler poked South in the ribs. South ignored him. He didn't answer Reice, either. Reice wasn't his favorite person among those he'd met since he'd come to Threshold.

After about twenty seconds, Reice said, "You say you've got that jump recorded? Want to boot it over here?"

"If I can." He checked with Birdy, who gave him a Transmission Ready signal. "Here it comes, if you can catch it."

He let Birdy send the sequence.

About the time that South's communications monitor was telling him Transmission Complete, Reice's voice came back: "Thanks, South." There was wonder in it. "Never saw anything like that in my life. I'd think it was a bogey reading, some weirdness in that geriatric ship of yours, but the time-framing's exact to when I lost contact. Those stupid kids. If they aren't dead, they could have been killed. Or killed somebody else. We're lucky that artifact didn't go with their ship into that hole—or even the whole spacedock."

"So they did punch a hole." South wanted Keebler to have his nose rubbed in whatever this was.

"Either they did or that kaleidoscopic ball did," said Reice sourly. "Or else we've witnessed the first spacetime tornado recorded by man and machine. I couldn't do that with my ship, not here. Not and survive."

"So these kids . . . are they all right?" South didn't care much. But he cared that he'd done Reice a favor, warning him about the hole. Although Reice didn't seem worried about falling into it the way South was. But then, Reice had never been to X-3 and nobody'd been interested in South's report on it.

"How do I know if the kids are all right? You see them around here? Their ship, maybe? I don't. Look, you better not get too close to that ball, not while space out here's so perturbed."

Keebler virtually howled a stream of objections in South's ear. South went visor-down and ignored him, for the moment.

"What about you, Lieutenant Reice? You going to fly right over that spot? What if the same thing happens?"

These guys knew more about this sort of thing than South did. Even Keebler knew more about it. South wasn't anxious to fall into some kind of spacetime quicksand or game pit, or whatever that was there. If there was any question of *STARBIRD*'s safety, Keebler could park by his find some other time. There'd be some way to make Director Lowe understand. ConSec, in the person of Reice, had ordered South not to get too close to the ball. And Birdy, as well as Keebler, had heard that order. Of course, "too close" was a term open to interpretation.

Reice transmitted: "I'm going to fly right over it, Captain South. Match their flight path. And hope to hell the same thing does happen. I really need to apprehend those particular fugitives. So you stay back, just in case I get lucky and it opens up and swallows me."

"You're not going to punch for it?"

"Punch—oh, like you guys did in the old days? Hell, no. First off, it's against the law to perturb populated spaces. Secondly, how the hell could you be sure you got the same hole they did? They didn't exactly log a flight plan. Thirdly, we use established lanes and perpetual holes, these days— places where it's easy to get in and out and you know where a hole will take you. If you want more lessons, you'll have to take a course. Now you do as I order, and stay back. I'd be grateful if you'd record my flight path, just in case something goes seriously wrong. If it does, send the log and my felicitations to ConSec. Copy?"

"You bet, Lieutenant." South was pleased with himself for having hailed Reice. Making yourself useful is never a bad thing. Performing this mission creditably was still uppermost in South's mind. He was demonstrating his skills for Director Lowe, the best he could. If he got Reice on his side, it could only help in future. Their first meeting had left a bad taste in both men's mouths that was going to be hard to wash away.

Blue Tick signed off and headed past South's ship on exactly the same course that the fugitive freighter had taken. Whoever was in that ship, ConSec wanted them very badly.

If anybody'd ever bothered to download South's log, maybe they'd have been prepared for holes opening up like that. Maybe they'd have been prepared for the sort of Northern Lights effect that South had seen on the ball, too. But maybe not. The ball, so far as South could see, was just a ball, now.

And the colors and the places and the memories that South had . . . those were recorded only in his dreams.

South toggled a parameter scan on the now-innocuous bit of spacetime that had swallowed the fugitive spacecraft.

Birdy brought it up as normal, with no anomalous readings whatsoever, the whole time that the ConSec vessel approached the coordinates where the perturbation had been.

The ball, too, was quiescent, now.

Since Birdy was keeping an eye on the ConSec ship, South let his stray to the artifact. What a strange damned coincidence, this thing looking so much like . . . what?

If somebody'd taken his X-3 log dump, would they have seen the colors he'd seen? The lavender and fiery striations and the strangely flowing pulses on the ringed planet in the purple haze. . . .

He shook his head. The planetary flyby was real enough. Birdy had that. The rest of it—his half-memories of landing somewhere achingly beautiful that looked nothing like home but reminded him of home, somewhere he watched a sunset with aliens standing by his side—those weren't real memories. At least they weren't the sort that would be in Birdy's memory.

He was watching the ball pensively for any sign of color and life when something poked him.

Keebler! He'd forgotten all about Keebler.

And Keebler was mad as a wet hen. Even before South retracted his faceplate and Keebler's demands for justice washed over him, he knew what the old scavenger was going to say:

"—no right to interfere wit' m' sanctioned examination of my personal property, that ConSec bastard! Y' kin see that nothin's happenin' that has anythin' to do with m' property! I was promised this opportunity, and I demand that we continue, or I'll talk to Missus What's Her Name, right now! And then we'll see. *Then* we'll see!"

"Easy, Keebler. Just calm down. We wait and watch what the ConSec ship does, and then we'll go on our way, just as we planned, if there's no trouble. Okay?"

Now that he'd had a moment to think it over, South didn't want to go back to Threshold having failed in his first mission, with an angry passenger who was going to raise hell about South's poor performance.

That was no way to resuscitate your career.

Keebler, who had Sling's black box in his hands and was shaking it under South's nose, was convincing him of that.

And Birdy wasn't afraid of a little old spongehole. They'd been trained to jump into the abyss with their eyes wide open, taking notes all the way.

Maybe these twenty-fifth-century pansies had to have road maps and boxed lunches; but where South was from, you paid your money and you took your ride. No questions asked, because there was nobody around to answer those questions.

So what if, these days, everybody knew the best routes through spongespace to get here or there or the other place? Those folks knew where they wanted to go, and why.

For Joe South and Birdy, it really wouldn't be so much of a loss if they slipped into oblivion and never found Threshold again.

They could never find their own century again, that was for sure. And nobody'd bothered to talk to him about that, as if he just should have realized that there was no way to compensate for the tricks that relativity was going to play on an X-class ship and her pilot.

Well, he hadn't known better. Nobody had. And, except for the fact that he didn't want to be stuck with Keebler for any significant portion of eternity, an unexplored spongehole wasn't looking like a bad option.

Since he hadn't known any better, he'd been considering that as one of his options all along.

All he had to do was get away from this local congestion, get up enough speed, and push his x-button. In a moment, he'd have left this time and place behind.

And if, the next time *STARBIRD* stuck her nose back into normal space, it was a few years down the line—or a few hundred—what difference did that really make?

"Sonny, are we goin' to park this tub o' bolts, or what?" came Keebler's crotchety voice.

Well, it would make a difference to Keebler. So South would play along, give things a chance to work themselves out. The least he could do was let the old guy off with his precious ball.

But he'd been expressly ordered not to do that. And South followed orders. Doing so had kept him alive all this time.

When you had two sets of orders, you took your pick. You chose what seemed the most survivable.

And, if nothing happened to the *Blue Tick*, then there was no reason not to finish his mission.

Punching out of here was still an option, just like heading for Earth no matter who tried to stop him.

A part of him envied the fugitives, whoever they were.

But the better part of him said: "Come on, Keebler, keep your shirt on, and wait until that cop out there forgets we're here. Then you can play with your box. Okay?"

Keebler came scrambling up beside him. "Okay, sonny. That's great. I knew y' weren't the kind to let a cop tell y' what to do."

South was watching his monitors. On them, the ConSec ship was flying the coordinates where the hole had been, and in the background, Keebler's silver ball seemed to be covered with some kind of purple haze.

And then it wasn't.

CHAPTER 26

▽

Goose Chase

The *Blue Tick* was the right tool for this job, Reice consoled himself as he flew the pursuit craft into the portion of spacetime that had so recently swallowed up his quarry. The *Tick* had all the capabilities a pilot could want when heading into the unknown: a zero-point apport pack that couldn't run out of power during a spongejump because it drew on the energy sea itself; asymptotic spacetime rectifiers and temporal navigation aids, which made sure that Reice's biological clock time and Threshold calendar time wouldn't get wildly out of sync, despite relativistic effects.

So what had happened to South could never happen to Reice.

Then why was he so damned nervous? He could jump out of whatever he fell into without losing a beat. That is, he could if nothing unforeseen went wrong.

Off his starboard bow, that weirdass artifact was purplish and hazy. He didn't like that one bit. There were still no guarantees that you wouldn't run into something, sailing the as-yet mysterious seas of spacetime, that nobody'd mapped.

But you didn't run into those things in the shoals of the home system. You didn't.

Almost unconsciously, Reice ran his upstretched hands over his fire controls. If something messed with him—if those kids did, or anything else did, Reice had enough firepower aboard the pursuit craft to hold his own.

But if the problem wasn't a hostile consciousness with a body and a ship, but some inimical force of nature, there wasn't a thing his weaponry could do to help him. You couldn't overpower nature. You had to think your way through it.

So, having put every pulse beam and KKD delivery system and vectored scalar grapple on stand-by, Reice had nothing else to occupy him. He could only fly over this one-time hole and wait to see if it sucked him up.

Hell of a note.

He kept a running log of his progress, keeping track of everything except his body's reaction to this kind of stress: no need to let the whole of ConSec know the way he was sweating this, if he lived to turn in his report.

Some men would have contacted Spacedock Control and kept up a continual stream of patter with the Emergency Controller, or even called back to Threshold for a conference before flying into . . . whatever this was.

But Reice wasn't going to let anybody know he was even a little bit nervous. He was going to treat this as completely routine and handle it all by his lonesome.

Having that Relic pilot sitting out there watching and recording everything was a lucky break, and one that satisfied the unwritten SOP for the unique: Whenever you were doing something life-threatening that hadn't been done before, you wanted somebody there for backup.

If South hadn't been a Relic, Reice might have kept an open channel to STARBIRD. As things stood, he was feeling almost comradely toward the antique pilot. South wasn't so bad to have around in a crisis. He sure didn't flap like a lot of these wet-behind-the-ears kids would, just because there wasn't a by-the-book way to handle something like this.

And South wasn't arguing with him about procedure and protocol the way anybody else would have: Reice finally admitted to himself that he wasn't calling into a ConSec station because, if he did, he'd get an argument about flying over the spacetime in question.

When you'd seen a set of coordinates turn into a sinkhole, the normal thing to do would be cordon it off and send in drones.

But Reice was betting that the kids had pulled this stunt on purpose, because they'd known he was back here and realized he was going to catch them and whip their spoiled asses (at least verbally) before he dragged them back by their freighter's ears to face discipline.

His rational mind was sure all this was a simple case of a couple of juvenile delinquents with a state-of-the-art spacecraft who'd grown up believing that the rules were for other, less privileged people.

Like father like son, as far as the Cummingses were concerned, for certain. If Reice could overfly the area and prove, right away, that there was no phenomenal problem here to blame the kids' disappearance on, then Cummings, Jr., wouldn't be able to tie everybody up in red tape and stymie any criminal proceedings with cries for massive searches and investigations into the possible culpability of spacedock authorities for ignoring a weakness in the fabric of spacetime out here.

Reice could just hear Richard the Second screaming cover-up. It would cost Threshold thousands of K-notes just to prove that there wasn't some nasty little sinkhole off Spacedock Seven waiting to gobble up unwitting children on joyrides.

So you flew over the spot and, if nothing happened, you'd shut down the argument—and the excuse—beforehand.

Reice wished the ball would quit changing colors like that. Then he'd believe he wasn't just comforting himself while he prepared to commit suicide.

He brought the ball into close focus once again, trying to ignore the fact that he was now entirely within the area that his mapping display defined as part of the recent deformation.

The ball was a plain old ball of silver, nothing special.

And his mapping display put him right in the center of the

recent disturbance. He watched that screen again while his palms sweated and the little blip representing *Blue Tick* crawled steadily across the funnel area, which was described by an overlay of crosshatched topological grid lines bending into a completely blank hole.

Reice was right in the middle of the hole, and his real-time display was reading no-problem: he had a clear readout in all modes and nothing, not a single parameter, was out of whack.

You just sat there with your heart pounding and listened to the tiny sounds of a spacecraft running like clockwork.

And you watched that ball for more purple haze.

Reice didn't know why he'd thought the ball was anything to worry about. It was South's prehistorical hysteria, getting to him. The ball wasn't squat. The ball was just some piece of crap that had come out of a white hole, the way a fin of an old ship might, or an ancient vid monitor might. White holes were nothing more than the sewer conduits of the universe.

Somewhere he'd heard that on old Earth there were big reptiles with huge teeth who lived in sewers because people flushed them down the waste recyclers. But the ball wasn't alive, and it wasn't doing anything in the least bit odd at the moment.

Reice dumped his view of the ball and went back to watching the topographical map. *Blue Tick* was now traversing the left-hand half of the diagrammatic hole, and nosing back into the spreading cone of the funnel.

Only a little farther, and he'd be able to say that he flew the distance without a single anomaly occurring.

He really wanted to be able to say that.

He brought up another topo scan, this one describing the actual spacetime he was overflying. Lidar mapped the real-time area and sent him back data with which *Tick*'s AI constructed a geometric display of the space around him, just as the ship sensed it.

Space was as calm here as it was around Threshold. There was actually less deformation, because Threshold had a lot more mass than spacedock and more artifically induced gravity as well.

About the time that Reice dumped the map of the hole that wasn't there anymore, South's ship called his.

"Yeah, South. What is it?" Reice wasn't glad to take the call. His voice was squeaky from the tension and he didn't like being bothered when he wanted, most of all, to go to the head and void his bowels, now that he had time to pay attention to his body.

South's transmission quality wasn't great, but it never had been. An antique was an antique. "Want me to boot this log over to you, Lieutenant?" the Relic pilot asked insouciantly.

"When I want you to do something, South, I'll tell you. You hold that log and take it, and the other one of the hole, over to Riva Lowe's office. Tell her I want it to go to Croft and Remson, ASAP. Got that: Croft and Remson?"

"Roger."

Roger?

"Well, get going, South. I don't want to send this stuff through normal channels. And I'm continuing my search. For all I know, that freighter'll pop back out right in front of me and try to get into a normal jump lane now that it thinks it's shaken me."

"Reice," said South's voice. "I'll hand-deliver your data, no sweat. As soon as I finish my mission."

Reice didn't give a fig about South's mission, whatever busywork it was. Riva Lowe had her own agenda where the Relic was concerned, and Reice knew better than to interfere with her where Customs matters were concerned. "Just don't take all week, Captain. Reice, out."

He didn't have the patience for the Relic. He had a freighter to find. If he couldn't find it, he wanted to be able to say he'd done his damnedest.

And he wanted to go to the bathroom. As he got up, his AI burbled and assumed complete control of the *Blue Tick*.

Reice couldn't ever remember being happier just to be alive. When he got ahold of those kids, he was going to make them wish they'd never been born. But until then, he was going to string out this search as long as he could.

Let the computer jocks back on Threshold try to figure out just what hole the fugitive freighter had accessed. If he were those kids, he'd be looking to get into a normal corridor so that they could jump for one of Daddy's outposts.

Maybe Reice could wangle a trip to five or six of NAMECorp's more exotic holdings. After all, Remson had given him a blank check to find the kids. And once he saw that log, which South had so conveniently provided, Remson was going to give Reice anything he wanted.

Anything at all. Because Reice, by providing Croft's office with that record of an unauthorized spongejump in a populated area, had given Croft the club that the Secretary needed to bludgeon both fathers into submission.

Not even rich, spoiled brats could commit felonies in the home system and get away with it. Not unless there was one hell of a horse-trading session involved.

The fines alone ought to shut both parents' mouths about Threshold's purported security failures. The log South had recorded was going to hit those fathers like cold water in the face.

And all thanks to Reice, who'd had the courage to overfly the spot where the kids disappeared, thus proving that it *was* the kids' doing, and no natural anomaly.

Now if he could just convince his bowels that everything was all right, he could get on with the business of gloating.

Maybe he could even parlay this into a promotion. Colonel Reice had a nice, substantial ring to it.

CHAPTER 27

Paradise

Rick Cummings braked into the planetary system as hard as he could. It had just suddenly . . . appeared . . . around them, as if the spongehole they'd come out of had dumped them out halfway into a solar system.

And what a solar system! He looked over at Dini, beside him, with a Brow asleep in her lap and her mocket curled up at her feet.

A grin tugged at his lips. If his father could see him now. But Richard couldn't see him. And for the first time in his entire adult life, Rick told himself that it didn't matter what his father thought.

Behind him, one of the other Brows reached up and tugged on his sleeve.

"Up," he whispered, not wanting to wake Dini.

The Brow jumped into his lap, turned around once, and instead of settling down, stood on Rick's thighs as if to look out at the planet that had just come up in his primary viewer.

The Brow stretched, its fingers clutching the console's bumper, and peered out the big viewscreen at the real-time display.

It began to whistle softly and its tail-tip quivered.

"You like this, don't you," he told it softly, and stroked

its back. Rick was almost ready to credit Dini's theory that the Brows had done this on purpose.

There didn't seem to be another explanation. He'd half-expected that, if the Brows had done it, the place they'd come out would be their home system.

But the planet in the primary viewer wasn't Olympus.

As a matter of fact, none of these planets looked familiar. So far as Rick Cummings and the freighter's AI could determine, this was a totally unexplored system.

Perhaps a totally uninhabited one, since he hadn't seen any man-made satellites as they came in. He'd asked the AI if there was a planet capable of sustaining human life without auxiliary life-support, and the AI had put up this one, the planet just ahead.

Beyond it was a ringed planet, sort of lavender and with a heavy atmosphere that made it luminous in the light of the distant sun.

This whole misadventure was strange, but not frightening, somehow. They could land on this planet, if they wanted. The freighter was transatmospheric. Maybe they'd honeymoon here, if the AI was right.

The Brow on his lap started lashing its tail furiously.

"What is it, boy?" He stroked the Brow to calm it.

Then Rick looked up at his monitors.

Out of the atmosphere of the planet that the AI had chosen, ships were coming. A swarm of them. Faster than anything he'd ever seen. And they were doing astrobatics as they came.

The ships were spherical. They swarmed and darted together like a flock of seagulls that Cummings had once seen at his father's Earthly beach house.

Rick couldn't imagine why they didn't hit one another, or what kind of power plants they might be using. He didn't see any afterburn. He didn't see any of the reddening glow on the spherical shells which should be there, if you were heating up as you came out of atmosphere the way those ships should be, zipping around like that.

He shooed the Brow off his lap and it hissed. Immediately, it jumped up beside its fellow on Dini's lap.

She woke up. "Rick! What's happening?" Dini knuckled her eyes. The second Brow, disturbed by the one who wanted to look out the viewer, nuzzled her and made that mewling noise of theirs.

"Happening? We're safely out of sponge and I've found us a beautiful planet. Take a look."

No use in scaring her.

He wasn't scared himself, and that was funny. Here was a bunch of ships, headed right for him in a flurry of impossible maneuvers—ships like he'd never seen before, from a planet nobody'd ever visited before, and he wasn't the least bit worried.

The Brow who liked to look at the stars was whistling softly.

Dini said, "Oh, it's beautiful. Look at the colors!"

The planet was beautiful. It was pastel and welcoming.

And the ships coming out of it had a rainbow finish to their hulls.

"I think we're going to have visitors. See, Dini. A welcoming committee."

"Oh. Here," she picked up the second Brow. "You look, too."

From down the corridor, the third Brow came hurtling and bounded onto Rick's headrest.

"Now don't you pull my hair!" he warned it.

But of course, that was exactly what it tried to do.

Then his com system beeped and he realized that the ships were trying to make contact.

He opened up his hailing frequency on wide band and his AI did the rest.

Rick heard "Welcome, travelers" in a whistly voice, and all the Brows suddenly went berserk.

They were jumping around—on his lap, off his lap, on Dini's lap, off Dini's lap, on the console, from there to the couch headrests, and back. And the whole time, they were whistling long, melodic strings and gesticulating with their little black hands.

"Ah—" Rick tried to think of something momentous to

say in return. After all, he was making contact with a spacefaring civilization—the first one that humankind had ever met. All the races they'd found had been technologically inferior, wherever humanity had gone. So he continued: "Greetings, from Earth, humanity, and North American Exploration Corporation, who's sponsored this visit." His father would like that.

But he wasn't sure that anyone could hear him, over the clamor of the Brows.

"You have brought our wayward children home, and we thank you," said the voice. "Will you allow us to make you welcome on our world?"

Dini looked at Rick. "Are they Brows? Brows with spaceships?" Her eyes were as big as saucers.

Rick tapped the viewscreen and toggled his AI's attention to the ships. A close-up of one showed him nothing new: a spherical spacegoing vehicle with a rainbow hull. He shrugged and put a finger to his lips; he didn't know if they were Brows or not, but he wasn't going to offend them.

"We'd love to visit with you, before we go on our way."

If only he could get video. But there was no video of his hosts to be had.

"Please let us assist you," whistled the voice. "Your craft must take its landing data from ours."

"Fine," Rick said. Don't rock the boat, so to speak. Dini's hand had found his and she was clutching him tightly. Her mocket was awake and whining softly, huddled in a corner under the console where the Brows wouldn't careen into it in their agitation.

All of a sudden, before he could tell his AI to prepare to take data from the ships outside, his control panels went crazy: everything went on and off and cycled through its parameters.

He tried to ignore it. He didn't want Dini to worry. He leaned forward and keypadded one of his monitors; at least he could still direct the ship.

What he'd asked for was a view of all four quadrants. He got it. There were sixteen of the spherical ships surrounding his.

Either it was a police escort or an honor guard. He didn't want to dwell on which. He kept telling himself that they'd been very polite, whoever they were.

"Rick," Dini said in a hushed voice. "Look at that."

He looked up to see all three Brows, standing on Dini's console, like three little people with tails, looking out the main viewscreen.

And on that screen, the impossible was being displayed.

The freighter must be swooping at unseemly speeds, down through a pink and lavender atmosphere. Clouds parted before them and Dini grabbed his hand tighter.

"Oh, Rick, it's like a dream."

The city that they saw when the clouds parted was hardly more than a town. There were white, gleaming buildings on hillsides and there were what seemed to be winding trails among gorgeously colored plots of vegetation, some of which looked like magnificent gardens of multicolored hue.

Rick glanced at Dini and she had tears in her eyes. He hoped they weren't tears of fright. Did she understand that this ship couldn't go this fast in atmosphere?

Again, he looked at his readouts. They made absolutely no sense. Physics were being violated here. But the spherical ships around them were doing the same thing.

He could see out the forward viewer that three of the ships were in front of them.

The ground sped by beneath, closer and closer, and suddenly he saw what must be a spaceport, if you could have a spaceport in a garden.

And then, without a bit of deceleration, g-force, or a single growl from his thrusters, or a shiver of torque, the freighter's nosewheel touched down. He hadn't even heard the landing gear descend.

He thanked his luck that the freighter was transatmospheric and capable of a landing at all. Yet something inside him told him it wouldn't have mattered.

Dini had the mocket in her lap and it was licking her face.

If the mocket was in her lap, where were the Brows?

"Dini, where are the Brows?"

"Oh, they went back to the cabin. Rick, they're so happy! I've never seen them like that before."

Neither had he.

Don't scare her. Maybe this is some wonderful adventure, just like she's been telling me.

"Do you think this is the 'wonderful thing' you've been expecting?"

"Of course it is. Woman's intuition." She sniffed and put her hand on her mocket's snout to stop its frantic licking. "Woman's intuition is never wrong."

"Good. Then you'll be ready to meet our host and be polite. We can't stay here too long, Dini. . . ."

"Why not?" She was unbuckling her safety harness as if they'd been coming here all along.

He tried to think of an answer. "Because . . . we have to get the Brows back to Pegasus before they run out of Leetles," he said triumphantly.

"They'll have enough Leetles," Dini said. "You watch. Those Leetles will breed just fine, as long as we don't eat them. We don't need to eat them," she said, her mocket in her arms. "Do we?"

She slid around him and started to leave the flight deck. "Well, are you coming, beloved?"

Dini was transported with a radiant excitement. She nearly skipped down the corridor.

Rick wished he could truly decide whether there was something awfully wrong here, or not. Maybe he should have a weapon. There were some basic weapons aboard, because freighter pilots always worried about piracy and rip-offs. You had to be ready to repel boarders.

But somehow he couldn't bring himself to get one. It would be wrong to meet his hosts with a weapon in his hand, wouldn't it?

Especially when they were capable of doing what they'd just done with this ship.

He could hardly believe they really had landed like that—so fast, so quietly, so safely, even though that kind of landing was far beyond the freighter's capabilities.

He hesitated, unwilling to leave the flight deck. He kept looking at his instrumentation. He reached over and tapped his AI. It was still functioning. It brought him full views of what was outside.

And so he saw the welcoming committee before Dini did.

Then he ran down the corridor to get the Brows and join her before she opened the hatch.

When he caught up with her, he took one Brow with shaking hands and coaxed it up onto his shoulder.

Then he straightened his spacesuit and stood beside his companion, who had a Brow in her arms and an excited mocket yapping at her feet. The third Brow was scratching at the lock determinedly.

"Ready?" he asked her.

"Oh yes," she said.

He pushed the lock's cycling button and they stepped into the air exchange chamber. The outer lock wouldn't open if, despite appearances, the air wasn't safe to breathe.

As he stood in that lock, Rick Cummings's pulse pounded in his ears. His eardrums actually ached from it.

The Brow on his shoulder was singing.

"Coming home," Dini crooned to it. "You heard them. We're bringing you home."

He didn't say anything, even though he'd seen the beings waiting outside. Dini would see them soon, and she'd make her own determination.

The Brows had had something to do with them coming here; Rick was now absolutely sure of that.

But it wasn't until the outer lock opened and the hatch came down that Dini saw the aliens.

Rick pushed her lightly forward, still balancing his Brow on his shoulder. He was thinking the most pleasant thoughts he could imagine.

They walked down the ramp and three of the aliens walked up, to meet them halfway.

When they stood toe-to-toe with the aliens, Rick held out his hand. As he did, the Brow on his shoulder jumped to the shoulder of the sad-mouthed, huge-eyed alien before him.

Its six-fingered hand touched his, and the feeling was strange: like touching your grandmother's hand; like touching your father's hand when you were very young. The hand seemed small and frail and yet bigger than his.

The aliens, too, seemed small and frail and yet large, immensely powerful.

"Welcome, children," said the alien whose hand he held.

And Dini looked at Rick for a moment with sparkling eyes, so that Rick knew she realized that it wasn't the Brows who were the wayward ones, coming home.

It was Dini, and Rick himself, whom the aliens had meant.

"I love you, Rick," Dini said. "I'll always love you."

"I love you too, Dini," Rick Cummings III answered.

The huge, sad eyes of the foremost alien, the one that still held his hand, went from Dini's face to Rick's as they spoke.

It nodded its delicate head and its huge eyes seemed to spin. "Welcome, all. We have much to show you."

Dini's Brow scrambled out of her arms and went racing around the feet of the three aliens on the ramp.

When Rick looked up, the sun was setting and a ringed planet was fading into view in the purple haze.

CHAPTER 28

Extravehicular Activity

The scavenger was throwing a full-blown tantrum. The box wouldn't work. South thought the old guy was going to bust a gut.

Keebler's face was purple and the veins bisecting his forehead looked as if they might pop right out of his skin: "I tol' y', sonny. I'm not satisfied! I'm not satisfied at all. It'll work, if'n it's close enough. It's this old piece-o'-crap ship that's screwin' things up! It's your relay system that's faulty. An' I'm gonna raise holy—"

"Look, Keebler," South said, though he didn't know why, "I can't let you out of the ship in one of my suits—it'd be irresponsible." Keebler started to yell again and South held up his hand. "There's nothing that says I can't take the box out and try it for you, if you'll be satisfied with that. I think I can rig up remote monitoring through the suit systems, so you'll be sure I did it right. Now, is that okay with you?"

Keebler chewed on that for a minute. Then he said, "Okay with me, sonny. So long's I c'n watch t' see yer doin' it right."

In the parking lights of *STARBIRD*'s flight deck, the old scavenger's face took on a diabolical cast for just an instant.

"Well, get out of the way while I set up for EVA, then," South told him. He'd better get this happening before he changed his mind.

The whole time he was coaxing Birdy into relaxing the trip-long prohibition against considering Keebler's suit as anything more than "Input B, to be ignored," South kept trying not to worry about what Keebler might do if left alone in *STARBIRD*.

"Now, Keebler, don't you touch anything on the flight deck. Is that clear?" South, in full kit for EVA, checked his seals one more time before he stepped into the lock.

"I hear y', sonny. What d'you think I am, an idiot? Anything happens to you out there, that crazy woman Director's gonna blame it on m' artifact. So y' come back safe, y' hear?"

Then there was nothing left but to do it. "We'll check out systems in the lock one more time. If you can't see or hear what you want, Keebler, now's the time to tell me—while I can do something about it. Not when I'm out there. Copy?"

"Copy, Cap'n," said Keebler with a broad, green-toothed grin.

"Then pull down your faceplate and sit on my damned bunk and, for God's sake, don't touch anything," South said and slapped the lockplate without another backward glance.

When the inner door closed behind him, he ran a systems check with Keebler. "Can you see the box through my helmet recorder?"

Keebler could.

"Can you read its status there in the lower left of your visor?"

Keebler could, thanks to Birdy, who ought to get a medal except that she was an AI and AIs didn't get medals, no matter how exemplary their performance was.

The air lock's status indicator told him it would open for him anytime. His MMU was topped off and ready. Under his right hand was the joystick for the jetpack on his back, which would allow him as much fine control as he wanted.

Nevertheless, he had a safety line on his belt.

He looked at the black box in his left hand. "Okay, Keebler, I'm going out."

South hit the exit button and *STARBIRD* opened up. Birdy cut the artificial gravity to the lock and he was weightless, with only the magnetized soles of his boots holding him down.

He pushed off. Test pilots got to hate weightlessness real quick. It told you that you were a lightweight. It told you that people didn't mean a whole hell of a lot in the cosmic scheme of things. South had flown early missions where you were in zero-g most of the time.

He hated free-fall.

And he hated EVAs. Always had. They scared the hell out of him. He didn't like feeling his guts floating around inside him.

Usually, you couldn't see much but stars, which was what EVAs were about.

Space ought to be full of stars, not big silver globes and commercial spacedocks in the background.

He was only five hundred yards from the ball. He'd kept parking *STARBIRD* closer and closer, trying to satisfy Keebler that distance wasn't the problem.

Sling had sworn that the box in South's gloved left hand wouldn't work. But the mission wasn't accomplished, so far as South was concerned, until Keebler believed it.

If he brought the scavenger back unsatisfied, it wasn't going to help his case with Director Lowe.

So he clipped his safety line onto *STARBIRD*'s hull and pushed off toward the ball, saying to Keebler, "I'm out and approaching. You getting all the signal you want?"

Keebler's voice came back, "Looks good from here, sonny."

South would rather be in intimate communication with Birdy, if he had to be out here nearly naked, but what could you do? He needed to give Keebler his money's worth.

It took only two taps on his joystick to bring him up so close to the ball's hull that he could touch it.

He didn't do that. He didn't want to do that.

The ball was so close, he could see his reflection on its mirrored surface. His helmet light made him look like an undersea diver; the floods from *STARBIRD* were so bright, he almost didn't notice the colors as they started to change. . . .

Joe South felt the prickle of his physiology kit and heard the whir as his suit's heater kicked down a notch, then another.

The ball turned purple and misty. Why was he feeling so damned strange? Euphoric, even. Like he'd found a way home after all . . .

When he realized what he was doing, South had one gloved hand on the ball and Keebler's voice was saying, "Sonny, y' don't have to try to bash yer way in with that box. Just push the red button and that's all she wrote . . ."

"Wrote?" But he was awake, or thought he was. Was he still dreaming? Euphoria during an EVA wasn't a great sign. Lots of good reasons why that could happen. He shunted his suit's technical data up where he could read it.

There wasn't anything wrong with his oxygen mix or his life support. Then how come he'd blacked out like that and come back to his senses to find himself nearly hugging the huge ball? On Birdy's log, he was going to look like an ant trying to lift a grapefruit.

Sweat was forming on his face and his suit was attempting to dry it before the moisture fogged the inside of his visor. The cool air circulating over his cheeks and eyelids felt good.

He pushed Keebler's red button and braced for whatever was going to happen.

An oblong seam of dark lavender appeared in the side of the ball. Then the oblong was drawing back, exposing a wonder of electronics and a flight deck within that looked almost familiar. . . .

The lavender oblong disappeared as the ball shut tight.

Simultaneously, South heard a voice in his ears say: "Hell with it, Cap'n. Never mind. Come on back. I guess I got took."

Keebler. Keebler should be howling with triumph and joy. . . .

Unless Keebler hadn't seen the ball open, let alone shut, and everything South had thought he'd seen was just his imagination.

Unless Sling had been right and the black box hadn't made anything happen.

South blinked and looked again at the ball. Then he had Birdy look at the ball. The ball was purely spherical, with no opening anywhere on its surface.

He had Birdy replay the last five minutes of his EVA as fast as he could watch it. There was nothing on the log that matched his memory. There was nothing at all there but a guy trying to make a box work, up against the side of a featureless ball.

None of what had seemed so clear to him was really there: no door, no internal components of the ball. Nothing. . . . South admitted to himself that he'd had another one of those half-dreams that seemed like a memory but was probably some psychological effect.

Keebler had been so sure that the ball would open that the scavenger's fantasies must have worked on South's admittedly shaky psyche like some sort of posthypnotic suggestion.

It was a good thing he hadn't said anything to Keebler, or to Birdy, which would have been a permanent part of the EVA record. Then everybody would have known that Captain Joseph South had a screw loose somewhere.

This way, nobody knew, not even Birdy, what South had thought he saw. Nobody knew he was still a little loopy. His suit said there was nothing wrong with him. His physiology package was pronouncing him fit as a fiddle.

"—sonny, I'm satisfied."

"What?"

"I said, come on in, sonny. I'm satisfied." Keebler's voice

was gruffly wistful, disappointed, and more embarrassed than angry.

"If you're satisfied, so am I," South managed thickly. Part of him wasn't really ready to leave. The ball was a mesmerizing surface that caught his reflection and did fascinating things with it. . . .

He punched his emergency line's retractor and let it drag him back as the spool on his belt rewound the line.

The whole time, he kept talking to Keebler: "I'm trying combinations three and four, from here." "I'll give this narrow band transmitter one more try." "I don't see any change . . . do you?"

Because he still wasn't sure that he hadn't seen what he thought he'd seen. If he had seen it, Keebler hadn't.

And what he'd seen, South knew, wasn't what Keebler was expecting. Or he thought he knew that.

When his retracted line brought him to *STARBIRD*'s hull, the lock was open, waiting for him. He didn't look back at the ball, just told Birdy to cycle him through.

He held on to the handrail for dear life until the lock had cycled and he was surrounded once more with all the life-sustaining comforts that Birdy could provide.

Inside, once he'd shrugged off the EVA harness, he handed the box to the waiting scavenger.

"Sorry," South said.

"I'm gonna bust that Sling's butt fer sellin' me this useless piece o' crap."

"Sling told you it wouldn't work. You just wouldn't listen." South squeezed by the scavenger. "You want to prepare to debark, Keebler? Time to go back to civilization."

Civilization, you bet. South was going to buy Sling a blue beer. If that ball was some kind of ship from a superior culture, South wasn't at all sure that people should be mucking around with it. As a matter of fact, whatever was in that thing ought to stay in that thing. The way he felt now was proof of that.

It took all of Birdy's competence and long hours of concentration on his flying to forget about those feelings. But

Birdy was absolutely sure that the ball wasn't any kind of threat, and *STARBIRD* was one seriously improved machine, since Sling had tweaked her, and all of that combined to help South shake off the spooky feeling that had overcome him when he was out at the ball.

It was just a ball, wasn't it?

Keebler still didn't think so. "I'll get into that ball yet, sonny. Gonna make me rich 'n' famous when I do. Y'll see."

"I believe you, Keebler," South said into the com channel that linked him to Keebler, back in his bunk. "You want to prepare for docking maneuvers now? I'm going to sign off until we're docked."

South really wanted to do a flawless entry into the Blue South docking bay, so that he could quit feeling like such an alien himself.

Once he did that, maybe he could shake these stupid aftereffects of his X-mission forever. It was just displacement trauma, after all.

Birdy patched him through to the controller and he said, "Yeah, Sol Base Blue, this is Customs Special *STARBIRD*, ready for final approach. You got a slot for me, Blue Base Control?"

CHAPTER 29

Telling Tales

When she got the call telling her that South wanted to bring the scavenger up to her office, Riva Lowe felt unreasonably relieved.

She told her secretary to squeeze them in before lunch and then realized that she'd only given herself an hour to prepare.

Then she wondered why she thought she had to be prepared. Her desk was stacked with paperwork and emergency requests because of the ongoing Medinan demonstrations in the conference zone and the extra security Croft's office had slapped on across-the-board.

Lowe pushed back in her chair, nibbled a fingernail, and said into her intercom, "I'm going to the lounge for a few minutes."

Then she shoveled everything on the top of her desk into her middle drawer and locked it. One didn't leave sensitive material lying around loose, not these days.

As she did, Remson's priority request for a change of status caught her eye.

She pulled it back out and sat down again. Vince wanted three recertifications: Ali-4, Ali-5, and Ali-7, imported provisionally for a three-week stay as equipment belonging to the Medinan delegation, needed to be recertified as human immigrants and issued visas and green cards.

Vince ought to be spanked, asking her to do all this, half of which wasn't the purview of her department. But there was a handwritten note on a card that had come with the hand-delivered sheaf of forms: *Riva: Help! Vince.*

Instead of going to the lounge, Riva Lowe called her opposite number in Immigration, and then a friend in the U.S. State Department (Threshold) office.

"I know it's irregular, but everyone else has come into line with Secretary Croft's request. Can't we have immediate provisional documentation? And I think that Secretary Croft himself would be grateful if you could manage a quick set of permanent documents on political grounds."

Riva Lowe listened for a moment, eyes closed, stylus between her lips. "Yes, certainly. Political asylum, under the circumstances, will more than cover all our needs. Thank you. I'll make sure the Secretary knows what a great help you were, and how quickly your department acted in this sensitive situation."

One might have thought that Remson could have done this himself. But on reflection, she knew why he hadn't: Vince Remson had taken these Alis under his wing. Concurrence from other department heads would bolster his case if there was a Medinan appeal.

She told her secretary to alert Remson's office that the "papers he requested for the Alis are coming up to him within the hour."

And her assistant replied, "Your appointment is here, Director. Shall I send them in?"

"Appointment?" For a moment she couldn't remember who or what might be waiting. Then she did. "Oh, yes. Send them in."

She still hadn't gotten to the lounge. She put Remson's request into her desk drawer and looked up.

There stood the scavenger. Her hackles rose. Why wouldn't the old fool just go away?

Beside him was the Relic pilot, looking tired and scruffy, but marginally presentable in Customs coveralls. The pilot closed the door. "Mission accomplished, Director."

All he needed was a helmet under his arm and jackboots to click as he saluted.

"Well, that's fine, Captain South. Mister Keebler. Won't you both sit down?"

"I'm not sittin' down. I'm leavin' right away," said the scavenger. "I'm just here t' tell y', y' ain't heard the last o' me." The scavenger stood spread-legged before her, his chin jutting.

Riva Lowe was prepared for Keebler. "I think you're wrong, Mister Keebler. I think I have heard the last of you."

She keyed her hard-copy generator and it spat out a prepared document. "Take this, Mister Keebler."

The scavenger stomped forward to snatch it as the hard copy rolled out of the document slot. South stepped aside and leaned against the curving blue wall of her office, his face impassive, as if he were pretending to be somewhere else.

"What's this?" Keebler wanted to know.

"That's a restraining order. It prohibits you from going near that ball again. We're confiscating it under Customs Ruling EU-48502a, which allows us to take into custody any unspecifiable object of alien origin. Your ball is now the property of the Threshold government, Keebler. So you see, I don't think you will be bothering me again."

"Y' can't do this! The Salvagers' Union'll never permit it. I got lawyers! I'll *get* lawyers. . . ."

Riva Lowe knew bluster when she heard it. Even the scavenger didn't have his heart in his tirade. He was seeming smaller, less threatening by the minute.

"Don't y' even want t' know what we saw out there?" the scavenger nearly whined.

"I'm sure I know what you saw. You saw the ball. And since it's our ball, what *you* think about it is no longer of interest. To anyone." She had to be careful. She couldn't let him create a loophole by tricking her into making a misstatement, not after all the work she'd done to find a pretext to confiscate the ball.

"You ought to listen to him," said the pilot, who was still standing by the door, leaning against the blue wall of her office.

"What?" The single word came out of her like a slap meant to bring South to his senses.

"I—" South began.

"Never mind Cap'n South, ma'am. He's just a crazy old codger, older than I am. A Relic pilot," said Keebler with a cunning that Lowe didn't immediately understand. "It's all in his ship's log, what we did and what we saw. Y'll be hearin' from me."

And the scavenger turned his back on her, stalked over to the door. The door drew back and he started through it.

South's arm shot out to bar his way. The two men exchanged a few words. Then South withdrew his arm and the scavenger left.

The door closed again, leaving her alone with the Relic.

She expected South's face to reflect the insults that Keebler had slung. It didn't. Nor did the pilot make any move to follow Keebler out the door.

"Yes, Captain South?" He flustered her, even now when he wasn't holding half of ConSec at bay from his ancient spacecraft.

"Before I deliver my report," said the pilot, "I've got a message from Lieutenant Reice that he said has to go to Remson and Croft."

What was this about Reice?

"You do? From Reice? Is he . . . all right?"

The pilot came up to her desk and put one hand on it. "I guess. He was chasing some ship and it went into a spongehole right between *STARBIRD* and the ball. The ball . . . changed colors during the event. Then the hole closed up and Reice flew over the area. He's gone on to continue the search. Says it's safe out there." South shrugged as if he wasn't sure he believed it. He reached into his coveralls' breast pocket and pulled out a data card. "Here's the log he wanted Remson and Croft to have. He's real adamant about them getting it, ma'am. We talked about hand-delivering it. . . ."

She took the card and turned it in her fingers. "Is there something else that's bothering you about this?"

Again, diffidently, the pilot shrugged. He had deep dark circles under his eyes, almost like bruises. "The scavenger said he didn't see the color change on the ball, but it's on the log tape. Maybe it matters, maybe it doesn't. Keebler couldn't get into the ball with the black box. . . ." He took his hand off her desk and straightened up. "I got the log on that, too, if you want it."

"Hold on to it. Later, if we have trouble with Keebler, we might need it. But we deal with so much information, Captain . . . I'm sure you understand."

He looked disappointed. "Yeah, I guess I understand."

Then Lowe thought she, too, understood. It was crucial to this man from the past to have done something relevant, something that was important, or at least acceptable: mission accomplished.

She'd sent him out there with the scavenger. He needed to know that what he'd done had mattered.

"I will want an abbreviated report. You can send one to my office, as soon as you get some rest."

"You bet." He was backing away.

"And, Captain South—nice job. We might really have had a problem with Keebler if you weren't around to make sure he was able to exercise his rights."

"Doesn't look to me like you needed much help or that he had a snowball's chance," said South under his breath, still retreating.

Snowball? Impulsively, Riva Lowe stood up: "Wait a minute, Captain. It seems we've got to deliver this data to Croft and Remson. You were on-site. They may want a verbal report. You have no idea how fortunate it was that you were around to bear witness to that freighter's disappearance."

And neither did she, until they got to Vince Remson's office and Remson viewed the log tape that the antique *STARBIRD* had made.

Vince looked South up and down, when he'd finished

viewing the log, and said, "Well, aren't you a gift from fate?"

Remson ran a spread hand through his pale hair and turned to her: "Riva, I can't thank you enough. With this log, we can convince both those fathers that they have no recourse under law to blame anyone but themselves. It may even stop these accursed demonstrations, if we play our cards right."

South looked at her, his brow furrowed. Of course, she realized, he couldn't possibly understand.

"We got lucky," she said modestly to Remson.

"Take your man, here, out to lunch on me. And, Captain South, if Riva doesn't treat you right, or you get bored in Customs, come see me. I can always use a man like you."

Vince Remson stood up to shake South's hand.

"Come on, South," said Riva Lowe. "Let's get that lunch."

The Relic was looking around Remson's office, which was filled with mementoes from out-system junkets. "I'll try to convince you to stay with us. I can't have Vince, here, picking off all my best officers."

"Yes, ma'am. Thank you, sir," said South, either confused or bemused, or some combination of the two.

On the way out of the U.S. Mission, South openly stared at everything until she said, "Are you all right, Captain?"

"Huh? Yeah, fine. That was a regular old American flag in that guy's—in Mr. Remson's office. And down here, that's the seal, right?"

"Right," she said, fighting the urge to chuckle. "You've done not only Threshold, but the U.S. government, a service."

"Nice to know we've still got one," he muttered, and turned around to walk backwards and crane his neck this way and that as she led him toward the doors.

"Let's go to my place for lunch," she said. "I'll have something sent in. You're tired and everything's still new to you." She kept forgetting how much must be strange for him. And he certainly wasn't dressed for a better restaurant.

Riva Lowe wasn't even the least reluctant to have him in her home until they got there and he stood on the balcony overlooking the government complex with his hands in his back pockets.

She was setting the table. The food and wine were on the way up. In her apartment was nothing to make anyone uncomfortable: good views of Earth—expensive, high-resolution shots of the Grand Canyon and the Maine coast—dominated the walls in the living room; excellent Epsilonian art hung in the foyer; the furniture was all antique, from the late Information Age.

She kept trying to make small talk but he wouldn't play along.

Finally she said, "Tell me about how you're making out. I do hope you won't jump ship and go work for Vince. He's a bit of an operator. . . ."

"I get funny flashbacks of someplace I was, or I saw, during my X-3 exploratory," he said, still looking over the balcony, his back to her. "I saw 'em again when I touched the ball."

She nearly dropped the water glass she was holding. "You—when you touched the ball. You weren't supposed to take Keebler out—"

He turned to face her and leaned against the railing. "I didn't take Keebler. I follow orders, lady—ma'am—Director. I went myself. If anybody bothered to look over a person's reports around here, you'd know that. I had to satisfy him—or I thought I had to. I didn't know you just wanted him out of the way until you could get your paper knife all sharpened up."

South wasn't stupid, she reminded herself through the shock she was feeling. She came around the round table and leaned against it. Their body language was nearly identical when she said, "I went out myself, you know. I touched that ball. And I saw . . . a ringed planet, kind of hazy—"

"Lavender mist. Sunset. Yeah." He dropped his eyes. "But you weren't out at X-3."

"No, I wasn't. Maybe I'll look at your log."

"Yeah, I'd like that."

"And all the rest of your data you think someone should see."

"Would you?"

"Absolutely."

A dozen years seemed to fall from the pilot. "I want to thank you for . . . giving me a chance."

"I want to thank you, for taking it and making something out of it," she said.

"About the ball—"

"The ball," she said firmly, "is government property. We'll have plenty of time to study it together."

The door chimed: their food had arrived. She straightened up. "Lunch is here. Will you get it? Just give them your Customs card."

And that reminded her, so when he came back with the containers and handed them to her, she said, "You know, I have no idea how or why you spent so much on that antique ship, but the next time it's that kind of money, clear it with me?"

He nearly grinned. Perhaps he did, for a second. "I knew I was going to catch hell about that," he said, putting down the final container and struggling to open it for her.

It was so domestic a moment that something inside Riva Lowe was totally disarmed. She went to help the Relic pilot with the container he didn't know how to use.

"You just push this indentation, and it breaks its own vacuum seal. See?"

But by then he had his hand on her waist and she knew that, unless she did something to stop him, he was going to kiss her and things would go on from there.

But she couldn't think of a single reason that held up against the hungry, vulnerable, determined look in the pilot's eyes.

A few moments later, she stopped worrying about Joe South's ability to reacclimate to modern society. He was going to do just fine.

CHAPTER 30

$\triangledown$

Model Citizens

"I don't think you're going to have any more trouble with Richard the Second or Beni Forat," Remson said with a wolfish grin as he came in, dressed for the evening's festivities.

"That would be nice," said Mickey Croft mildly, straightening his tie in his dressing room mirror. Only Vince would have the stones to barge into Croft's very bathroom to report. "What about the demonstrations?"

"Take a look outside." Vince Remson was trying unsuccessfully to restrain himself, which in itself was unusual.

So Croft left the dressing room and strode across his adjoining library to a window overlooking the street.

The demonstrators who had become a constant fixture of his existence and whose presence had been so unutterably depressing . . . nearly all of them were gone.

A few people in tribal headgear were picking their way desultorily through the litter, which, at last, sanitation crews were starting to clear. ConSec vans were pulled up, loading force-field generators and yellow police barricades.

"You know, Vince," Croft said dryly to the man standing behind him, "I've told you before that it's disconcerting to have you working unannounced miracles while I'm in the bath."

"Yes, sir," Remson said crisply. "Sorry, sir. It won't happen again."

239

Croft turned around and added, deadpan, "Until we need another miracle, it had better not." Then he let his pleasure show, and his big security chief dropped his eyes in bashful pride.

"I hope you're not going to make me beg for an explanation, Mr. Remson."

"No, sir." His eyes came up and locked with Croft's. "I took the liberty of treating Mr. Cummings, Junior, and Mr. Forat to a session with your modeler."

"You *what*?" Croft wasn't sure whether he should laugh or cry. The modeler wasn't to be used publicly, ever. But the result . . .

"I had the log that the Relic ship made of the kids' spongejump in the NAMECorp freighter at Spacedock Seven. You knew about that."

"Yes, you told me you had something of the sort."

"I took the log, edited it slightly, and invited both parents to the modeler room to watch it. At the same time, I showed them models of both their children, each of which told the father that they'd do anything they had to in order to get away together, alive."

"That must have been touching."

"Embarrassing, I believe, is the word. At that point, Cummings knew he'd lost any chance of blaming this whole mess on Forat, or on us. And once he caved, Forat fell into line. . . . The political repercussions alone made my case."

"You mean you didn't tell these poor parents that you wouldn't—couldn't—release the modeler data?"

"I sure didn't, sir." Vince was looking at his highly polished dress shoes concertedly.

Croft rubbed his chin with one hand and said, "Vince, you're not telling me everything."

Remson looked up with an air of exaggerated, wounded innocence. "I'm telling *you* everything."

"Oh, you didn't. Heaven preserve us, you didn't . . ."

Remson's white teeth flashed and he nodded his head.

". . . fail to explain to those two parents what a modeled image is, Vince. You let them believe that they were talking to their actual children?"

"It really wasn't that hard, sir. The questions they asked, and the way the models responded, just lent themselves to allowing the parents to make those assumptions. Which they dearly wanted to believe: that their children are alive and well and simply hiding out somewhere. You know parental guilt. . . . I didn't have the heart to tell them they were making their separate peace with a couple of AI-generated images."

For a moment, Croft's calm snapped: "And what's going to happen when they do find out?"

"Then we'll be surprised and apologetic that they didn't realize what they were seeing. And talking with. We can't be responsible for technological illiteracy and its results. How could anyone not realize it when they're in a modeler room?"

Croft's legs were weak. He felt behind him and then sat very gingerly on the window seat. "But the risk, Vince . . ."

"I don't see it as significant. Either the kids are alive, somewhere, or they're dead. Either way, the models were adamant about making their own lives together and not giving the parents the opportunity to destroy those lives. So, unless and until the kids show up, alive or dead, as it were, we're in good shape. The demonstrations are over; Cummings owes us an apology; Forat is a born-again moderate, rethinking the whole concept of ritual beheading—and women's rights."

"What did we trade for all this moderation?"

"Well, we're sealing the kids' files: no subsequent drug or smuggling infractions in five years, and we wipe those files. I've done as much for less reason."

"And a few concessions on your Alis?"

"I was getting those anyway. But yes, Forat won't obstruct the humanization legislation, as long as we don't release the log of the kids' escape or any of the . . . model . . . comments to the news services."

"Vince, remind me never to cross you."

"I won't have to do that, sir. Ever. Now, if you're ready, I've come to take you to the evening's festivities."

"I'll just get my coat, Vince." Croft still felt numb. This morning, he'd been fighting an impossible battle and there was a single straw of hope in the shape of an accidental recording of those children escaping in a wild and dangerous fashion.

Not to mention an illegal one.

When he'd fumbled his dress coat from his closet, Croft said, "And what about the Leetles?"

"Leetles. Cummings isn't going to try to fight us on the Leetle Control Act. And he's accepted that the Brows' species is nonexportable."

"A pity. I rather think I'd have liked to own one."

"Mickey, you're dangerous enough as it is."

"All thanks to you, dear boy. All thanks to you."

And off they went, to the dinner held in honor of the conference attendees, in the selfsame hall where the pilgrims had completed their journey in a simulated Mecca.

Croft had been deeply worried that this dinner would turn into a fiasco. The presence of so many unbelievers in a place which had, only yesterday, been holy, combined with the hostility that the Medinans had whipped up, might have been disastrous.

But when they entered the videodrome module, it was as placid and festive as could be.

On the circular wall was projected a moving montage of scenes from the hundred worlds who'd sent representatives. The UNE emblem dominated the arched ceiling, and below the entry balcony, people were mixing and eating and chatting and drinking as if this were the most successful conference ever held on Threshold.

And well it might be, considering that, despite the difficulties, great strides had been made in human rights legislation, as well as subhuman and alien rights legislation.

Human rights were always the most difficult to agree upon, since people could hold such disparate views of right and wrong, good and bad, freedom and slavery, moral and immoral.

Their entrance was announced, and he and Remson walked

down the long sweeping staircase into the middle of the crowd.

Normally, in a group as varied and thus as explosive as this, Croft entered with a stomach full of butterflies. Tonight, his stomach was settled, his lips were moist, and his heart was beating a quiet, calming rhythm.

Most of this, assuredly, was due to his faith in Remson. But some was an assessment of his own performance. He'd done a good job of keeping a lid on things. A fine job.

Beni Forat came over and told him so. And thus Croft knew that it was true, once he'd seen the capitulation on the mullah's hawk-nosed face.

"Everyone learns a thing or two, yes, Croft?" said Forat.

"We learn by listening to our own hearts," he told the leader of Medina. "Not by listening to anything else. And so what we learn can be trusted, because the source is true." Croft mentally asked forgiveness from all of mankind's philosophers for brandishing truisms in the name of diplomacy.

"Yes, that is exactly it," said Forat. "We are growing into adults, all of us. All the time."

"Generosity of spirit is never a mistake. We of Threshold applaud your decision to grant your women full and equal status with men under Medinan law."

Might as well go for the brass ring.

The hawk-faced man suddenly dropped his mask: "If you hear anything of my daughter, you will send word to me. And you will tell her that not only is all forgiven, but every woman on Medina—and every bodyguard—will bless her name as a liberator."

"I will certainly do that," Croft promised Forat. "I surely will." So that was how Forat was handling this mess, to save face. Rather neat.

Over the Medinan's shoulder, Remson wriggled his eyebrows: Did Croft want to be rescued?

Croft tugged on his earlobe, giving a sign that meant, *Yes, please.*

In between an Epsilonian female whose low-backed dress displayed the beads wound into the hair on her humped spine, and a Russian diplomat with a medal-spangled chest, came Remson to the rescue.

"Sir, I have someone who's been waiting to meet you, if Representative Forat will excuse us?"

Croft had thought that Vince was simply fabricating a likely excuse until he was shepherded over to Riva Lowe. She had a gaunt, youngish man with her who obviously felt a bit awkward. He had his hands in his pockets and his expression was dazed, as if he were a child wearing an itchy suit at a grown-up's party.

"Secretary General Croft, this is Captain Joseph South, the Relic test pilot who made the recording, which came in so handy, out at Spacedock Seven," Vince said, as if he had personally masterminded the entire escapade.

"I hope they've told you, these two—," Croft eyed Riva Lowe and cocked his head at Remson, "—how you saved their bacon—and mine—on this one, Captain South. It's a pleasure to have you in our service." He held out his hand and the Relic pilot pumped it briefly.

"Thank you, sir," Joseph South said in a husky voice.

Then something occurred to Croft. "He is, I hope, in some one of our services, people?"

Remson scratched behind one ear with his index finger and looked at Riva Lowe from under his brow.

"The captain's in Customs, sir," she said determinedly.

"Is that so? Well, Captain South, if there's ever anything I can do . . ."

"Yes, sir. I'd kinda like—"

The test pilot's accent was old American. It was like listening to a historical vid show. "Yes, Captain?"

"Well, my original mission was to—"

Vince Remson nearly stepped between Croft and the pilot, saying, "In case you think we dropped a stitch, Captain South, we went over that ship of yours with a fine-tooth comb when it first came in. We took a transcript. We've analyzed that transcript and filed it with other, similar data. And we're aware that the globe out at spacedock has some characteristics in common with other classified, related phenomena—"

"Globe?" South said.

"He means the ball, Joe," said Riva Lowe. And: "Classified, Vince?"

Then Croft realized what must be said: "We're putting together a study team to look at the . . . artifact in light of all previously gathered information. From what you're not saying, Vince, perhaps the captain should be on that team."

This was no place to discuss the matter further.

Riva Lowe knew that. There was a look of quiet desperation on her face that lingered until Remson said, "Mickey, I think that's a fine idea. If Riva concurs?"

"I certainly do, gentlemen. Now if you'll excuse us, I'm trying to take this opportunity to show Captain South as much as I can, while there are so many visitors on hand to give him a taste of what the UNE's really about."

The Customs director nearly dragged the Relic pilot away.

"Vince?" Croft wasn't completely sure that he'd done the right thing; anomalies were Remson's department.

"It'll be fine, Mickey. I was going to suggest it to Riva at some point anyway. South is wasted in Customs, where what he knows is useless."

"And what does he know?"

"That's what I'm going to find out. Come see how Ali-7's doing as a free citizen on his first big night out."

Croft let Remson cut yet another path through the crowd. Vince was proud of what he'd done for the Alis. And so was Croft.

Remson had a penchant for strays.

Ali-7 was proud to attest to that, when they found him.

When the ex-Medinan bodyguard said, "Lord Secretary Croft, I am calling myself Michael Ali, if you will allow this," Croft was truly touched.

"That's very flattering," he told the bodyguard. "I'm honored."

And he was. Their batting average tonight was impressive. Croft turned away from the Ali and looked above the crowd to the UNE emblem overhead.

For the first night in too many nights, Mickey Croft was

beginning once more to enjoy his job. Around the UNE emblem was a starfield. He fancied he could identify uncharted reaches, places where man hadn't yet ventured.

They had it all, did the diverse races of humanity, if they could just refrain from fighting among themselves. And since it was Croft's task to keep the peace that made everything else possible, he took that task very seriously.

Too seriously, he chided himself when Richard Cummings, without a glint of rancor in his eyes, came up to tell him a joke about an Epsilonian lady and a whirlpool bath.

When he'd told the joke, Cummings said, "I want to bury the hatchet, Mickey. Permanently. Let's try working more closely from now on."

If Cummings's declaration hadn't been prompted by the loss of his son, Mickey's triumph at that moment would have been without blemish.

But everything costs. Cooperation costs dearly. If someone had asked him, at that moment, Mickey Croft would have said the future was worth any price.

"Drink? To our future," Richard Cummings, Jr., said, as if reading Croft's mind, as a waiter came by with a tray of blue champagne.

"I'd be delighted to drink to that," Mickey Croft said, and he was.

CHAPTER 31

<hr>

Aftermarket Rendezvous

Sometime after South had lost track of Riva Lowe, Lieutenant Reice came to the party and dragged him out.

"I want to talk to you, but not here," Reice said.

South was sure that the lieutenant was drunk. South was drunk. It was that blue stuff. You had to stay away from the blue stuff, South reminded himself blearily.

"Reice, where are we going?"

None of the streets they'd crossed, or this tubeway they were entering, looked familiar.

"Shortcut," Reice said. He was in civilian clothes.

"You find the freighter?" South asked when a single car whined up a levitation track and stopped before them. It opened. There was nobody else inside the little four-place car.

"Get in and don't ask questions."

South got in and Reice followed, closing the door and stabbing at the destination keypad as if he had a personal grudge against this piece of equipment.

"Did you find the freighter?" South asked again.

"Are you drunk, South?"

"Yep."

"Well, so am I," Reice said. "No, I didn't find the freighter, but I got orders to jack my butt back here, posthaste. You have anything to do with that?"

"I dunno." South was trying to blink away the extra image of Reice he was seeing. "I delivered your message, and the log. The way you said."

"That's probably what did it," said Reice morosely.

They rode along in silence.

Eventually South asked, "Where are we going?"

"Down to Blue South, the priority way."

When they got there, Reice wanted to go aboard *STARBIRD* and see the log again.

South said okay and they ran the log three times, until South couldn't watch it anymore. At least his vision was clearing.

"What's this?" Reice wanted to know, pointing under the console.

"Black box."

"I can see that, Captain. What kind?"

"Aftermarket, Lieutenant."

"I can see that too. What's going on here?"

"Don't get all police-like with me. That was the scavenger's box. He left it. Remember the mission I had?"

Reice didn't.

South told Reice what he thought he should about taking the scavenger out to see the ball.

"You mean those funny colors—you saw them, too?" Reice asked.

"Yeah. It's not the first time, either." Then he remembered what Remson had said at the party about the ball being classified. Maybe he shouldn't be talking about this with Reice.

Maybe he was too drunk to talk about it.

So he told Reice about Sling instead.

Then Reice wanted to go see Sling.

"It's awful late, isn't it?"

"Depends on your sleep cycle," Reice said. "Come on. Let's take this with us."

So off they went, black box in hand. "That's Keebler's black box," South protested weakly as Reice strode toward the ConSec docking bay's kiosk. "What if he wants it back?"

"I'm not confiscating it. I just want to know how it's put together, and why it was put together that way."

South told Reice that Sling had sworn the box wouldn't work. Reice wanted to go anyway.

It wasn't until they were almost to Sling's shop in the Loader Zone that South remembered how Sling felt about ". . . government officials. So don't tell him you're from ConSec if you want to get anything out of him."

Reice chuckled nastily.

Reice was just a mean drunk, South decided.

And he thanked his lucky stars that Sling wasn't home. Or wouldn't open up if he was.

Reice said, "I need another drink."

South couldn't argue with that. They ended up in the bar where South had first met Sling, and Sling was sitting there, pulling on his braid.

He saw them in the mirror and turned on his bar stool: "Hey, South. Who's your friend?"

Sling never seemed to get really drunk. His eyes were on the black box that Reice held.

"Ah—Reice, meet Sling."

The two looked each other over.

"Reice wants to know what the specs are on this box," South said, easing onto the stool beside Sling's. The bartender came over, and South remembered that he'd wanted to buy Sling a blue beer. So he ended up getting three, one for each of them.

"Why do you want the specs?" Sling asked Reice point-blank. Then, to South: "Did it work?"

"Hell, no."

"Then why do you want the specs?"

"Curious."

"You've got the box," Sling observed. "Take it apart, Reice."

They drank their beers and then Sling said, "I knew it wouldn't work all along."

Reice said, "But you built it for the salvage guy anyhow?"

"He paid me good money." Sling started twirling his braid in his fingers, as if Reice was beginning to make him nervous.

Reice could make anybody nervous.

South said, "Well, Sling, you did fine, so far as I'm concerned. And what you did on my ship—that was primo. The best. I want you to do some more . . ."

So they started talking about what could be done to *STARBIRD* to bring her up to date, like dropping a zero-point power plant into her.

Somewhere about the fifth blue beer, Sling promised Reice that, if he wanted to come along to the shop while South and Sling worked up a price for *STARBIRD*'s retrofit, then Reice could open up the box on Sling's worktable.

"If that'll make you happy," Sling said to Reice.

It would, and they did.

South was feeling pretty happy himself, what with all the new goodies Sling was promising to give *STARBIRD*.

Well, not give, exactly. And South had to use his Customs card to pay Sling for the work, if Sling was going to get started right away.

As soon as he sobered up, South promised himself, he'd call Riva Lowe and clear it with her.

After all, *STARBIRD* needed to reacclimate to Threshold society as much as he did. They were going to be here a long, long time.